MURDER AT THE MAYFAIR HOTEL

A CLEOPATRA FOX MYSTERY, BOOK 1

C.J. ARCHER

WWW.CJARCHER.COM

ABOUT THIS BOOK

It was the most fashionable place to stay in London, until murder made a reservation. Solve the puzzle in this new mystery from USA Today bestselling author of the Glass and Steele series.

December 1899. After the death of her beloved grandmother, Cleopatra Fox moves into the luxury hotel owned by her estranged uncle in the hopes of putting hardship and loneliness behind her. But the poisoning of a guest throws her new life, and the hotel, into chaos.

Cleo quickly realizes no one can be trusted, not Scotland Yard and especially not the hotel's charming assistant manager. With the New Year's Eve ball approaching fast and the hotel's reputation hanging by a thread, Cleo must find the killer before the ball, and the hotel itself, are ruined. But catching a murderer proves just as difficult as navigating the hotel's hierarchy and the peculiarities of her family.

Can Cleo find the killer before the new century begins? Or will someone get away with murder?

CHAPTER 1

LONDON, DECEMBER 1899

*M*oving into a luxury hotel in the world's most dynamic city was just the tonic I needed. If I had to live with relatives I hardly knew, what better place than The Mayfair Hotel? From the look of its magnificent façade, I wouldn't have to worry about bumping into them at every turn.

I planted a hand on my hat and tipped my head back to take it all in. Like most old mansions, it was both elegant and imposing; a grand dame that inspired admiration and awe in equal measure. The top of the fifth level appeared to butt against the dense gray clouds, and I counted seven arches spanning the width of the ground floor.

I headed for the central arch, sheltered by a burgundy canopy printed with the hotel's emblem of an M inside a circle. I recognized it from the stationery my aunt used for her infrequent letters.

"Miss," said one of the two doormen. "Miss, can you hear me?"

"I'm sorry, were you speaking to me?" I asked.

The doorman regarded me down his nose. "Are you sure you're at the right place?"

"Is this The Mayfair Hotel?"

"It is."

"Then I am at the right place." I frowned. "Why would you think I'm not?"

His gaze held mine a moment longer than necessary. He was assessing me, no doubt trying to determine how a young woman alone could afford to stay in a luxury hotel when she wore a black cloak with frayed cuffs and a hat that was at least two seasons out of fashion.

I did not look away.

"Would you like to put down your luggage? I'll have it sent to your room with your trunk." The doorman gave a pointed look at my battered brown leather bag, his mouth turned down in distaste.

The bag had belonged to my grandfather. Thinking about him brought tears to my eyes, but I breathed through my sorrow until they disappeared. He may have died three years ago, but I'd thought about him a lot this last month.

"Miss?" The word came out as an irritated hiss.

I clutched the bag tighter. "Thank you, but I'll keep it with me."

The doorman signaled to an extraordinarily tall porter dressed in a smart red jacket and a rimless hat. The porter picked up my trunk and hat box and placed them on a trolley. Another doorman opened the door for him to push it through. I adjusted my grip on my bag and hurried after the porter.

I stopped in the foyer, suddenly out of breath, not from the exertion of a few steps, but from the spectacular sight. I didn't know where to look first; there was so much to take in, and the space was vast. A Christmas tree festooned with glass baubles, garlands and candles stood proudly in the center of the tiled floor. It reached an impressive height but still fell short of the crystal chandelier suspended above it. Three chandeliers hung in the wide foyer, all ablaze with what appeared to be electric bulbs. The bright light staved off the mid-afternoon gloom and reflected on the shiny tiled floor. Several armchairs in burgundy leather were positioned here and there. Two of them were occupied by elegantly dressed ladies chatting amiably to one another. Roses arranged in large black vases trimmed with gold added a splash of pink to the foyer's cream, black and burgundy color scheme. Considering roses were not in season, the displays were even more impressive.

The tall porter cleared his throat. He stood with my luggage at a counter behind which another man stood, smiling patiently.

"Would miss like to check in?" he asked.

I approached the counter. "Yes. Or no. I'm not quite sure."

"Perhaps I can assist you to make up your mind. The Mayfair Hotel is a boutique family-owned establishment of one hundred well-appointed rooms. We pride ourselves on our friendly service, family values, and modern amenities."

The porter's head turned to the front desk clerk and an eyebrow arched ever so slightly. The clerk kept his gaze on me and his smile didn't waver, but I suspected he knew the porter silently challenged his spiel. I couldn't determine which of the points made by the clerk was in question. Perhaps it was all three. From what my paternal grandparents had told me of my mother's relatives, family values were in short supply here.

"The Mayfair offers all the comforts of home and more," the clerk went on.

A small laugh bubbled out of me. I couldn't help it. If he'd known my previous home was smaller than the hotel's foyer, he would have found it amusing too. But he did not. The smile disappeared and a blush infused his cheeks. He looked to the porter, who merely blinked at me.

I pressed my lips together until my smile flattened. "I'm sorry for my outburst. I'm sure the hotel is wonderful. I am very impressed with what I've seen so far, and the service is excellent."

The porter puffed out his chest and the smile returned to the clerk's face.

"However, you don't need to sell the hotel's qualities to me any further. I won't be going to one of your competitors. I have no choice but to stay here."

A small crease connected the clerk's dark brows. "No choice?"

"I am Miss Fox."

The clerk glanced down at his reservation book. "Did you telephone ahead? I recall a Miss Fox…"

"Miss Cleopatra Fox," I clarified.

He flipped the page and ran his finger down the first

3

column. "No Miss Foxes here. Perhaps there has been a mistake. A very rare mistake, you understand. This sort of thing almost never happens." His frown returned. "Although your name certainly rings a bell." His gaze slipped past me and he stood straighter. "Mr. Armitage, sir, would you mind offering your assistance in the matter of Miss Fox. It seems she telephoned ahead and made a reservation, however I have no record of it."

I turned to see a dashing figure dressed in formal black coat with tails. He was tall with dark hair brushed back off a face that an admirer would call chiseled and a detractor call sharp. I couldn't imagine he had too many detractors, however. Certainly not of the female variety, and particularly when he gave them his full attention, as he did now to me.

"Miss Fox." He held out his hand and I shook it. "I'm delighted to meet you. We've been expecting you."

The clerk frowned down at his reservation book again, only to emit a soft "Ah". He'd realized why my name sounded familiar yet wasn't in the book. It seemed he'd forgotten about my arrival. Mr. Armitage had not.

"I'm Harry Armitage, the assistant manager. Welcome to The Mayfair Hotel."

"Thank you. It seems my arrival has confused your staff. I am sorry," I said to the clerk. "I was about to tell you that I don't have a reservation because I've come to live here, but you summoned Mr. Armitage before I had the chance. I hope you forgive me."

The clerk blushed again. "Yes, Miss Fox, you are certainly forgiven. In my defense, I'd like to point out that you're a day early."

"No, I wrote that I would arrive today, Christmas Eve."

"I was told Christmas Day." The clerk's gaze flicked to Mr. Armitage.

Mr. Armitage signaled for a second porter to join us. "Please inform Mrs. Kettering that Miss Fox has arrived. There appears to have been a mistake and she is a day early."

"Actually, I'm on time," I said as the second porter disappeared into the wing of the foyer. "I wrote to my aunt that I would arrive on the twenty-fourth."

"Your aunt?" the clerk asked. "Lady Bainbridge? Well then."

I waited for more, but the clerk merely blushed again as Mr. Armitage turned the full force of a stern glare onto him.

"Thank you, Peter, you have a guest waiting," Mr. Armitage said.

Peter the clerk nodded quickly then turned on his smile for the next guest. I stepped aside so he could serve the newcomer.

Mr. Armitage instructed the tall porter to take my trunk and hat box up to my room. I passed him my bag, feeling somewhat foolish now for refusing to do so outside. It wasn't going to be stolen in a place like this. The porter headed off with my things, but not to the nearby stairs. He disappeared around the corner at the far end of the foyer. If my things were to be taken *up* to my room, why did the porter not take the stairs?

"May I offer my deepest condolences on the loss of your grandmother," Mr. Armitage said.

The warmth in his eyes and voice almost undid me, then and there. I muttered my thanks and quickly looked away, determined not to cry in the middle of the hotel foyer. It helped to change the subject.

"Why did Peter not seem surprised by my aunt's mistake about my arrival?"

The assistant manager blinked, caught unawares by my question. "I'm very sorry for the mix up. You won't find us usually so flustered."

"You don't appear flustered, Mr. Armitage. You seem quite composed."

"This is my flustered face."

I laughed softly. His face hadn't changed in the least. He still smiled and regarded me as if I were the most important person in the foyer. His smile widened just a little, however.

I leaned in conspiratorially. "Nice avoidance tactic."

He tilted his head to the side, all innocence. But there was no innocence in his dark eyes. He'd deliberately tried to use his handsome face and charms to distract me from my pursuit of an answer. I suspected it worked on most women. It wouldn't work on me.

"It's quite all right," I said. "You don't have to answer if you don't wish to. My aunt is married to your employer, and I wouldn't want you to jeopardize your position by gossiping about her."

He drew himself up to an even more impressive height. "My position wouldn't be jeopardized. It's my principles I prefer not to compromise. I don't gossip, Miss Fox. I'm sorry if that frustrates you."

"As I said, it's quite all right. I'll get to know my aunt soon enough and will be able to make my own judgements about her."

"I'm sure you will," he said with a sharp edge to his tone.

I sighed. This wasn't going at all well. I wished I'd kept my mouth shut. In my defense, I wasn't ordinarily so prickly, but it had been a long day—a long month—and part of me wanted to see Mr. Armitage's smooth façade crack just a little.

"We've got off on the wrong foot," I said. "I'm sorry. Perhaps I wrote the wrong date in my letter to my aunt. It certainly is of no consequence to me that I wasn't expected until tomorrow, but I feel awful that your staff have been put out. I do hope Mrs. Kettering isn't too inconvenienced. I'll apologize to her and to Peter again too."

My speech seemed to have achieved the desired effect of thawing the frostiness in Mr. Armitage's gaze. "Don't worry about Mrs. Kettering. The head of housekeeping is the most efficient woman I've ever met. Her maids might curse you, however—entirely under their breath, of course." He leaned down and lowered his voice. "Mrs. Kettering is a task master, so they tell me." He straightened. "As to Peter, it's almost impossible to get off on the wrong foot with him. He's the friendliest member of staff. That's why he's on the front desk."

Mr. Armitage's gaze moved past the couple checking in at the desk to another desk further afield where a staff member attended to a tall woman with a large hat trimmed with every type of trim imaginable, from lace and velvet to ribbon and feather. The long feathers fluttered as her head bobbed. The entire effect was of a hen pecking at the poor man.

Mr. Armitage emitted a small, almost imperceptible sigh.

"Is there a problem?" I asked.

"Not at all," he said, suddenly giving me his attention again.

"It's all right, Mr. Armitage. You don't have to treat me like a guest. If I am to make my way here, I'd like to be treated as one of the family, as someone with a purpose. I don't yet know what role I can do, but I ought to learn as much about hotel life as I can so that I may find that role."

He stared at me for several moments, his lips slightly ajar as if he'd been about to say something but the words had suddenly escaped him, or he'd thought better of speaking them.

"You might as well tell me which are the difficult guests and what can be done about them," I went on. "I assume family members are called upon from time to time to assuage them."

"I, uh, I see. Assuaging guests is the role of myself and the manager, not the owner's niece."

"That's a shame. I'm quite good with people. For some reason, they seem to trust me."

That smile returned, but this time it wasn't the practiced one of an assistant manager of a luxury hotel. It was more genuine, and softer. "I don't doubt it."

I would have asked him what he meant, but a passerby caught his attention. "Mr. Hobart, do you have a moment?"

Mr. Hobart was dressed in a tailcoat too and wore the same practiced smile the assistant manager had used to greet me. That was where the similarities between them ended. Where Mr. Armitage was tall and dark, Mr. Hobart was balding, shorter and older. I guessed him to be in his late fifties, whereas Mr. Armitage could be no older thirty, and perhaps younger. Mr. Hobart had a friendly face, with bright blue eyes that sparkled and a web of red veins across rosy cheeks.

"Allow me to introduce you to Miss Cleopatra Fox," Mr. Armitage said.

There was no confusion in Mr. Hobart's demeanor. He knew my name instantly. He gave a brief bow, and when he straightened, his smile was kind. "Delighted to meet you, Miss Fox. Welcome to The Mayfair Hotel. I see you've met Harry already."

"Mr. Armitage has been very kind clearing up the confusion surrounding my arrival date."

"I'm very sorry you weren't met at the station. Sir Ronald wanted one of the porters to meet you in a hotel conveyance and assist with your luggage. He'll be disappointed you had to make your own way here."

"It wasn't terribly difficult. The cab driver knew the way."

Too late, I realized that wasn't what the manager meant. He meant that my uncle wanted me to be met at the station because I was representing his family now, and a Bainbridge lady shouldn't have to catch a hackney cab from the station and organize such mundane things like porters herself. She had staff to do that for her. I could practically hear my grandparents' voices saying as much. In our household, the Bainbridge snobbery was legendary.

The more I thought about it, the more I realized that was why the staff were so concerned about such a trifling matter as my early arrival. They were worried my uncle might hear that my room wasn't ready or that I wasn't greeted properly. I also now understood the odd look Mr. Armitage had given me when I'd mentioned finding myself a role within the hotel. It was likely my aunt and cousin Florence had no role here except a decorative one.

Even more reason for me to be of use. I needed a task, something that would not only stave off the boredom, but also take the burden of supporting me off my uncle's shoulders. I didn't want to owe him a thing.

"I'm sure Lady Bainbridge will be delighted to see you," Mr. Hobart went on. "Harry, if you'd be so good as to inform her ladyship of Miss Fox's arrival. Miss Fox, would you care to wait in the main sitting room just through there until your room is ready?" He indicated the door at one end of the foyer. "One of the waiters will be happy to serve you refreshments."

I thanked him and went to move off but Harry did not. "I think I'd better see to Mrs. Cavendish-Dyer." He nodded at the woman with the elaborate hat, still pecking at the young man. "You'd better speak to Lady Bainbridge, sir. She prefers you anyway." He flashed a quick grin that seemed quite at odds with his formal smoothness. Perhaps he'd already decided to drop the façade in front of me, considering I wasn't a guest.

The manager looked a little uncomfortable by this change in his assistant, though not cross. More awkward than anything, as if he hadn't quite made up his mind how to act in front of me. It seemed none of us were sure where I fitted into the hotel's community.

Mr. Armitage strode off towards Mrs. Cavendish-Dyer, and Mr. Hobart departed too, so I made my way to the sitting room. It was a large airy space, filled with comfortable chairs, sofas and tables. A three-piece ensemble played in the corner, the sound soft enough that conversations could still be had but loud enough that one group couldn't eavesdrop on another. The décor was lighter than the foyer, with no burgundy or black vases in sight. It was mostly cream with some gold and more splashes of pink from the roses in the white marble vases. It was the epitome of elegance. Grandmama would have loved it, although she would have felt out of place. Grandpapa would have liked the two rooms off the sitting room. The door to one was labeled LIBRARY and the other labeled WRITING ROOM. My father would have liked those rooms too. My most vivid memories of him were with his nose in a book in his study.

A waiter dressed in crisp white waist apron greeted me and guided me to a spare seat in the bay window. It looked out over the side street with a bookshop opposite. My father would definitely have liked this place. My mother even more so. She would have taken the hotel's elegant grandness in her stride. It was easy when one was born into luxury as she had been.

"May I bring you a cup of tea?" the waiter asked. "Sponge cake?"

I was about to enthusiastically agree. My stomach felt hollow after not eating anything since breakfast in Cambridge. "Just a cup of tea," I said, however. Until I spoke to my uncle, I didn't know what he expected me to pay for out of my allowance and what was free.

I eyed another passing waiter carrying a tray with slices of cream sponge cake and cups of tea. The cake did look delicious, but no doubt it was expensive in a hotel like this. I needed to save every bit of my allowance if I was to become independent.

The waiter brought over the tea on a tray and asked me for my room number.

"I don't have a room yet. The housekeeper is having it made up now." I bit the inside of my lip, considering how to proceed. I didn't want to boast that I was the hotel owner's niece, yet I didn't want to cause the waiter embarrassment as I'd caused Peter.

I was saved by a pretty young woman with strawberry blonde hair and a delicate spray of freckles across her pug nose. Her blue eyes were the color of a summer sky and matched her dress.

"Is it you?" she asked in a girlish voice. "Are you my cousin Cleopatra? Mr. Hobart said I'd find her here and you are the only female sitting alone."

"I am. You must be Florence." I stood but was almost knocked off my feet by her enthusiastic hug.

She drew away and caught both my hands in hers. "I am so thrilled to finally meet you!"

It was a relief to receive such a warm welcome. Until this moment, I hadn't realized how worried I'd been about seeing my relatives. If the rest of the family were as friendly as Florence, perhaps the knot in my chest would finally loosen. It might be too much to ask, however. From the way this girl's parents had treated my mother after she married my father, I was quite sure their reception would be different.

"Do sit down and enjoy your tea, Cleopatra. Gregory, would you mind bringing me a cup too? And a slice of cake each, of course. The sponge here is the airiest in London," she added as Gregory headed off. "Now, Cleopatra, tell me all about yourself. I want to know everything."

"Call me Cleo," I said. "Cleopatra is such a mouthful."

"And you must call me Flossy." She reached across the space and patted my knee. "We are so alike, you and I, are we not? I could see the family resemblance immediately. You have my brother's coloring and he takes after mother, so I suspect you must take after your mother." She suddenly gasped. "Oh dear, I forgot. My condolences on the death of your parents and grandparents. I know your parents' deaths occurred many years ago and your grandfather was last year—"

"Three years ago, actually."

"But your grandmother's is very recent." She patted my knee again. "It must still feel raw."

I swallowed the lump threatening to clog my throat. Raw wasn't a strong enough word to describe the overwhelming sense of loss I'd felt all month. There was a measure of trepidation mixed with the grief, too. Ever since learning I had to leave my home in Cambridge and move in with an uncle and aunt I'd met only once—and at my parents' funerals at that—I'd been anxious. Flossy's enthusiastic greeting and sympathetic gaze went some way to easing my mind, but it wouldn't be completely at ease until I'd gauged my uncle and aunt's reactions to my presence and dependency.

"Thank you, Flossy," I said. "You're very kind. Everyone here has been kind so far." Except the doorman. The wicked part of me was quite looking forward to seeing his face when he learned I lived here now.

"You clearly haven't met everyone then." She wrinkled her nose. "The housekeeper, Mrs. Kettering, is the devil incarnate. I think even Father's afraid of her. Obviously you met Mr. Hobart, the manager. If Father is the head of the hotel, Mr. Hobart is its heart. He's been here from the beginning. The Mayfair couldn't run without him at the helm. He knows everything there is to know about this place, and probably some things there aren't to know." She pulled a face. "That doesn't make sense, but you know what I mean. Ah, our cake."

Gregory handed us plates with slices of sponge and poured a cup of tea for Flossy before quietly melting away. There was no mention of room numbers.

Flossy murmured her approval of the cake as she took her first bite. "I adore the sponge here. I could eat a slice a day, but of course I mustn't. Just on special occasions such as this."

This was information I needed to know if I were to live here. "Is there a restriction on how often family can partake of the afternoon tea?"

She giggled into her hand. "No, silly. You can come in here and eat cake to your heart's content. I only mean I can't have

11

a slice every day or I'll get fat. You won't have to worry, of course. You're so slim! How do you manage such a tiny waist?"

"I don't eat cake as good as this every day," I said.

Flossy giggled again then finished the rest of her slice before setting the plate down and picking up her teacup. "Mr. Hobart mentioned you'd met his nephew."

"Have I?"

"Harry Armitage."

"I didn't realize Mr. Armitage was his nephew. Neither of them mentioned it."

"They would have eventually. They like to act profession-ally in the presence of guests, so they refer to each other as mister this and mister that, but all the staff know. Harry has worked here for years, not always as assistant to his uncle, though. He's devilishly handsome, don't you think? All the maids are in love with him."

"Are they?"

She set down her teacup and clasped her hands. "Isn't this lovely? I've always wanted a sister; someone to share all my secrets with, go shopping together... We're going to have so much fun, Cleo. It's wonderful that you made it in time for Christmas. Oh, and I can't wait to show you off at the ball."

"Ball?"

"Our New Year's Eve ball." She tilted her head to the side. "Mother didn't tell you, did she?"

"Our correspondence has been very brief."

"I'm sure it has." Her ominous tone was the first sign of seriousness she'd displayed. The spark also briefly left her eyes, but it quickly returned again as she cast aside whatever bothered her. "I do hope you have something to wear to the ball. There isn't enough time to get a proper gown made."

"I don't own any ball gowns," I said with an apologetic shrug.

Her assessing gaze took in my simple dress and her nose wrinkled ever so slightly. She was probably wondering how someone so plainly clothed could have anything remotely pretty in her luggage. She would be right. I didn't own anything as fine as the silk dress trimmed with white lace that she wore. Like all the ladies in the hotel sitting room, her clothes were in the latest style. My mourning outfit might be well made, but it was certainly not in the current fashion.

"I have several ball gowns," she said. "You can wear one of mine. We'll have one of the maids take it in to fit you. We're a similar height but our figures are quite different." She thrust out her considerable bosom, just in case I hadn't noticed it.

"That's kind of you, but unless it's in black, I'll have to decline."

"Yes, of course, you're in mourning." She studied my outfit again. "I'm sure one night off from black won't matter, will it? Ah, here's Mr. Armitage, come to solve our dilemma." She smiled up at the assistant manager as he approached.

"I'm happy to help in any way I can, Miss Bainbridge," he said, using the formal politeness I thought he reserved just for guests. Despite having known one another for years, there was no casual familiarity between them.

"It's all right for Cleo to take one night off from wearing mourning, isn't it? Her grandmother died a month ago, and Cleo is quite young, after all. It ought to be a sin for someone so young to be in full mourning for anything longer than a week or two. You agree with me that she ought to wear something nice to the ball, don't you?"

Mr. Armitage had a tightrope to walk. Disagreeing with Flossy would likely upset his employer's daughter, but disagreeing with me would go against societal rules. I was rather looking forward to seeing him traverse it and gave him my full attention.

His gaze slid sideways to me before returning to Flossy. "I believe six to nine months is the usual mourning period for a woman for her grandparent, but you're right, Miss Bainbridge. It would be unfortunate to see someone as young as Miss Fox in full black at a ball."

Flossy beamed. "So you agree."

"I think the decision should be left to Miss Fox."

I felt like applauding him. He'd navigated the tightrope perfectly.

"The point is moot anyway," I said. "I won't be attending. It wouldn't be right."

"But she died a month ago!" Flossy declared.

Mr. Armitage gave the fleetest of winces.

Flossy didn't seem to notice. Her cherry pink lips formed a pout and a crease connected her brows. "Do give it some thought, Cleo. Nobody will mind, certainly not your grandmother."

I pressed my lips together to suppress a smile. I found it harder and harder to take Flossy seriously, although I didn't think she was trying to be amusing. She was right in that Grandmama would have encouraged me to attend a ball, even one thrown by people she despised. She would also most likely be bellowing with laughter right now, listening to Flossy bumble her way through the conversation without realizing she was bumbling.

Out of the corner of my eye I saw Mr. Armitage watching me with the most curious expression on his face. I couldn't quite make out what it meant. It certainly wasn't a negative one. Indeed, I quite liked it when he looked at me like that, with something akin to surprise.

"Your room is ready, Miss Fox," he said when he realized I was watching him. "I'll show you the way."

"I'll take her," Flossy said, rising. "I'm sure you have lots of other tasks on your plate."

Mr. Armitage bowed. "As you wish, Miss Bainbridge." He handed me a key. "Room four eleven. I hope you like it, Miss Fox. All the rooms on that side have a nice view over Green Park."

"He's very efficient," Flossy said as we walked out of the sitting room behind him. We both watched as Mr. Armitage joined a gentleman near the Christmas tree who appeared to be asking him something.

Flossy stopped alongside a sliding wooden door where a woman wearing a cloak trimmed with fur also stood. She didn't appear to notice us as she peered in Mr. Armitage's direction. After a moment, she lifted a pair of spectacles hanging around her neck and peered through the lenses.

"How odd," she murmured, frowning. "So very strange to see him *here*."

I waited for Flossy to say something, but it seemed she didn't know the woman. Flossy pressed a button beside the door and a distant bell rang.

"He looks so different, so much older," the woman went

on. "It *has* been several years. Ten at least." She shook her head and her frown deepened. "He shouldn't be here."

My curiosity almost got the better of me, but I refrained from asking her why Mr. Armitage shouldn't be here. Indeed, she might not have been referring to him at all. There were another two gentlemen in the vicinity.

The door slid open before I gave in to curiosity, revealing a short man with a pencil-thin moustache dressed in the same uniform as the porters. He stood inside a room no larger than a wardrobe. At the back was a bench seat upholstered in burgundy velvet with a large letter M inside a circle, embroidered in gold thread. Mirrors on all the walls made the tight space appear larger than it was. This was no ordinary room, I realized. This was a lift to take us up to the higher floors. I'd never been in one before and wanted to know how it worked, but I once again forced my curiosity down. I didn't want to seem unworldly in front of my cousin.

"Good afternoon, Miss Bainbridge," the lift operator said to Flossy. "Level four?"

"Yes please, John." She introduced us as she ushered me into the lift.

John welcomed me with a friendly smile and rested his gloved hand on the door. "We have room for one more, madam."

The woman lowered her spectacles and, still frowning, entered the lift. "Level three."

He closed the door and pushed the lever attached to the circular device on the wall. The room rose and my stomach lurched, more from the anxiety of the strange sensation than the speed at which we ascended. The lift was so slow I could have climbed the stairs faster.

John eased off the lever and we stopped at level three, where the woman got out, then we continued up to the fourth floor. I expelled a breath once my feet were firmly set on the corridor's carpet.

"Thank you, John," I said.

"My pleasure, Miss Fox. And don't worry. Everyone finds it a bit unnerving their first time." He winked and closed the door.

Flossy had already moved off, and I rushed to catch up

15

to her. "This level contains the hotel's suites rather than single rooms," she said with the direct manner of a tour guide at a historical monument. "Each suite has a bathroom as well as a sitting room. Some have more than one bedroom, to accommodate families, and dressing rooms. The entire floor is reserved for our family and distinguished guests. We don't have any staying at the moment, but some should arrive shortly for the ball. Father has invited several important people." She strode down the long corridor, pointing out the door to her parents' suite, then her brother's, her own and finally, mine. "Here we are, room four-eleven."

I unlocked the door and entered. Despite the open curtains it was rather gloomy until Flossy flipped a brass switch on the wall by the door.

"Electric lighting!" I squinted up at the bulb but had to quickly avert my gaze away from the brightness. "How marvelous."

"The entire hotel has been electrified." She frowned at the word. "Electricalled? Electrically wired? Anyway, all the rooms have a little switch like this to turn on the central bulb. We had it installed a few years ago—at enormous cost, so my father likes to remind me whenever I ask him to increase my allowance."

It would have indeed cost a fortune to install electricity throughout the hotel. Few homes had converted from gas lighting, although many streetlamps were now electric, as well as some underground trains, public spaces and buildings. I supposed the hotel had to modernize if it was going to tout itself as a luxurious place to stay.

"So, what do you think of your room?" Flossy asked.

The suite was as elegant as I expected it to be, based on what I'd seen of the hotel so far. Not only was the bedroom three times the size of the one I'd had in Cambridge, but the sitting room was enormous too, and the bathroom was very modern with a large bath.

The rooms contained everything I'd need, from a fully stocked writing desk, sofa, armchairs, dressing table, and a bed in which three people could comfortably sleep. More pink roses cheered the rooms in white vases edged with gold.

My luggage, waiting beside the wardrobe doors, looked out of place amidst all the grandeur.

I passed a hand over the warm wood of the desk and looked out the window. Mr. Armitage had been wrong. The view wasn't simply nice; it was spectacular. I could look through the window over Green Park all day, even with its winter-bare trees.

Flossy joined me. "There's hot and cold running water in the bathroom, but I'm afraid that's where the modern amenities begin and end." She glanced at the lamp. "Well, that and the electric lights. I wish we could have telephones in our rooms. Father has one in his office, of course, as does the reception and Mr. Hobart's office, but we're quite behind the times here compared to newer hotels. I once asked Father when the family's suites would get telephones and he ranted and raved for a full twenty minutes about my laziness. He said if I wanted to stay in touch with friends, I ought to write or visit." She ran her fingers along the windowsill as if checking for dust. They came away clean. "He's so miserly and quite the bear at times. Just wait and see. You'll meet him soon. Anyway, you have to make do with the speaking tube." She pointed at the brass mouthpiece on the wall. "It connects to the kitchen. If you want something sent up, just ask for it. Breakfast must be ordered the night before, but if you forget, you can simply go to the dining room in the morning."

Again I wondered what I must pay for, but I would leave those questions for my uncle. I suspected Flossy wouldn't have a clue.

She departed with a little wave of her fingers and closed the door, leaving me alone to freshen up and change after my day of travel. Cambridge wasn't too far by rail, but I felt exhausted. It was probably the accumulation of a month's worth of mourning for my grandmother and everything else that needed to be done afterwards—selling what I could to pay off debts, giving away her personal things to her friends as well as packing, and finally giving back the keys to the landlord for the house we'd moved into after my grandfather's death three years ago. While it had never quite felt like home, I had fond memories of precious time spent there with my aging grandmother. Moving into that house had signaled a change in our relationship. The previous house had been the one my grandparents moved into as newlyweds. It had been full of warmth and love at a time when I desperately needed it. They'd taken care of me in that house, and made sure I'd had a good life despite the tragedy of losing Mother and Father when I'd been just ten.

But after Grandpapa died and we realized the two of us couldn't afford to stay there, after the full extent of his debts were revealed, we'd rented a smaller place. His death and learning of his debts had been the beginning of the end for Grandmama. It were as if part of her had died with him. Our roles reversed in a matter of weeks, and for the last three years, I'd taken care of her as her body and mind became more fragile.

When she died, my Uncle and Aunt Bainbridge had written and offered me the opportunity to live in London with them. Despite not having seen them in years, and my very strong reservations, I took the opportunity. It was the only way to free myself of the last of Grandpapa's debts. The only way to begin anew. Besides, I'd always wanted to see London.

I only wished I didn't have to depend upon my mother's family. Her own parents had criticized her, severed all contact with her, and cut her out of their will when she'd married my father. Her younger sister, my aunt, had inherited a vast fortune upon their deaths, and my mother had received nothing. Not even a personal token. Aside from the single appearance of my aunt and uncle at my parents' funeral, I'd had no contact with them until I received the letter from my aunt after Grandmama died. And now I was utterly dependent on their goodwill. A goodwill I wasn't entirely sure they possessed. They believed in duty, apparently, or I wouldn't have been invited here, but if they had a caring heart between them, we would never have become estranged in the first place.

A light knock on the door shook me from my melancholy thoughts. "Sir Ronald will see you now," said the footman.

I bristled. I didn't like to be summoned, and I almost told him I'd be five minutes, just to make my uncle wait. But I was here thanks to his charity and couldn't afford to stand on principles. Besides, the footman might get into trouble too.

"Is Lady Bainbridge with him?" I asked.

"No."

I grabbed my room key and locked the door. With a steadying breath, I followed the stiff-backed footman along the corridor. I wished my aunt would be present. Not because I especially cared to meet her, but because I didn't want to be alone when I faced the man who held my immediate future in the palm of his hand.

CHAPTER 2

*S*ir Ronald Bainbridge hadn't changed in the thirteen years since my parents' funeral. Aside from patches of gray amid the red-gold hair at either side of his temple, he was exactly as I remembered him—a short man with a pug nose and steely eyes that quickly took in my appearance. Whatever his assessment of me from that brief glance, his expression didn't give it away. He greeted me with a benign smile and a handshake, as if I were a business partner.

That was how I preferred it. I didn't want to be pecked on the cheek and fussed over. It had felt genuine from Flossy, but anything this man offered other than the simplest condolences would fall flat.

He indicated I should sit in the chair opposite and clasped his broad hands on the desk in front of him. "I was very sorry to hear about your grandmother. I expect it didn't come as a shock to you, however."

"No," I said.

"I'm glad you accepted my offer to come and live here." *His* offer? Not my aunt's?

"Thank you for making it. I'm very grateful." Despite going through this conversation dozens of times in my head, I still hesitated, unsure how to proceed.

"I expect this change in your situation is difficult for you, but I'd like to make it easier somewhat. You are family, after all." He reached for a sheet of hotel stationery then picked up a pen and dipped it into the inkwell. "By my estimation, an extra five pounds should suffice. If you'd like to see how I reached this figure, I'd be happy to show you my calculations."

I frowned. "Pardon?"

He opened the top drawer of his desk and pulled out a book. He opened it to a page and handed it to me. "I've used Florence's expenses as a guide, and taken into consideration the amount you're already receiving."

I stared at the page with its neat columns of figures. Every possible item a woman of my age could need was written down with an amount beside it. Indeed, there was far more than I would need. A new hat every month and new gown every three was excessive, but if he'd used Flossy as a guide, it was clear how he'd reached the figure. I suspected economizing was a foreign notion to her.

Neither the items nor the amount was what confused me the most, however. I put down the ledger and fixed my uncle with a glare. "How do you know the amount I'm already receiving?" It wouldn't surprise me if he'd bullied his way into my banker's good graces and coerced the knowledge from the poor fellow. My uncle's ruthlessness was legendary.

He tilted his head to the side. "I pay your allowance, Cleopatra."

My jaw dropped.

"You didn't know?"

"No," I murmured. *He* paid my allowance?

"They kept that from you?" He leaned back in the chair, moving his clasped hands from the desk to the top of his stomach. He stared at me, and I suspected I stared back with the same confused expression.

"I don't understand," I said. "How long have you been paying my allowance?"

"Ever since you were born."

My jaw dropped again. Any more surprises and it was in danger of unhinging altogether. "For twenty-three years! But...why did no one tell me?"

"That is a good question, but one I suspect I know the answer to. Your family didn't like me. Or, more specifically, they didn't like your mother's parents. Not telling you the

21

source of your allowance was one small way they could obliterate them—us—from your life."

"I don't understand," I said again, rather stupidly. "My maternal grandparents died before I was born. They were never *in* my life. Why withhold information from me about the allowance? What did it matter?"

My uncle flattened his moustache with his thumb and forefinger. His shoulders heaved with his sigh as he sat forward again. "I suspect there's much you don't know, Cleopatra, and hearing the truth might cast some of your family in a poor light. Are you prepared to hear it?"

I gripped the chair arm to steady myself. I suddenly felt as if the chair were floating away, taking me with it. I had never shied away from the truth. Indeed, I believed the truth, however hurtful, should always be revealed. I'd witnessed my parents' deaths; I'd heard their arguing voices moments before our gig veered off the road. Knowing that fact about the accident helped me move on.

On the reverse side, there was Grandpapa's secret debts. Grandmama had been deeply hurt when she'd learned of them. Nothing good came of deceit.

But I wasn't convinced that my uncle was speaking the truth. I would hear his version, however. "Go on," I prompted.

"Do you know that your mother's parents left their entire fortune to her sister, your Aunt Lilian, when they died?"

"Yes. They didn't like that she married my father against their wishes, so they removed my mother from their will, and their lives."

"That's a fair summary. I married your Aunt Lilian shortly afterwards, and her inheritance allowed me to turn my ancestral home into this hotel." He spread out his hands. At least he admitted that his wife's money had led him to become the wealthy hotelier he now was. I hadn't expected him to, and I gave him credit for it.

"Soon after our marriage, I wrote to your parents and offered them an allowance. It never felt right to me that Lilian should inherit it all. Your parents refused my offer."

He offered no reason, thankfully. I suspected stubbornness

and pride played large parts, but that didn't mean I wanted this man to point it out.

"When you were born, I offered again," he went on. "The granddaughter of a gentleman who'd been one of the nation's wealthiest merchants shouldn't be brought up in…reduced circumstances."

I bristled. "We weren't poor."

He held up his hands. "My apologies. No, you weren't poor by the average man's standards. But you were by ours." He indicated the walls surrounding us, with the rich wood paneling and the paintings in gilded frames. "Academia doesn't pay well, unfortunately. Your father was a very clever man. The cleverest I've ever known. But sadly, our maker doesn't distribute money along with brains. I knew there'd be little left over from his wages after the necessities had been paid for. Your parents agreed to a lesser amount than I offered —for your education and future dowry, so their letter stated. I've been paying that amount into a bank account in Cambridge ever since, but I am well aware that it isn't enough for a young lady entering London society." He tapped the ledger with a blunt finger. "Shall we agree to an extra five pounds a month?"

He was wrong, surely. It must be a lie to make himself look generous. There was an easy way to find out. "What amount was paid monthly?"

"Four pounds."

"Which bank was it paid into?"

"The National Commercial on the first day of every month unless the first was a weekend or bank holiday then it was paid on the next business day. The manager's name at the Cambridge branch is Mr. Arnold. I never met him, so I cannot describe him to you, but he has been the manager the entire time, so is likely my age or older."

The allowance went into my account on the first of every month and it was indeed four pounds. Prior to my grandfather's death, I had not been allowed to access it without his signature, but after his death, I was given full access. I'd always assumed my father set up the allowance in the event of his death; an event that had unfortunately come to pass. If

Uncle Ronald were to be believed, it had been paid by him and from the day I was born.

"It will be easy enough for me to check," I told him.

"Yes, it would." He smiled, but there was a hint of sadness tugging at the corners of his eyes. "You remind me so much of your mother. You have her spirit." He cleared his throat and reached for the pen again. "You have your father's practical common sense, however, so I suspect you will accept the raise to your allowance without objection."

It wasn't a question, yet he didn't immediately sign the letter. Reading it upside down, it was indeed a letter addressed to Mr. Arnold at the National Commercial bank, stipulating my allowance should be raised by the amount of five pounds a month and that I would henceforth be drawing on the funds from London.

"I have already informed Mr. Arnold of my relocation to London," I said. "I met him for the first time prior to my departure. He's older than you, has poor eyesight, and no hair on his head but an abundance on his face in the form of long gray whiskers."

My uncle's smile returned. He set the paper aside. "I'll draft another and remove that paragraph. It'll be sent by the last post of the day."

"No."

"What?"

"No, I don't want an additional allowance. Not from you. I mean, not from anyone," I added quickly. "Thank you, I appreciate the offer but the four pounds I already receive will suffice."

"But...are you sure?"

If I was to make my own way here, I couldn't rely on his money. Not more than I already was, anyway. Discovering that he had been paying my allowance all these years made me feel somewhat sick; I couldn't stomach it if he more than doubled it.

"I'm sure, sir."

He picked up the letter to the bank manager and appeared to be re-reading it when he suddenly screwed it up into a ball. "Call me Uncle Ronald." He tossed the ball into a rubbish basket. "If you change your mind about the extra allowance, just come and see me." He indicated the photograph of a newlywed couple in the oval frame on the corner of his desk. The man was a younger version of Uncle Ronald. "I want to assure you that your Aunt Lilian and I are very happy to have you with us. We hope you'll be a steadying influence on Florence."

"She has been very kind to me today," I said.

"She's a kind-hearted girl, if a little flighty at times. But you seem sensible, steady, Cleopatra."

"Call me Cleo. Everyone does."

"There, you see? Sensible."

His reasoning was lost on me, but I went along with it and nodded. "May I ask you some questions about my stay here?"

"Of course. I imagine you have several."

I cleared my throat. "I don't want you to think me ungrateful for the offer." I indicated the rubbish basket. "I am very grateful. However, I need to know what things cost here. Are there menus with prices on them?"

He frowned. "You're not expected to pay for anything. All hotel amenities are free for family."

He couldn't possibly understand me. "What about tea and cake in the sitting room? And breakfast and dinner?"

He smiled. "All free."

"What?" I blurted out. "All of it?"

He chuckled, producing a fan of wrinkles from the corners of his eyes. "Even dessert. I don't expect you to pay for food, Cleo. As your uncle, I'm supporting you."

"So…it's not coming out of my allowance?"

"Your allowance is yours to do with as you wish. Spend it on hats and shoes, or save it. I don't care. As I said earlier, the inheritance ought to have been shared between your mother and your aunt upon their parents' deaths. It never sat well with me that your mother received nothing. While I can't afford to give you her entire half, I can give you a little every month. I think that fair, don't you?"

I blinked hard. This conversation was not going as I expected. Ever since I could recall, my grandparents had told me that my Uncle Ronald was greedy, that he'd married my aunt for her inheritance. To be honest, they didn't really know him. After all, they knew him about as well as I did—and that was not at all.

"Thank you." It sounded rather weak, so I said it again, just to be sure he understood I was truly grateful. "I don't wish to be a burden on you for long, however. I want to be useful."

"Useful?"

"I'd like to find a role for myself within the hotel."

He waved off the suggestion. "You don't have to work, Cleo. Work is for those who need the money. You don't. Not anymore."

"Is there nothing I can do? Some task, no matter how small? I'm good with mathematics, but I quite like people too and am happy to help the manager. Or the steward, perhaps, although I know very little about restaurants."

He gave a stiff shake of his head. "Bainbridge women don't work."

I bit the inside of my cheek to stop myself from retorting that I was a Fox not a Bainbridge. My uncle's thinking was no different to my father's or that of most other men and many women too, and I shouldn't let it rankle. Yet it did.

"Well then, let me assure you I won't be a burden on you for longer than necessary," I said. "I plan to move out of the hotel one day."

"Of course. When you marry, you'll want to make your own home. That's only natural."

"I don't plan to marry."

He made a scoffing sound in the back of his throat. "Of course you will, my dear. A pretty girl such as yourself will find a husband. There are many eligible bachelors coming through the hotel. You will have your pick of gentlemen, both English and foreign."

I bit the inside of my cheek again. I was going to have quite the sore spot there soon. "Thank you, but I really don't intend to marry."

"But—"

"I will work. If not here in the hotel, then elsewhere. I don't yet know what I will do, but I'm sure something will crop up. Perhaps I'll be an authoress or teacher, or a private secretary to a lady. Perhaps all three," I added with more cheerfulness than I felt. He was looking at me as if I had grown horns so I found myself wanting to drive the point home. "I'm an independent woman, Uncle, and I plan to stay that way. As I see it, there is only one way to remain independent and that is to find work. I can't accept your allowance forever."

He continued to stare at me with the same look on his face that was part horrified, part fascinated.

"Of course I will honor your rules while I live here," I went on. "I hope you won't find me to be a burden or come to regret your decision to allow me to stay."

He quickly got to his feet as I rose, and rounded the desk. "No, no, I don't think I will. Indeed, I think we shall get along quite well." He took my hand and gave it a shake and a pat, as if he couldn't decide whether to treat me as a business associate or a niece.

"Do you know when my aunt will be available to see me?" I asked.

He glanced at the clock on the low bookshelf. "My wife suffers from headaches. I believe she is suffering from one today. If she feels better, she'll summon you."

I waited in my rooms for the summons, but it never came. Flossy arrived, bearing a verbal invitation to dine with the family at eight, then left to get ready even though it was only five.

I sat at the desk and wrote letters, both to Mr. Arnold the banker and a friend in Cambridge with whom I'd stored another trunk of clothes. I'd only brought black outfits with me and my underthings. The second trunk I'd left behind, assuming I wouldn't need other clothes for some time. But Flossy's reasoning had taken root, and there might come a day in the not too distant future when I'd want to wear colors again. I had a gray dress with white trim that looked fetching. Gray would be acceptable to wear soon. As Flossy said, young women weren't expected to wear full black for long.

I took my letters downstairs and asked at the front desk what to do with them.

Peter the clerk pointed at a counter diagonally opposite. "The post desk appears to be unmanned at the moment. You could leave them on the counter or wait. He has probably just stepped away for a few moments."

I decided to wait by the counter rather than leave the letters unattended. It gave me an opportunity to explore this side of the foyer. Next to the post desk was a billiard room where two gentlemen played. On the other side of the billiard room was a corridor with several doors leading off it. Some were offices, labeled for the manager, assistant manager, steward and housekeeper, while others were unlabeled. A potted plant occupied the space between the manager and assistant manager's offices, but otherwise the corridor was clearly not meant for guests to venture down, given its utilitarian appearance. The dimmer lighting, lack of marble and other adornment meant the foyer sparkled by comparison.

I was about to return to the post desk when the door to the steward's office opened an inch. Someone peered through the gap then the door opened wider. Mr. Armitage the assistant manager emerged.

"Good evening, Miss Fox," he said cheerfully as he locked the door behind him and pocketed the key. "Are you lost?" His friendliness was at odds with his furtive peek through the gap.

"Merely being nosy. I wanted to see what was down here. I'm sorry, am I not supposed to be here?"

"You can go wherever you want. The entire hotel is available for family to explore." He hesitated then checked his pocket watch. "Would you like a tour?"

"Yes, please."

"Then let's begin here." He pointed to each of the labeled doors. "These are the offices for the senior staff. You won't often find us in them, however, since we're usually attending to matters within the hotel. Beyond them is a service lift, usually used by the porters, and our private chambers."

"You live here?"

"Only the unmarried senior staff do. That's myself, Mr. Chapman the steward, and Mrs. Kettering the housekeeper." He put a hand to the side of his mouth and whispered, "She's actually *Miss* Kettering, but housekeepers are always called Mrs, so I'm told. Apparently it gives them the appearance of authority."

I laughed softly. "I won't tell anyone. And the manager?"

"Mr. Hobart lives with his wife off-site."

I cupped the side of my mouth with a hand as he had done and lowered my voice. "You can call him Uncle in front of me. I don't mind."

His lips tilted with a disarming lopsided smile. "My uncle has already left for the day. My aunt likes him home for dinner."

"So you're in charge in the evenings?"

"Sir Ronald is in charge. I'm merely his lackey."

"I can't see you being anyone's lackey." It just slipped out without me thinking. I hardly knew Mr. Armitage, but I suspected my observation was correct.

"I admit that asking me nicely rather than ordering me does get better results. Something most people here understand."

We left the corridor and returned to the foyer. A staff member stood behind the post desk so I gave him my letters and he promised to see they made the last collection of the day. Then Mr. Armitage continued with his tour, taking me to another sitting room, smaller than the one I'd taken tea in, as well as pointing out the luggage room, a small parlor used by staff, the vestibule leading to the dining room where diners could wait for their friends in comfortable chairs, and finally the dining room itself. Waiters wove between tables, setting places for dinner, while Mr. Chapman the steward rearranged a vase of flowers. He pinched off a rosebud and poked the stem through his buttonhole.

"That's all the areas the guests are allowed access to, but I want to show you everything on this level and below," Mr. Armitage said. "Do you have time?"

"An abundance of it .I'm not dining with my family until eight."

"Including your aunt?"

"Of course. Why wouldn't she join us?"

He watched me and I watched him back, waiting for an explanation. None came. A small crease appeared between his brows, however, as if my confusion confused him in turn.

"No reason," he said simply. "Sometimes she suffers from headaches. I assumed your aunt and uncle's letters had informed you. Or that your cousin's letters would. Miss Bainbridge seems like she would blurt out all sorts of secrets to her only cousin."

"We've never exchanged letters," I said.

His brows arched. "Never?"

I shook my head. "My aunt and uncle were estranged from my parents."

"I'm so sorry. I had no idea."

"You weren't to know."

"I feel as though I've stumbled my way through this conversation and thrust my nose in where it shouldn't be."

"Call it even, given I was lurking in the staff corridor."

He laughed softly and led the way past tables to the corner of the dining room. "So you've come to London to live with people you don't know?" he asked as he pushed open a door.

I nodded and almost told him more, about my grandfather's debts, my dire financial situation, and the reason my mother fell out with her family. Part of me wanted to tell him. But it wasn't something one blurted out to a man one hardly knew, particularly given he was an employee of the uncle supporting me.

"That's very brave," he said. "I hope your family are kind to you."

What an odd thing to say. "Thank you."

"And if they're not, just come and see me."

"Oh? You'll box their ears on my behalf?"

He brushed past me to lead the way. "Are you mad?" he teased. "I'll lose my position as assistant manager. They might demote me to porter. I was a porter in my first year here, and I swear my shoulders became more stooped with all the carrying. I'm sure they still are."

I was quite sure they were not. His shoulders looked impressively wide within his well-made suit. "Very rounded," I said with mock seriousness. "Such a pity. You would be at least another two inches taller if only you weren't so stooped. It must be such a trial, being so short now." Mr. Armitage may not have been as tall as the porter, but he wasn't much shorter. My nose only reached the middle of his chest.

"So you agree, there will be no fisticuffs between myself and your uncle or cousin. When I said come and see me if your family are unkind, it was because I have the key to the cellar. You can drown your sorrows in fine wine."

I laughed. "Is it all very fine?"

He grinned. "The most expensive money can buy. Apparently that makes it the best."

The rest of our tour took in the service rooms including a still room, an enormous kitchen in the basement that we quickly left before we got in the way of the busy chefs, another service lift, the scullery, pantry, and finally the cellar, filled with rows and rows of wine bottles.

"This could drown a lot of sorrows," I said.

"It would be a shame if it came to that." His deeply melodic voice rumbled in the confines of the thick stone walls.

I glanced at him and caught him watching me from beneath lowered lashes. He quickly looked away.

"I'd better return to work," he said, switching off the cellar light. "Can you make your own way from the dining room? I have to speak to the steward about Christmas luncheon."

* * *

My aunt's headache had not vanished by the time the rest of us sat down for dinner. We were given the best table, positioned at one end of the grand dining room. The large space looked different with people seated at the tables, although it was only half full and the tables were set well apart. When Mr. Armitage had given me the tour, the lights had blazed from the three large chandeliers hanging from the high ornate ceiling, but now the lighting was not so bright. Even so, the silver cutlery and crystal glassware sparkled. There was just enough light to read the menu. Each dish was written in French, but thankfully an English translation accompanied it.

"So what do you think of your new home?" asked my cousin Floyd.

He was the same age as me, and Flossy had been right when she said we looked alike. Our hair was a similar shade of light brown, and we both had high cheekbones and green eyes. It was difficult to tell what his character was like yet. The dinner was subdued and quite formal so far. Even Flossy's vibrancy had been turned down like a gas flame. I blamed their father.

Uncle Ronald had said very little to us since sitting down. He seemed pre-occupied with something and gave his children and me very little attention.

"The hotel is beautiful," I said to Floyd. "Every room is a piece of art in itself. There is something different to admire in each. The foyer is very grand and looks wonderfully festive with the Christmas tree in the middle."

A slow smile stretched Uncle Ronald's moustache, proving he had been listening after all.

"Everyone has been nice to me," I added.

"Of course they have. You're the owner's niece." Floyd tempered the spiteful comment with a smile that transformed his face from handsome to mischievous.

"Hopefully they'll be less reserved around me once they know me better," I said.

Flossy looked appalled. "You don't want the staff knowing you *too* well. They already gossip about us too much."

My chest pinched as I recalled what I'd told Mr. Armitage about not knowing my family. But the feeling of panic dissipated just as quickly. Not only would the assistant manager be unlikely to gossip about his employer, he didn't seem like the type to take joy in the exchange of titillating information.

Floyd leaned closer to his sister. "Perhaps Cleo wants people to like her for her character, not because she can have them dismissed."

"Why would she want anyone dismissed? They all do such a splendid job. They wouldn't be here if they didn't."

Floyd rolled his eyes. Neither his sister nor father saw it.

Our soup course arrived along with a group of carolers from the nearby boys' home who sang Christmas carols before being led out by their teacher. When the musicians resumed their regular playing, we resumed our conversation. We chatted easily enough about Cambridge and my life there, and about the features of the hotel that I needed to know. It seemed nothing was off limits to me. I could go where I pleased.

"The staff don't live here?" I asked. Mr. Armitage had mentioned only the senior staff lived on the ground floor. He hadn't spoken about the rest.

"Unmarried staff were moved off-site into residence halls years ago," Uncle Ronald told me. "They used to be accommodated on the top floor prior to that, but installing the lifts meant those rooms could be renovated and turned into guest rooms. Five flights of stairs was a little too much to ask of the guests."

But not the staff, apparently.

Flossy pulled a face. "It used to be exhausting going up to our rooms on the fourth floor."

"You can't possibly remember that," her brother said. "You were very young when the lifts were put in."

"Old enough to remember. Anyway, the fifth floor now has some of the best rooms. Not as good as the fourth floor suites, naturally, but the guests like the view."

"Except for Mrs. Cavendish-Dyer," Floyd said, reaching for his wineglass again. "The old bat isn't satisfied with anything."

"Floyd," Uncle Ronald bit off. "Don't speak that way about a guest."

"No one can hear me, and Cleo is family." Floyd drained his glass and beckoned a waiter standing nearby to refill it.

Uncle Ronald didn't take his hard glare off his son, but Floyd pretended not to notice. He raised his refilled glass in salute to me.

"The ball," Flossy said suddenly and rather loudly. "You must both convince Cleo to attend and to wear something other than black. An exception to the rules of mourning should be made for balls, don't you think?"

Her breezy chatter didn't hide the fact that her father and brother were waging a silent battle with one another, but it did lead them to call a truce. Both men turned to me and, taking Flossy's side, tried to convince me to attend the New Year's Eve ball.

"Perhaps I'll defer to my aunt on this matter," I told them. "I'm sure she'll be able to guide me." As a means to shutting down the conversation, it was successful. But mention of my aunt brought a taut silence and everyone gave their desserts a great deal of attention.

Uncle Ronald went to speak to Mr. Armitage after dinner while Floyd, Flossy and I waited for the lift. Once his father was out of sight, however, Floyd broke away.

"Well then, I'm off." He turned, blew us both a kiss as he walked backwards, beckoning one of the porters to fetch him his cloak.

Flossy clicked her tongue. "I wish he'd take me with him, but he flatly refuses."

"Where does he go?" I asked.

"Out with his friends. I'm not sure where, but at least it's out. Living here can be so stifling. Father never lets me go anywhere."

I watched her retreating brother as the porter handed him his cloak and hat. He looked like a man with a world of opportunity at his fingertips. Given he was wealthy and male, he had no reason to think otherwise.

"Father doesn't like Floyd going out all the time, but he tolerates it. Some of Floyd's friends are the sons of very influential people, many of whom are our guests when they come to London." Flossy pressed the Call button again and looked up. "It must be stuck. This wouldn't happen if we installed a new one."

I waited a few more moments then gave up. "Shall we take the stairs?"

Flossy wrinkled her little pug nose. "I'll wait. John will have it fixed soon."

I didn't want to wait and headed up the stairs, only to stop on what I guessed to be the landing between the second and third floors when I heard a woman's raised voice coming from somewhere above. I peered up the stairwell and could just make out two women talking far above.

"You should not be here," the woman scolded.

"Sorry, Mrs. Kettering." I had to strain to hear the younger voice. If we hadn't been standing in a stairwell, I suspected her voice wouldn't have carried.

"You should be on the second," Mrs. Kettering said. "Why were you on the fifth?"

"I lost count."

"You can't count to two?"

"No, Mrs. Kettering. I mean, yes, I can, I just got confused."

Silence, then, "I know your kind, Edith," Mrs. Kettering went on, her voice a guttural snarl. "If I catch you somewhere you ought not to be again, you will be dismissed. Is that clear?"

I imagined the girl named Edith cowering beneath the housekeeper's glare as she muttered something I couldn't hear.

"Go and turn down the beds on level two," Mrs. Kettering snapped. "It's getting late."

Blazes! They were coming my way and we would pass one another on the stairs. I stepped heavily to warn them I was there and gave a smile and a nod as I passed the maid named Edith and then Mrs. Kettering, some steps behind. One set of footsteps continued on but the second set stopped. I could feel Mrs. Kettering's glare on my back, but I kept going. I preferred to meet her officially another time, when she wasn't so riled and I wasn't feeling guilty for eavesdropping.

I exited the staircase on level four. There was no sign of Flossy as I headed along the corridor. I stopped abruptly outside my door. It was ajar. Who would enter my room while I was at dinner? Indeed, who had a key, for I was quite certain I'd locked it?

I pushed the door open wider. A woman hummed, the sound coming from the bedroom. I tiptoed through the sitting room to the bedroom door and let out a pent-up breath. A maid plumped up a pillow. She stopped humming when she spotted me.

She smiled broadly. "Good evening, Miss Fox. I wasn't sure if you wanted your bed turned down, since I haven't received your instructions yet, so I took the liberty of doing so anyway. I hope you don't mind."

"Thank you, that's very kind, but there's no need."

Her large black eyes blinked back at me. "Are you sure? It's no trouble. I do all the rooms on this floor when it's my evening. All of the family want their beds turned down."

"Then by all means you should do mine too. Thank you…"

"Harmony." She beamed again and continued plumping. "How has your first day at The Mayfair been?"

"Very pleasant, thank you. All the staff seem nice."

"So you haven't met Mrs. Kettering yet."

I laughed and she smiled back, although looked confused by my reaction. "I overheard her scolding a maid just now in the stairwell," I said. "She was supposed to be turning down beds on the second floor but had met Mrs. Kettering on the fifth."

"That would be Edith on level two tonight. If she was on level five, she probably deserved a scolding." Harmony frowned. "What was she doing all the way up there? And what was Mrs. Kettering doing, I wonder?" She smoothed down the turned edge of the bed cover then straightened. She was tall, probably about my age, with a slender figure and black hair pulled severely into an arrangement beneath her white cap. A few springy curls had escaped and brushed her forehead. From time to time, she pushed them away with the back of her hand.

I wasn't sure what to do while Harmony went about her work of turning down the bed so I sat at the desk and pretended to write a letter. After a few minutes, the maid cleared her throat. I turned to see her standing in the doorway to the bedroom.

"Would you like me to unpack your things?" she asked.

"I've already unpacked."

"Then I'll put your bag away for you."

"That's all right. It needs to go up high. I'll ask one of the men to do it."

Instead of returning to the bedroom, she headed for the front door. "We don't need men."

She left the suite and returned a moment later with a step ladder. She opened the door of the floor-to-ceiling wardrobe and set the ladder in place then hefted my empty bag and hat box up to the top shelf.

"The trunk can be stored elsewhere in the hotel," she said, stepping down. "You won't be needing it." She dusted off her hands and folded up the ladder. "Anything else? Do you require something to eat?"

"I just ate."

"A cup of chocolate? Our chefs make the most delicious hot chocolate." Her eyes half-closed in pleasure. "I've tried it twice when there was some left over."

"Perhaps later. Flossy told me I can use the speaking tube and order what I want and a footman will deliver it from the kitchen." I pointed at the brass mouthpiece.

"You can, but I thought since I'm here I might as well be useful." She carried the ladder through to the sitting room and looked around. After a moment, she leaned the ladder against the edge of the desk and assembled the papers I'd left scattered about. She set them down in a neat stack and flipped the lid closed on the inkwell.

She turned to me and smiled. "Anything else?"

"All is in order, thank you, Harmony."

"Do you have any mending? I'm very good with a needle and thread."

"No mending."

"Would you like me to air out your clothes for the morning?"

"I'll be wearing this again."

Her smile slipped a little. "But it's Christmas Day. Do you have something special to wear?"

"I'll put some ribbons in my hair."

"Oh. Well then, perhaps I could help you undress and put on your night clothes."

"I can do it myself, thank you."

"What about your hair?" She stepped closer and, thanks to her height, inspected my arrangement from above.

"I can also do my hair myself," I assured her. "It's not complicated."

She sighed.

"I appreciate your offer, Harmony, but there's really no need to fuss. I'm used to taking care of myself. I've never had a maid before."

"You haven't? But you're a Bainbridge."

"Actually, I'm a Fox. We're the Bainbridges' poor relations." I attempted a laugh but it fell flat when Harmony gave me a blank look. I supposed her notion of poor and mine were quite different, and it wasn't fair of me to call myself that when I was living in a luxury hotel where she worked.

"I just want to be of use," she said before I could change the subject. "We don't have many guests at the moment, and I find myself idle most evenings back at the residence hall. I like to do a little sewing or spot cleaning while we maids chat until bedtime. Some guests require my assistance of an evening, but most ladies bring their own maids. It'll be busy closer to the ball, of course, but until then..." She shrugged and her darting gaze looked around the room again. Suddenly her face brightened. "I could fix your hair in the morning. Something a little more elaborate."

I touched my hair. Elaborate had never really been something I could manage on my own, and my grandmother hadn't been any help. She preferred old fashioned simple styles. Fortunately I rarely attended events that required complicated arrangements.

"Please say yes," Harmony said. "I can come in after my early duties are accomplished and before I have to clean the rooms."

"You work long hours."

"I have two half days off a week, which is more than most maids at country manors. Well? Shall I do your hair each morning? Your cousin has hers done, and Lady Bainbridge too, when she leaves her room."

"Very well. But only if you don't have too much work to do. I don't want to add to your burden."

She smiled and picked up the ladder. "I'll see you at eight tomorrow, Christmas morning. Goodnight, Miss Fox. I hope your first night in your new home won't feel too strange."

I smiled back. "Thank you, Harmony. I think I'm going to like it here."

* * *

IT WAS CLOSER to eight-thirty when Harmony knocked on my door in the morning. She rushed in, a little out of breath, her dark eyes huge.

"I'm sorry for my lateness," she said, a hand to her stomach.

"You look flustered. Is everything all right?"

She shook her head. "Something terrible has happened. Mrs. Warrick from room three-two-four died overnight."

"How awful. What did she die of?"

"That's the terrible thing. They're saying she was murdered."

CHAPTER 3

I directed Harmony to my sitting room but she refused to sit on the sofa. "I'm all right. Just a little shaken."

I poured her a glass of water from the jug and handed it to her. She wrapped both hands around it and drank.

"Better?" I asked when she passed the glass back.

She rose and smoothed down her apron. "Thank you, Miss Fox. Now, come and take a seat at the dressing table, and let's do something pretty with your hair. Lord! I almost forgot! Merry Christmas."

"Merry Christmas to you too, although there's nothing merry about it now. That poor woman."

Harmony still looked shaken, but her hands were steady enough as she brushed out my hair. Her gaze, however, seemed unfocused. "I don't understand, though," she said, as if we'd been in the middle of a conversation. "Why would one of the staff want to poison her?"

"Poisoned!"

"The police are questioning Danny, the footman who brought her hot chocolate last night."

"They think he did it?"

"It seems so."

"Does he have a motive?"

"Motive?" she echoed.

"A reason for killing Mrs. Warrick?"

She scooped my hair back with the brush, letting it cascade over her other hand. "She reported him after he spilled hot chocolate on her fur coat the night before last. He ruined it, so she said. She demanded the money to replace it be taken out of his wages." She clicked her tongue. "It would take Danny a year to replace something so valuable. He was cross with her, and quite rightly so, but not enough to kill her." She stopped brushing and her gaze connected with mine in the mirror. "I'm worried the police will think it is reason enough. Lord knows, men have hanged based on less evidence."

"I'm sure the manager will vouch for Danny."

She put down the brush and started parting my hair. "Mr. Hobart is a good man."

"So the police are here now?"

She nodded. "They've inspected the room and taken the cup away for testing. They're about to interview staff."

"That's promising. It means they're keeping an open mind and don't blame that particular footman."

"True, but what if they come up with another suspect amongst the staff? No good will come of this for us," she warned. "We'll all be tainted now, from the lowliest scullery maid right up to your uncle. The bad publicity will cause all sorts of problems, particularly if the killer isn't caught before the ball. Can you imagine if the ball is canceled? That's our major event of the winter. If it's canceled, the reservations will follow. It could be a disaster for the hotel."

My uncle must be very worried. The newspapers would relish splashing details of the murder across their front pages.

Harmony placed some hair pins between her lips and spoke around them. "Sir Ronald will want the killer caught quickly to minimize scandal. I'm afraid the police won't be thorough enough in their search for the killer, and will blame the easiest culprit."

"Danny." I handed her more pins as she used up the last between her lips. "Don't worry about an elaborate arrangement this morning, Harmony. The sooner you're done, the sooner I can find out what's happening."

It might not be my business, but I wanted to know more details. My uncle could railroad the police into rushing their investigation for the sake of the hotel's reputation. And as Harmony feared, the person to suffer could very well be an innocent employee.

* * *

I FOUND Floyd yawning in the corridor just outside his father's office. Low voices could be heard on the other side of the door, but other than being male, I couldn't determine who they belonged to.

"Merry Christmas," Floyd said wryly. "By the look on your face, I suspect you've heard."

"I did. How awful."

"Father is beside himself with worry. He's talking to the police now, but they're refusing to make an arrest without more evidence."

"I'm glad they're being thorough."

"Thorough?" He grunted. "I wish they'd just bloody get on with it. The sooner they arrest someone, the better. The hotel can't afford for this to drag on."

"Surely it's only better if the *right* someone is arrested."

He grunted again.

A door opened further along the corridor, and Flossy emerged, her hair down around her shoulders and a dressing gown thrown over her nightdress. "My maid just told me what happened," she said as she rushed towards us. "Poor Mrs. Warrick. And on Christmas Day, too."

"You knew her well?" I asked, taking the hand she stretched out to me.

"Only by sight. I'd never met her. She was the lady waiting at the lift with us yesterday."

I remembered her. She'd talked to herself about a man she'd seen who was out of place in the hotel. She'd been looking in Mr. Armitage's direction as she said it.

Floyd indicated his father's office door. "Now that we're all together, we might as well get this over with. The police want to question the three of us about our movements last night."

"Us?" Flossy clutched her nightgown closed at her throat. "Why?"

42

Her brother waggled his brows at her. "Because they think one of us did it."

She gasped, and he chuckled.

"They're just following a process," I assured her. "It doesn't mean anything. They'll probably ask all the staff what they were doing at the time of the murder."

Flossy went pale. "Murder," she whispered. "It's so awful to have the hotel's good name dragged through the mud like this, and just before the ball, too. What if our friends get wind of it and don't come?"

I expected Floyd to tease her to make light of it, but he just muttered, "Indeed."

He knocked and opened the door. A uniformed constable stood beside the bookshelf, a notebook in hand. A second man, dressed in a dark gray suit, sat at the desk opposite Uncle Ronald. He looked familiar, but if it weren't for his distinctive bright blue eyes, I wouldn't have guessed why. What was a relative of Mr. Hobart's doing in Uncle Ronald's office after a murder?

"Ah, the rest of the family," he said, rising. "Come in, come in. The sooner we get these interviews over with, the sooner we can move on and enjoy Christmas festivities, although it'll be difficult to get into the spirit, I imagine." He extended his hand to Floyd. "Detective Inspector Hobart, Scotland Yard."

"Hobart?" Floyd glanced at his father.

"Your manager is my brother," the detective said.

"Delighted to meet you," Flossy said, putting out her hand. "Please excuse my appearance."

The detective inspector grasped her hand loosely and seemed unsure whether to shake it, kiss it, or bow over it. He let it go quickly and shook mine when I extended it to him as Floyd had done.

"You must be Florence," he said to me. "I see the resemblance with your brother."

"I'm Cleo Fox," I said. "Sir Ronald's niece. Flossy is Floyd's sister." I indicated my cousin.

The inspector put up his hands. "My apologies to you both."

"Get on with it," Uncle Ronald growled. "This is a waste of time, anyway. None of us did it."

"Perhaps one of you saw something relevant. Telling me where you were last evening might bring important evidence to light."

"Approximately what time did the murder take place?" I asked.

"I'd rather not speculate here and now. I'm inquiring about everyone's movements throughout the late afternoon and evening, just to be sure."

"Did she dine in the dining room?"

"If you wouldn't mind detailing your movements, Miss Fox."

I told him I'd written letters then been taken on a tour by Mr. Armitage, which produced a small smile on the detective's lips. "I dined with my uncle and cousins at eight, then retired to my rooms. I went to bed a little before eleven. I awoke at seven-thirty this morning, but didn't hear of the murder until just now when a maid mentioned it."

The constable scribbled furiously in his notepad throughout my retelling. Flossy recounted her evening next, but it was as uneventful as mine. She sat with her mother after dinner then went to bed. Uncle Ronald worked in his office until midnight after having a brief discussion with Mr. Armitage at the conclusion of our dinner. Floyd said he went out.

"Where did you go?" Detective Inspector Hobart asked.

"To a gentleman's club."

"The name of the club?"

"You wouldn't know it. It's very private."

"Nevertheless." The detective waited, his face friendly and eyes sparkling in the pale morning light filtering through the window.

"Does it matter?" Uncle Ronald spat. "My son isn't the murderer. He wasn't here. None of us poisoned Mrs. Warrick." He flicked his hand towards the door. "Do your job, Inspector, or I'll have you replaced. I want this matter resolved today."

"I'll do my best, but it's unlikely we'll have an answer today. There are a lot of staff and guests to interview—"

"Do *not* talk to the guests! Is that understood? They are not to be bothered."

The inspector pursed his lips, neither agreeing nor disagreeing. The two men entered a glaring match until the inspector departed the office. The constable followed.

Floyd flopped onto a chair. "Incompetent fool. Clearly our Hobart got all the brains in the family."

Uncle Ronald glowered at him from beneath the deep shelf of his brow. Floyd swallowed heavily and rose. He left the office. Flossy and I followed.

While Floyd and Flossy returned to their rooms, I joined Detective Inspector Hobart and his constable at the lift.

"The stairs are faster," I said.

"So I discovered on the way up." The inspector smiled at me. "You've just arrived at the hotel, I believe."

"Yesterday afternoon."

"What a shocking introduction to your new home, and on Christmas Day too, a day of peace and goodwill. I hope this doesn't reflect poorly on The Mayfair in your eyes. The hotel has an exemplary reputation."

"I didn't think murders happened very often here, but thank you for the reassurance."

He chuckled. "We'll take the stairs, Constable. The lift doesn't seem like the most efficient device."

"May I join you?" I asked, following anyway.

The stairwell was quiet, but I knew from experience that voices echoed so I kept mine low. "Is it true you suspect the footman who delivered Mrs. Warrick's hot chocolate last night?"

The detective's step slowed. "I'm keeping an open mind at this juncture."

"That is a relief because I have it on good authority that he's not the type to commit murder just because Mrs. Warrick accused him of ruining her fur coat."

"In my experience, people who are not the type commit murder all the time." He softened his harsh statement with a smile. "But I don't expect an innocent young woman such as yourself to know that."

He quickened his pace, perhaps in the hope of leaving me

behind. I picked up my skirts so as not to trip over them as I kept up.

"Was the poison definitely in her pot of hot chocolate?"

He hesitated. "The pot and cup have been taken away for testing, along with the teacup delivered by the maid who discovered the body this morning."

That was neither confirmation nor denial. Surely if the chocolate cup held the poison, it could be smelled or a residue had been left behind.

"Have you questioned the footman who delivered it?" I asked.

"I have."

"And the chef who made it?"

"Yes."

I waited, but he offered no more information. "I assume they both deny adding poison to the pot of chocolate." Again, I waited, but he said nothing. "Did anyone else handle the pot in the meantime?"

"That is not yet clear."

"I don't understand. Was the chocolate unattended between the chef making it and the footman collecting it or was it not?"

He stopped on the top step of the next flight. By my estimation, we were somewhere between the second and first floor. "You ask a lot of questions."

"I simply want to understand how it could have happened that a guest was poisoned and no one knows who put the poison into her cup."

"As do I, Miss Fox. As do I."

He continued on and I almost let him go. Almost.

"I thought of one more question," I said.

"Only one?" he muttered. The constable snickered, but it withered when the inspector glared at him.

"I appreciate your patience in answering me, Inspector," I said in my sweetest voice. "You've been most indulgent. My question is, was there any sign the door to Mrs. Warrick's room had been forced? Was the lock broken?"

The silence was peppered with the taps of our footsteps on the stairs, and finally broken by the constable clearing his throat.

"If it were forced open," I went on, "that means the footman didn't do it. Mrs. Warrick would have let him in if she was expecting him."

"Is that so?" the inspector asked. I detected a hint of humor in the idle question. I wasn't sure if my attempt at detecting amused him or he was laughing at my lurching to conclusions. He gave no hint whether my conclusion was correct or not. I needed to find out.

"So it *was* forced," I said, watching him closely.

He stepped into the foyer. "If you'll excuse me, Miss Fox, I have staff to interview."

Damnation. He'd given nothing away. He'd not so much as flickered an eyelash.

The inspector and constable were met by a very grave looking Mr. Hobart who directed them through to the vestibule. I followed at a distance, but Mr. Hobart closed the doors to the dining room where a number of staff waited. The manager did not join them.

"Is something the matter, Miss Fox?" he asked. "Did you have something to tell the inspector?"

"You mean your brother?"

"Ah. He told you."

"Yes, but he didn't have to. You're very alike and have the same surname. Is there no one else you're related to? The prime minister, perhaps?"

He smiled, and for the first time, it seemed genuine. "I don't think you'll come across more of us, unless my wife pays a call on me here. Sometimes she stops by if she's out shopping. She likes to see Harry. He doesn't call on us at home as much as he ought."

"He gets fed too well here, I suspect. You know what young men are like. Once they grow up and leave home they only return for their mother's cooking—or their aunt's, in your instance."

"I suspect you're right. The food here is better than what he'd get at home." Mr. Hobart nodded at the closed dining room door. "His parents often scold him for not visiting on his days off. I don't think my brother has seen him yet, but I suspect he'll receive just such a scolding when it's his turn to be interviewed."

"The detective inspector is Mr. Armitage's father? But their surnames are different."

He signaled that I should walk with him out of the vestibule to the foyer. "Harry is an orphan. He was taken in by my brother and sister-in-law at aged thirteen, but he wanted to keep his real name. He'd grown used to it, I suppose."

It was quite a story, and I wanted to know more, but Mr. Hobart spotted a guest trying to attract his attention and excused himself.

I watched him greet the guest with a smile. Now I knew why he looked nothing like Mr. Armitage, although there was a similarity in their manner. They both had a way of putting others at ease, yet there was a quiet authority about them too. Instead of being a family trait, that manner must have been learned by Mr. Armitage as he studied at his uncle's side all these years. Mr. Armitage would be a worthy successor to the role of hotel manager when Mr. Hobart retired.

The guest to whom Mr. Hobart spoke moved off. He looked somewhat familiar, but it took me a moment to place him. He'd been speaking to Mr. Armitage yesterday afternoon when Mrs. Warrick muttered to herself about a man who ought not to be in the hotel.

It was quite a strange comment to make, now that I thought about it. *Who* shouldn't be in a hotel? Anyone could walk into the foyer.

On the other hand, not everyone would walk into the foyer of a *luxury* hotel. The rude greeting I'd received from the doorman upon my arrival was testament to that. Or, perhaps Mrs. Warrick was referring to a luxury hotel in *London*. There were so many things she could have meant. She had also mentioned he looked different and it had been years since she'd seen him.

There'd been three men in her line of sight—the guest who was now leaving the hotel clutching an umbrella, Mr. Armitage, and another man. Hopefully when I saw him again, I would recognize him. It might be important.

Or it might not. Perhaps I was seeing potential suspects where there were none. Grandmama called my imagination vivid, and my father had gently chastised me on more than one occasion for daydreaming instead of studying.

"That's a wistful smile," said a familiar voice. I looked up to see Mr. Armitage striding towards me. "There aren't too many smiles around the hotel this morning, despite it being Christmas Day."

"You're right, it's insensitive of me. Poor Mrs. Warrick."

"That's not what I meant. There's no need for you to stop smiling. You didn't know her."

"Did you?"

He looked taken aback by my earnest question. "I met her when she checked in, and again when there was an incident with one of the footmen."

"Danny, the one who is now the prime suspect?"

"Is he?" The sudden change from friendly to steely wasn't lost on me. "Has the detective inspector confided in you?"

Despite being disappointed with the change my questions had produced in him, I forged on. Answers were more important than flirting. "Your father confide in me? No, of course he hasn't. But I've heard from one of the maids that Danny delivered the poisoned cup of hot chocolate to Mrs. Warrick and that she had a prior grievance with him."

"That grievance was resolved before her murder, and there was no poison residue left in that cup, I believe."

It seemed the detective had confided more to his son than he had to me. Mr. Armitage realized he'd said too much. He crossed his arms. "Leave the detecting to the police, Miss Fox."

"I'd be glad to."

Mr. Armitage's gaze narrowed. "My father is very thorough."

"I'm sure he is."

His gaze narrowed further. "You're agreeing with me too readily."

"I'm sorry. Do you want me to disagree with you?"

He sucked in a breath between his teeth. It seemed to dissolve his frustration with me somewhat. His smooth smile returned again, but his eyes held none of their earlier warmth. "Enjoy your morning, Miss Fox. Please don't hesitate to ask one of the staff if you require something." He bowed and walked off.

I sighed. I had enjoyed seeing a more relaxed side to Mr. Armitage before our little confrontation, but it would seem my questions were not welcome. Truly, I hadn't thought I'd been attacking his father's reputation, but it must have come across that way. Perhaps I ought to apologize.

Then again, I wasn't sure I had anything to apologize for. Mr. Armitage had simply read more into my responses than had been there.

"Cleo! There you are." Flossy hurried towards me from the direction of the lift. "I've been looking for you everywhere. Come with me. Mother is awake and wishes to see you."

Finally, I would meet her. I followed Flossy back into the lift and we headed up to level four. She knocked on the door to her parents' suite and a voice inside bade us enter.

A thin woman sitting on the sofa smiled and held out a bony hand to me and another to Flossy. "You must be Cleopatra. Merry Christmas, my dear."

She inspected me, giving me an opportunity to inspect her in turn. Instinctively, tears welled in my eyes. There was a remarkable resemblance to my mother, despite Aunt Lilian's gaunt features and my memories of my mother being several years old. The sea-green eyes had been my mother's most remarkable feature and were the same for my aunt. The gray streaks in her hair didn't completely override the natural almond shade and her skin resembled the finest porcelain. Her high cheekbones would have given her a regal air if not for the hollows below. She was an older, thinner version of my mother.

"You look so much like her." The words could have easily come from me but it was my aunt who whispered them. Her eyes shone as she patted the sofa beside her. "Come and sit with me, Cleopatra. Flossy, the gift."

"She goes by Cleo," Flossy said as she handed a small box to her mother.

Aunt Lilian gave it to me. "Merry Christmas."

"Oh, I can't accept it," I said. "I'm afraid I didn't get you anything."

Aunt Lilian thrust the box into my hand. "It's just a trinket. We were going to exchange gifts all together but your uncle informed me he's too busy now, thanks to that poor woman's murder. He might not even join us for luncheon."

I opened the box to reveal a silver brooch in the shape of a butterfly, its wings made of blue enamel. I certainly wouldn't describe it as a trinket. I pinned it to my dress. "Thank you. It's lovely."

She smiled. "It looks very fetching on you. Now, tell me everything about your life. I've missed so much of it. And you've missed so much of ours, too. Has Flossy been a good cousin while I've suffered with my headaches? Have you met Floyd? Dear Floyd, such a rascal, isn't he, Flossy? In a good way, of course. And what do you think of the hotel?"

Flossy laid a hand on her mother's shoulder. Going by Aunt Lilian's wince, she squeezed it quite hard.

I tried to answer all of my aunt's questions while she listened. There wasn't much to say about my life, but I gave her an account of the years since my parents' deaths. Despite being a short retelling, my aunt seemed to lose concentration. Her gaze darted about the room and it took Flossy clearing her throat to bring her focus back to me.

Despite the too-thin figure and drawn features, she was a vibrant woman with considerable energy. She found it difficult to sit still, and when I finished speaking, she suddenly rose.

"Shall we go downstairs?" she said. "Or perhaps for a walk. Would you like to shop with us, Cleo? Flossy, don't you think Cleo would like some new things?"

"The shops are closed," Flossy reminded her. "It's Christmas day."

Aunt Lilian laughed. "Of course it is. Is it time for our feast yet?"

"Almost," Flossy said. "But I'm not sure we ought to leave our rooms. There's a murderer about."

"Nobody will try to murder us, dear." Aunt Lilian flashed a smile and in that moment, I saw the famous beauty she'd supposedly been her in youth. "I would very much like to go out before luncheon. Where are my gloves? Flossy, have you seen my tan gloves?"

Flossy fetched gloves and hat for her mother, and she and I fetched our own things while her mother waited in the corridor. When I emerged from my suite, Aunt Lilian was pacing the floor near the stairs.

"We'll walk down," she said. "The lift is too slow."

Flossy sighed.

Outside, we walked for an hour at a brisk pace that had Flossy puffing heavily and me feeling nicely warm. All the shops were closed for Christmas Day, but Aunt Lilian pointed out their favorites, commenting on why such-and-such was the best for parasols, or so-and-so made the finest boots.

We walked through Hyde Park and returned to the hotel from the opposite direction from which we'd left. Although Aunt Lilian set the brisk pace, she seemed to deflate very quickly. By the time we reached the hotel, she claimed she had a headache and needed a rest. Without being asked, Flossy led her away. She mouthed an apology to me over her shoulder as the doorman greeted them and opened the door.

The doorman waited after they disappeared through it, staring straight ahead.

"Merry Christmas," I said to him. "Do you remember me from yesterday?"

"Yes, Miss Fox." His cheeks pinked, but still he did not look at me. "Merry Christmas to you too."

The porter who'd taken my bags the day before smirked and rocked back on his heels. He was enjoying this. The doorman was not, if his increasingly reddening cheeks were anything to go by.

The doorman swallowed. "I'd like to apologize for my greeting last time we met. It was unforgiveable. Let me assure you, it won't happen again."

I sighed theatrically. "I will *try* to forgive you. That's all I can promise at this point."

He bowed stiffly. "You're very generous. Very generous indeed."

The porter made a snorting sound as he tried to cover his laugh. The doorman's jaw hardened.

"It seems I'm at a disadvantage," I went on.

"No, Miss Fox, I assure you there is no disadvantage intended," the doorman said. "If there is some way I can make you feel less at a disadvantage, please allow me to perform the task."

"There is, as it happens. You can tell me your name."

He went quite still. "Why?" He must suspect I was going to inform the manager of his ill-mannered greeting yesterday.

"Because I didn't catch it."

"I, er…"

"He's Frank, miss," said the porter, stepping forward. "And I'm Gilbert, but everyone calls me Goliath."

"I can see where the moniker comes from. I've never seen anyone as tall as you."

He puffed out his chest, earning an eye-roll from Frank.

"May I say something that should have been said yesterday?" Goliath asked me.

"Of course. What is it?"

"Welcome to The Mayfair." He bowed deeply.

Frank eyed the porter as if he'd stolen money right out of his pocket.

"Thank you, Goliath." I strode past Frank, still holding the door open. "And thank *you*, Frank."

"Me?" he blurted. "Why?"

"For holding the door. You do it with such aplomb. May I offer some advice, however?"

"Please do."

"A smile wouldn't go astray."

He gave me a hard smile, revealing crooked front teeth.

"Perhaps with a little less ferocity, however." I winked at Goliath and he chuckled. Frank continued with his forced smile as I passed him and entered the hotel.

* * *

AUNT LILIAN WAS FULLY RESTED by the time we sat down to luncheon. Uncle Ronald managed to join us after all, and we enjoyed a feast of turkey, ham, and mince pies in the dining room, along with the hotel guests. The pop of Christmas crackers, chatter and laughter seemed out of place considering a murder had taken place overnight just upstairs.

Indeed, it was the strangest Christmas day I'd ever experienced. I hadn't gone to church as I usually would in the morning, and my family spent much of the luncheon exchanging pleasantries with guests rather than each other. They even sought out particular guests between courses. The only times all five of us sat together was to eat, and even then their attention often diverted to one neighboring table or another as if deciding who they'd speak to next. It lacked the intimacy and warmth I was used to. I'd never missed my grandparents more, and my parents too.

I retired to my suite after luncheon and was reading a book when Harmony sought me out. I needed little convincing to go with her to the staff parlor where Danny the footman waited. Apparently she suggested he tell me everything he'd told the inspector. When I asked her why, she merely said she suspected I would put in a good word for him.

"I collected her chocolate pot and cup from the kitchen, same as every other night," Danny said.

Like all the footmen and waiters I'd seen in the hotel, he was handsome and young. But Danny's youthful good looks were marred by an anxious frown. He hadn't been arrested, thankfully, but he'd been ordered not to work, and a constable stood outside the parlor door. Danny was essentially a prisoner in the hotel.

"How did you know it was Mrs. Warrick's pot of chocolate?" I asked. "I assume there are pots of chocolate going from the kitchen up to the guests all the time of an evening."

"From the label."

I gave him a blank look.

"Mrs. Warrick's hot chocolate is a regular order," he explained. "She doesn't have to call down to the kitchen. Regular orders get made as necessary and a footman collects them. The chef writes the guest's name and room number on a label and leaves it with the tray. There were only three of us footman working last night, and we're always coming and going. I saw the pot and cup when I entered the kitchen, read the label, and took it up to Mrs. Warrick."

"And she was definitely alive when you delivered it?"

"Yes! She scolded me for being late, but I swear I wasn't. Ugly old bat." He all but spat the words. "I placed the tray on the table and asked her if she required anything else. She didn't even answer me. She just kept complaining that I was late with the hot chocolate. She was alive the whole time, I swear to you." He lowered his head and dragged a hand through already ragged hair. "The detective mustn't believe me or he wouldn't be asking everyone where they were *before* eleven, which is when I saw her. He's even asking what everyone was doing in the late afternoon! Why? Can't he check if she ate dinner in the dining room or in her own room?"

Harmony squeezed his shoulder. "It's all right, Danny. We believe you, and Miss Fox is going to help the police find who really did it."

I blinked at her. "I don't—"

"Thank you, Miss Fox." Danny gave me a wobbly smile. "It means a lot to me to have one of the Bainbridges on my side."

"I'm sure they're all on your side, Danny," I said. "Everyone wants to find the truth. Nobody wants a murderer roaming around the hotel." The thought chilled me. My words weren't empty ones. I did want to find the real killer. Like Harmony, I didn't think Danny was the type.

But as Detective Inspector Hobart said, killers did not have a type. Anyone was capable of murder, and poison was the weapon of choice for absentee murderers.

"Mr. Hobart and Mr. Armitage believe you're innocent," Harmony assured Danny. "Mr. Hobart told us so this morning, in the dining room, when we gathered to be interviewed by his brother the detective."

"Thanks, Harmony." Danny glanced at the door. "The sooner you find the killer, the sooner I can get back to work."

"And the better we can avoid scandal." Harmony squeezed his shoulder again.

It didn't cheer Danny up. "Will this affect the ball?"

"It might, if we don't find the killer soon. No one will want to stay here with a murderer roaming about, like Miss Fox said."

We went to leave, but I paused at the door. "Did you notice anyone in or near the kitchen last night who shouldn't have been there?"

Danny shook his head.

Harmony and I left, giving the constable smiles of thanks as we walked towards the stairs. Instead of going up, we went down.

When Mr. Armitage had taken me on a tour, we'd not stepped very far into the kitchen. Today, Harmony and I ventured beyond the door into the hot, pulsing, noisy space. Chefs dressed all in white worked at long counters or by the stoves, some shouting orders with others hurrying to carry them out. A robust man with red cheeks sang an operatic tune as he chopped potatoes, while the sweating chef next to him downed the contents of a tankard in one gulp. Shelves stacked with pots and pans ranged against the back wall and electric bulbs hung from long wires over the benches to better cast their light in the windowless basement. A short fellow with curled moustache ends strolled between the other staff, hands at his back, inspecting the work of each man and sometimes tasting the contents of a pot.

"The *chef de cuisine* calls it the heart of the hotel," Harmony said with a nod at the short man, "but I think it should be called the bowels, seeing as it's located in the basement and all the food is processed here."

"He's the kitchen manager?" I asked. "We should speak with him."

She grasped my arm and held me back. "Lord, no. He'll order us out." She waited until he'd moved further into the kitchen, his back turned, then she beckoned to one of the other chefs. "Victor is one of the junior cooks. He'll talk to us."

Victor's soft features would have given him a baby-faced appearance if not for the white scar across his cheek. He sauntered over, carrying a large knife, and greeted Harmony with a curt nod. He gave me a very thorough inspection as Harmony introduced us and I too received a nod.

"Were you working last night?" Harmony asked.

Victor tossed the knife and caught it by the handle without taking his gaze off Harmony. "Aye."

"Miss Fox wants to ask you some questions."

He tossed the knife in the air again, catching it deftly, before repeating the motion over and over. He didn't once look at the knife whereas I couldn't take my gaze off it. "Who're you, Miss Fox?" he asked in a Cockney accent.

"Sir Ronald's niece," Harmony said through a clenched jaw. "Honestly, Victor, you should get out of the kitchen sometimes."

"Why would I want to do that?"

Harmony thrust a hand on her hip. "Will you stop doing that?"

"Doing what?"

She indicated the knife as he tossed it again. "It's very distracting."

"No, it ain't. It's calming. A properly made, well balanced knife is real soothing to handle." He threw the knife up again, but this time caught it on the back of his hand, horizontally. It didn't so much as wobble. "Want me to show you a trick?" he asked me. "Put your hand down on the table and spread your fingers wide."

Harmony gasped. "Do *not* show her that trick! Put your own fingers at risk if you want to show off."

Victor twirled the knife with his fingers then thrust it into the knife belt slung around his hips. Now that his hands were still, I could see the burn scars on his right and the missing tip of his index finger on the left. "So what do you want to know?"

"Did you make the hot chocolate for Mrs. Warrick last night?" I asked.

"Nope, that was Jack, but I was next to him the entire time." He indicated another man by one of the stoves. "The police have already asked me this, but I'll tell you too, Miss Fox. No one came near the pot and Jack ain't the type to poison someone."

"Did anyone else go near Mrs. Warrick's pot of chocolate after he filled it and before Danny collected it?"

"Not that I saw, but I wasn't watching the entire time. After Jack filled it, he wrote the name and room number on a card and placed it on a tray then left the tray on this table." He indicated the table beside the door where a tray with a covered plate on it awaited collection.

"Did you see anyone in or near the kitchen who shouldn't have been there?" I asked.

"Nope, but it's busy in here. Anyone can walk in and out without being noticed."

"You! Go!" shouted someone in a French accent.

I looked up to see the *chef de cuisine* striding towards us. "We just needed a word with Victor about Mrs. Warrick's hot chocolate," I assured him.

Harmony tugged on my arm. "We should go."

"There was no poison in the chocolate!" the chef snapped. The other chefs looked up. The operatic one fell silent. The chatter, shouts and chopping ceased. The only sound came from the bubbling pots. "My kitchen does not have poison! I tell the policeman this, now I tell you, Miss Fock."

"Fox," I said with as much sweetness as I could muster as the head chef bore down on us.

"She's Sir Ronald's niece," Harmony added.

He withdrew a knife from his belt and charged forward, pointing the blade at me. "I do not care if she is queen of England! She does not belong here! There is no poison in my kitchen!"

Harmony and I turned and fled. We raced up the stairs and didn't stop until we reached the warren of service rooms on the ground floor.

Harmony fell back against the wall, puffing, her hand on her stomach. "That was close."

"He wouldn't really have stabbed us," I assured her.

"He wouldn't stab *you*, but I'm fair game. He stabbed one of the cooks once, when the poor fellow dropped a pot of sauce on the floor. Chef later claimed it was an accident, but the other cooks weren't convinced." She pushed off from the wall. "Anyway, we got some answers from Victor."

"Not really. All we learned is that he saw no one out of place in the kitchen and didn't think Jack put poison in Mrs. Warrick's chocolate."

"That's answers, isn't it? So what shall we do next?"

"If we truly want to know if Danny is telling the truth about seeing Mrs. Warrick alive when he delivered her chocolate, we ought to find out if she was at dinner first. One of the waiters will remember her."

"If they don't, she would have given her name and room

number. Mr. Chapman the steward will have that information in his book. We could sneak into his office—"

"Harmony! We are not sneaking about the hotel. Besides, I'm not sure we should continue. You said yourself that Mr. Hobart doesn't believe Danny did it. I'm sure his brother, the detective, will come to the same conclusion too, if he hasn't already."

"You want to stop investigating?" she asked with a pout in her voice.

"I think we ought to leave the detective work to Scotland Yard. I see no reason for them not to be thorough."

"But do you *want* to stop?"

I bit the inside of my cheek. Harmony's eyes were bright, eager. She was enjoying this endeavor. As was I. "We *must* stop," I said. "We don't want to get in the way of Inspector Hobart's investigation."

She crossed her arms. "I thought you were like me, that you wanted answers. I thought you wanted to *do* something."

She was referring to wanting to help Danny, but I couldn't help thinking about my suggestion to my uncle that I hoped to be of some use within the hotel. Even so, I saw no reason to continue with our separate investigation.

"Inspector Hobart will find the killer, Harmony. Don't worry about Danny."

She drummed her fingers on her arm and, for a moment, I thought she'd argue with me. Then she lowered her arms. "I suppose you're right. I better return to work anyway before Mrs. Kettering catches me."

She headed off to the service lift while I returned to the foyer. I spotted Mr. Hobart disappearing into the corridor that housed the offices and private chambers of the senior staff. He walked with Mr. Chapman, the steward, at his side. Now was as good a time as any to ask the manager if there were some small task I could do for him.

He opened the door to Mr. Armitage's office and entered, Mr. Chapman at his heels. Beyond them I could just make out Mr. Armitage, Mrs. Kettering and the detective inspector, all crowded into the small space. Their Christmas luncheon had been as brief as ours, and they'd already returned to the hotel, if they'd even left. I felt sorry for both Mrs. Hobarts, not getting to spend the entire day with their husbands.

I didn't want to interrupt their interviews so I waited outside, my back to the corridor wall.

The door closed but I could still hear the inspector's voice asking where each of the senior staff had been yesterday afternoon and evening. It seemed he still didn't trust that Danny spoke the truth about seeing Mrs. Warrick alive at eleven.

They each answered, but it was Mr. Armitage's response that had me pressing my ear to the door to hear better.

"I dined in my office at about eight as I looked over the day's accounts," he told his father. "I finished around ten, retired to my rooms where I read for an hour before falling asleep."

"And earlier?" Inspector Hobart asked.

"I took Miss Fox for a tour of this level then spoke to Mr. Chapman in the dining room. Following that I spent some time in maintenance, assisting with the lift problem."

"Isn't that a maintenance issue?"

"I was idle and felt like doing something with my hands."

"And prior to your tour with Miss Fox?"

Mr. Armitage paused. "I was in my office, going over today's arrivals and departures. I heard a noise in the corridor and saw Miss Fox wandering about, looking lost."

The liar! He hadn't been in his office when he saw me. He'd been coming out of Mr. Chapman's office. Indeed, he'd done it furtively, opening the door a mere crack and peeking through before emerging. He was checking the coast was clear first. Clear of what? Or whom? Mr. Chapman?

The detective inspector sounded as though he was about to dismiss the group so I hurried away. I didn't want to be caught eavesdropping. I didn't want Mr. Armitage or anyone else offering me polite smiles and innocuous conversation. I needed time to think about what I'd heard, and consider what possible reason Mr. Armitage could have for lying.

But there was only one explanation I could come up with —he was hiding something.

I ought to inform the inspector. In ordinary circumstances, I would do just that. But Mr. Armitage was the inspector's son. If Mr. Armitage turned out to be the murderer, Hobart would cover it up. It wasn't just the lie about his whereabouts before he met me that concerned me. There was also Mrs. Warrick's muttered words as she stepped into the lift—she'd recognized someone. Someone who shouldn't be in the hotel.

And she'd been staring directly at Mr. Armitage as she said it.

CHAPTER 4

I climbed the stairs to retire to my room and think, but by the time I reached the fourth floor, there was only one thought in my mind and I couldn't shake it. If Mr. Armitage was the killer, Detective Inspector Hobart would protect his son. He might even look for an innocent man to blame instead.

A hollowness settled in the pit of my stomach. I liked Mr. Armitage. I liked his uncle, Mr. Hobart, too. But both men were hotel employees and I was their employer's niece. Of course they'd been friendly towards me. Even if I didn't deserve their kindness, they'd bestow it upon me anyway. So if I couldn't trust their outward manner, why should I trust them at all?

It seemed I'd been too hasty in telling Harmony that I wouldn't conduct a separate investigation. I ought to find her and inform her of my decision to resume. She would be the only one I'd inform, however. The fewer people who knew I doubted the inspector's impartiality, the better.

"Cleo! I'm so glad I found you." Flossy waved at me from further along the corridor. "I'm in need of good company. Father is in a lather over the murder." She whispered the word as if speaking it aloud made it more horrid. "Poor Floyd is taking the brunt of his anger since Mr. Hobart has been busy helping Inspector Hobart. Mother is resting and I'm in desperate need of an outing, but I can't go shopping so we'll have to settle for a walk."

Now that I'd made my decision to investigate the murder, all I wanted to do was get on with it. At the top of my list was to talk to the guests who'd been near Mr. Armitage when Mrs. Warrick uttered her damning statement. Unfortunately I couldn't think of an excuse and Flossy hustled me towards my room.

"Get a coat, hat and gloves," she said. "I've already got mine."

I did as ordered and locked the door again. "Do you know all the guests currently staying in the hotel?" I asked her as we waited for the lift.

"Good lord, Cleo, there are so many! We're not terribly busy, admittedly, but there must be…" Her lips moved as she did calculations in her head. "Tons. Too many to know individually. Why?"

"I was curious. Do you know who would know them all?"

"Mr. Hobart and Mr. Armitage. Father once scolded Floyd for not doing as the managers did and study the reservations book each night to learn the names of the guests arriving the following day. Peter would know too, of course, but *after* each guest checks in." The lift arrived, its floor perfectly level with the corridor. John opened the door and smiled. "John knows all the guests too, of course," Flossy added.

"Only those who travel by my ascending room," he said, patting the door as if it were a loyal pet. "Not those who take the stairs." This last he said with a pointed look in my direction as he pushed the lever.

"I like the exercise," I muttered.

"Was there a guest in particular you wanted to know about?" Flossy gave her hands a little clap. "Oh, I know! There's a dashing foreign count staying on level two. You ought to know he's married, Cleo. Not that he's here with his wife." She winked.

I had no idea how to interpret the wink, but John smiled. I felt as though I were being left out of a joke.

"Did either of you notice the gentlemen standing near Mr. Armitage yesterday when we got into the lift?" I didn't want to mention Mrs. Warrick's name in case it led either of them to suspect I was investigating her murder.

Neither could recall the gentlemen, and I decided to try Peter. Unfortunately he was busy at the main counter where four guests stood. Goliath and three other porters waited nearby with luggage, and Mr. Armitage and Mr. Hobart spoke to the guests. Peter looked worried as he accepted the key off a gentleman.

"Oh no," Flossy muttered. "It has started."

"What has?" I asked.

"The exodus. Father's fears are being realized. We managed to get through luncheon before word about the murder got out, but it seems it's out now."

We headed to the luggage counter to collect umbrellas. "I wouldn't go outside, Miss Bainbridge," said Goliath as we passed him. "The newspapermen are like hungry pigs."

The front door was suddenly pushed open and a cacophony of voices surged through along with a figure drenched from head to toe. The door closed behind him, but not before I saw Frank the doorman trying to urge a cluster of men to move along.

The newcomer's sharp gaze settled on Flossy and me. He strode towards us, leaving a trail of drips behind on the tiles. "Excuse me, ladies, can I have a word? What can you tell me about the murder that took place here last night? Did you know the victim?" He reached into his inside coat pocket and whipped out a pencil and notepad.

Flossy shrank away from him. "Leave me alone!"

Mr. Armitage approached, his face set hard, dark eyes flashing. "Get out or you'll be thrown out."

The man put his hands up in surrender. "I'm just trying to make a living, same as you."

"You are not the same as me. Leave."

The towering form of Goliath overshadowed us. "Want help, Mr. Armitage?"

"It's under control, thank you, Goliath. This man was just leaving." Mr. Armitage grabbed the lapel of the journalist's coat and forced him towards the door.

Goliath opened it and Mr. Armitage pushed the man through. He stumbled into the other journalists.

"I think Frank could do with your help," Mr. Armitage said to Goliath.

Goliath touched his forehead in acknowledgement and joined Frank outside. "Move along!" Frank's voice boomed.

"Are you all right?" Mr. Armitage asked us. His gaze quickly danced over Flossy and lingered a little longer on me.

I dipped my head, suddenly feeling guilty for thinking him involved in the murder. Surely he couldn't have done it. He seemed far too honorable. But why had he lied to his own father when he'd questioned him about his movements yesterday afternoon?

"Yes, thank you," Flossy said with a tilt of her chin at the door. "Horrible people, journalists."

"They're just doing their job," Mr. Armitage said.

Flossy seemed a little put out to have her opinion brushed off, but he didn't notice. He watched the guests at the counter, his features still set, fists clenched at his sides. The smooth man who'd greeted me the day before was nowhere in sight.

"Are they all due to leave today?" I asked.

"No."

"They're frightened," I said.

Flossy shivered and rubbed her arms. "I don't blame them."

I put my arm around her. "We'll be all right. The killer chose Mrs. Warrick for a reason, and now that she has been silenced, he has no reason to strike again."

She leaned into me. "Thank you, Cleo. You're probably right. It must be such a comfort being so sensible all the time."

I smiled, despite myself. "Some say comforting, others say dull." I looked up to see Mr. Armitage giving me a strange look. The tightness of his features had softened somewhat, but his eyes were still dark beneath the lowered lids.

He strode off to assist his uncle, attempting to talk the guests out of their early departure.

"I don't feel like going for a walk now," Flossy muttered.

"I don't particularly want to pass those journalists either," I admitted. "Besides, it's raining."

She sighed. "I have an hour before I ought to get ready."

"Are we dining together again?" I asked, not quite sure if it was a regular event for the family.

"Oh, I am sorry, Cleo, I forgot to tell you." She nibbled on her lower lip and frowned prettily. "I'm dining out with Mother and Father tonight. Friends of my parents came to London for Christmas and this was the only evening they had free. It was arranged ages ago, probably before we even knew you were coming. Mother and Father want me to marry their son, you see. They've been trying to throw me into his path for a while now, but haven't managed it until this invitation arrived."

"That sounds painful," I said, smiling.

"Oh, it is. Very painful indeed. He's so awkward and a terrible bore. I tried to get out of it by feigning a headache but mother is insisting and told me she'll drag me along, no matter what." She sighed. "I wish you were coming with me so I had someone amusing to talk to. The first time I met him, he spoke *all* evening about an archaeological dig he'd been on. He loves antiquities."

It sounded quite interesting to me, but I suspected she didn't want to hear that so I merely nodded sympathetically. "And Floyd?"

"You won't see him. The moment we leave, he'll be off too. Don't tell Father, though. I suspect Floyd has told him he'll be here all evening keeping an eye on things. Not that it's necessary, with Mr. Armitage always present after his uncle leaves of an evening, but Father likes to think Floyd is in control when he's not here. So what shall we do for an hour?" she finished.

"Read? Write letters?"

She wrinkled her nose. "Perhaps I'll start getting ready early."

Harmony's face appeared around the corner near the stairs. Spying me, she signaled me to join her.

"I think I'll see what books are in the library," I said to Flossy.

We walked together to the lift where I left Flossy and headed to the main sitting room that contained the hotel's library. I waited, dismissing the waiter who asked if I wanted to take a seat, and watched while Flossy got into the lift. As soon as the door closed, I retraced my steps and joined Harmony near the staircase.

"Come to the parlor," she said. "There's something you should know."

"There's something you should know too," I said, following her. "I've decided to continue investigating. But don't tell anyone."

She didn't break her stride as we made our way to the staff parlor. "I thought you would change your mind, but I didn't think you'd change it until you heard what I have to tell you."

"What do you have to tell me?"

She pushed open the door to reveal Victor the cook perched on the edge of a table, flipping his knife in the air. "Victor!" she snapped. "You're not in the kitchen now."

Victor slotted the knife into his belt in one continuous motion.

"You're very skilled with it," I told him.

He crossed his arms over his chest. "I am."

"Did you learn to do that here?"

"Nope. Found my first knife when I was a boy and taught myself some tricks."

"Found?" Harmony made a scoffing sound. "Stole it, more likely."

Victor merely crossed his legs at the ankles and regarded her coolly.

She thrust out her chin. "We have terrible news, Miss Fox. Danny was arrested. They've put him in prison!"

"A holding cell at Scotland Yard," Victor clarified.

"It's the same thing."

"No, it ain't."

Harmony turned her back to him. "I'm so glad you've decided to investigate, after all. We'll help, of course." She indicated Victor.

Victor patted a chair back and invited me to sit. "Want some tea while you think?" He indicated a teapot and cups on the table.

"Thank you," I said.

Harmony poured tea into three cups and Victor handed one to me. "So, where shall you begin?" she asked.

I sipped slowly, gathering my thoughts, then lowered the cup to my lap. The door suddenly opened and Goliath entered. He paused when he saw me.

"Keep moving, you big bloody giraffe," said someone behind him.

Goliath stepped aside to reveal Frank the doorman. He saw me and flushed.

"Sorry for my language, Miss Fox," he muttered. "I didn't see you there."

I rose. "It's all right. It's my fault, I'm intruding. This is your space to relax for a few moments."

"Please stay," Harmony said. "Miss Fox is helping investigate the murder," she informed the men.

"Then you've got to stay," Goliath said. "They arrested Danny."

"The police will find the killer," Frank told him.

"The police will find whoever the most convenient suspect is," Harmony said darkly. "They want this wrapped up quickly and quietly. I know all too well what the police are like, Frank."

"Mr. Hobart won't let his brother convict Danny. Have some faith, Harmony."

She sniffed. "It doesn't hurt to have another mind investigating. Miss Fox is clever. Have faith in *her*, Frank."

If Mr. Armitage weren't their immediate superior, I would have told them my suspicions about him and my doubts that his father would investigate thoroughly if he knew his son killed Mrs. Warrick. I wouldn't tell anyone my suspicions until I was absolutely sure, however.

I sat again as Goliath poured himself a cup of tea.

Victor withdrew his knife from his belt. "Are the journalists gone? Want me to go out there and frighten them off?"

"Two constables are outside now," Frank said. "That got rid of all but a few determined ones. Mr. Armitage said me and Goliath can take ten minutes in here while he helps defend the fort outside."

"Looks like he and Mr. Hobart convinced those guests to stay too," Goliath said.

"Probably by telling them the killer had been caught," Harmony said with a glare at each man. "Mark my words, they're going to blame Danny. I don't want to see my friend hang for something he didn't do. Do you?"

Frank shuffled his feet and shook his head.

Goliath puffed out his chest. "No, ma'am, I do not."

Victor ran the blade edge along his finger. "So what do we do next, Miss Fox?"

They all stared at me. How had I become their great hope? I'd done nothing to deserve it except show an inquisitive nature. Harmony seemed to have decided that I could be trusted to find the truth, but I wasn't sure what that decision was based upon.

It could simply be because I was a relative of the hotel owner. I could access places the staff could not, and talk to people who wouldn't give Harmony the time of day.

"The police are at a disadvantage," I told them. "They're not allowed to question the guests, but I think the guests should be questioned. Some of them, at least. For one thing, someone might have seen Mrs. Warrick during the evening, or could have witnessed Danny speaking to her when he brought the hot chocolate."

Harmony sat forward on the chair. "I did discover something that may be of use. It answers the question as to why the police are asking everyone where they were in the early evening and late afternoon. I found out that none of the waiters remembered seeing Mrs. Warrick in the dining room. Nor could Mr. Chapman find her name in his book. He notes down guest names and room numbers when they arrive," she told me. "The cost of the meal is added to their final list of expenses to be paid when they check out."

"No meal was delivered to her room, either," Victor added. "I checked after I spoke to you this morning, Miss Fox."

"Could she have dined out?" I asked.

"She didn't leave the hotel," Frank said.

Goliath pointed his teacup at Frank. "Maybe you were looking the other way when she passed."

Frank's lips pursed. "I notice everybody. Not a single soul can get past me."

"That journalist got past you today."

"No one can get past me *unnoticed*. Unless Mrs. Warrick

used a disguise, she didn't leave the hotel."

Harmony nodded thoughtfully. "A disguise is a distinct possibility. But why employ one?"

The door opened and Peter walked in with one of the maids. I recognized her as the young woman who'd endured a scolding from Mrs. Kettering in the stairwell. She paused when she saw me and bobbed a hasty curtsy. Harmony introduced her as Edith.

"I really shouldn't be in here," I said, rising. "I don't want to get in your way."

"You ain't in the way," Victor said, pushing a spare chair towards Edith.

She slid onto it, her head bowed, hands in her lap.

"Miss Fox is helping solve the murder," Harmony explained.

I winced. I wished she'd stop announcing it.

"Edith discovered Mrs. Warrick's body this morning."

"How awful for you," I said. "Shouldn't you go home and rest? You've endured quite a shock."

Edith looked up, her eyes huge. They were her best feature, particularly when she blinked innocently like that. If it weren't for her big blue-gray eyes she'd be a little plain. I'd thought her young, but now that I got a proper look at her face, I could see the telltale signs of age at the corners of her mouth and eyes. She must be near thirty.

"I'm all right, thank you, Miss Fox. I'd rather be working. So you don't think Danny did it?"

"No," chimed several voices as one.

"I'm so glad you're going to help him," she told me. "But who do you think poisoned Mrs. Warrick?"

"I'm not sure. But we need to keep this investigation between ourselves," I told them all. "Don't tell the senior staff, or any other staff, unless it will help us find answers. Edith, are you up to talking about the body? It's all right if you're not."

"Do you think it will help free Danny?"

"It might."

She drew in a fortifying breath and let it out slowly. "What do you want to know?"

"Tell me what you told the detective inspector about your

movements before and after discovering Mrs. Warrick."

"I was delivering her tea at seven this morning, as I have done ever since she arrived. She has a regular order, you see; tea delivered at seven by a maid, not a footman. She doesn't want men seeing her in her nightgown."

"A regular order, just like her cup of hot chocolate," I said.

Edith nodded. "I knocked on her door, but there was no answer. I'm sure I knocked loudly enough because I awoke the gentleman in the room directly across the corridor. He came out and picked up the newspaper that had been left by his door. I knocked on Mrs. Warrick's door again, then when there was still no answer, I used my key."

"Is it usual for you to enter with your own key?"

"Not very, but I just thought she was in a deep sleep. I didn't want to leave the tea at the door because I know she likes it hot. It was only in a cup with a cloth cover, not a pot and it would have gone cold very quickly."

"Do you always carry keys to all the rooms you deliver tea to in the mornings?"

"Just for the rooms I clean."

"Tell me what happened after you stepped into her room."

"I put the cup down on the table beside the empty pot of chocolate, opened the curtains, and turned around to greet Mrs. Warrick. That's when I saw her…covered in her own sick." She shuddered and clutched her throat. "It was awful. I'll never sleep tonight with the memory of her ghastly face in my mind."

Harmony touched Edith's hand, and Goliath squeezed her shoulder.

"I came straight outside and told the other guest still reading his paper that Mrs. Warrick looked dead. He went into her room to check while I ran to tell Mrs. Kettering."

The poor girl. No wonder her hands still shook. I wasn't sure I'd still be able to work if I'd discovered a dead body just that morning.

"You mentioned you have a key to the rooms you clean," I said. "Who else has access to room keys?"

"Mr. Hobart and Mrs. Kettering each have a master set of keys," Peter said. "If a guest loses their room key, I have to ask one of them to unlock the door. It doesn't happen often."

"Mr. Armitage doesn't have keys?"

"He uses Mr. Hobart's set if the need arises."

"Who do you think could have murdered her?" Goliath asked. "She was at the hotel alone, wasn't she?"

Peter nodded. "She checked in two days ago. I recall her saying she was looking forward to the ball and seeing old friends."

"Had any of those old friends arrived yet?" I asked him.

"I don't know."

"Peter, do you recall yesterday afternoon when Mr. Armitage spoke to a gentleman beside the Christmas tree? There was another man also nearby, reading the newspaper."

"Just after you and Miss Bainbridge came out of the sitting room?" Peter nodded. "I remember."

"*He* doesn't miss anyone," Goliath said with a smirk at Frank.

Frank looked like he wanted to retort, but he pursed his lips and hunched his shoulders. Goliath chuckled into his teacup.

"The man Mr. Armitage spoke to is Mr. Hookly, room five-oh-five," Peter said. "Nice fellow, cheerful, receives a lot of parcels from various shops. The one reading the newspaper was Mr. Duffield, second son of a second son of an earl, or something like that. Bit of a snob but doesn't give us any trouble. He's staying on the third floor."

The same level as Mrs. Warrick. "Do you know what they're doing in London?"

Peter shrugged. "They came for the ball, I suspect. They must have decided to come a few days early. The unmarried ones without family like to spend Christmas Day here."

"Do you know anything about where they're from? What they do for a living?"

"No, but I can find out their addresses. Everyone has to leave one when they check in. It's recorded in the reservation book."

"If you could get them for me, that would be marvelous."

"Why?" Goliath asked. "What have these men got to do with Mrs. Warrick's murder?"

"She recognized one of them, but I don't know which." I didn't tell him that she could have been referring to Mr.

Armitage. If I did, would these staff defend their superior's honor? "It could mean nothing," I went on. "It's just a line of inquiry I want to follow."

"You're very thorough," Harmony said, taking my empty cup and placing it on the tray.

Edith suddenly got to her feet with a gasp. "Look at the time. I'd better return to work."

Harmony glanced at the small clock beside a stack of periodicals on the shelf. "I thought you'd finished for the day, like me."

"Mrs. Kettering asked me to do something for her."

"Or are you really going off to see your beau?" Goliath asked with a wink.

Edith blushed and lowered her head.

"Leave her be," Harmony scolded.

Frank plucked the empty teacup from Goliath's fingers. "Just because no one loves you, Goliath, there's no need to be jealous of those of us with paramours."

"Those of us?" Goliath snorted. "I don't see women lining up outside the hotel to get a look at your ugly mug."

Frank placed the teacups down with a loud clatter. "Nor yours."

Edith opened the door to go, but I laid a hand on her arm. She jumped. "Speaking of Mrs. Kettering," I said gently, "remember not to breathe a word of my investigation to her. Or to anyone."

"I won't, and certainly not to that dragon." Edith put more spirit into the word than she had the rest of her words combined.

"That was unexpected," Harmony said with a laugh after Edith departed.

Victor threw one of his knives in the air and caught it. "Calling someone a dragon seems normal to me. From the way Mrs. Kettering talks to you girls, I'm surprised someone hasn't poisoned *her*. I'd wager you've dreamed about it on more than one occasion."

"You are a strange man." She picked up the tray and shoved it into his chest, choosing the moment between him catching the knife and tossing it again. "Take this back to the kitchen. This *girl* has finished for the day."

Victor steadied the tray as Harmony marched out of the parlor. "What'd I say to deserve that?"

* * *

I SPOTTED Mr. Hookly while I sat in one of the chairs in the foyer, pretending to read a book. He emerged from the lift and headed for the smoking room. I followed five minutes later, the book tucked under my arm.

There were only three gentlemen in the smoking room and all looked up upon my entry. The two elderly smokers held cigars while the third, Mr. Hookly, stood side-on to the fireplace, a slender cigarette dangling between his fingers. One of the cigar smokers gave me such a look of disgust that I wanted to run from the room. The second shook his head, as if my presence saddened him. Only Mr. Hookly welcomed me.

"May I try one of those?" I asked, setting my book on the mantelpiece and pointing to his cigarette.

"Of course." He reached inside his jacket and pulled out a silver case.

I removed one of the cigarettes and held it between thumb and forefinger while he lit it for me. He watched, smiling, as I placed it between my lips.

"You're supposed to inhale," he said, his smile widening.

I inhaled and promptly coughed as the smoke hit the back of my throat.

Mr. Hookly poured a sherry from the decanter on the sideboard and handed the glass to me. I gratefully sipped and the coughing eased.

"First time?" he asked.

"How can you tell?"

He chuckled. "You're either very brave or very foolish." He glanced pointedly at the two older gentlemen mumbling around the cigars plugged into their mouths. Considering the only women who smoked were prostitutes or some of the more extreme activists for the women's emancipation movement, it wasn't surprising they looked upon me as an aberration. To them, my presence in their masculine domain was either an act of defiance or promiscuity.

I wondered what Mr. Hookly thought of me. From his smiles, I gathered he realized I was neither and that smoking was a new endeavor. Considering my second inhalation produced another round of coughs, it was an easy conclusion to draw.

"So which is it, Miss...?"

"Fox." I held out my hand and he shook it, introducing himself as Mr. Hookly. "Perhaps I'm a brave fool," I said. "Or simply adventurous."

He acknowledged this with a shallow bow. "So now that we've established why you're in the smoking room, tell me what brings you to The Mayfair. You don't look like their typical guest."

"Don't I? And what does a typical guest of The Mayfair Hotel look like?"

He nodded at the gentlemen. "Older."

"You're not old."

He was indeed not. I gauged him to be in his middle to late thirties going by the dashes of gray specks in his sideburns. He was also handsome, but not in an overt way. He wasn't a man that women would gush over, but his features were pleasingly arranged and there was an air of refinement about him and in the way in which he held my gaze. This man did not lack confidence.

"Perhaps I was being unkind to my fellow guests. Not all are stuck in their ways like those two. I've seen some younger ones coming and going. I hear Sir Ronald's son brings in a younger crowd."

"Is that so? I wouldn't know. I only arrived yesterday."

"Alone?"

I gave him an arched look, and he instantly apologized.

"Forgive me, the question was too personal, but innocently meant." He offered me another bow, deeper this time. When he straightened, his smile had vanished and he did indeed seem apologetic.

I decided to be honest. If I wanted him to trust me enough to tell me about himself, I had to give something of myself in return. "I arrived alone but I live with my family on the fourth floor. Sir Ronald Bainbridge is my uncle."

He paused, the cigarette halfway to his lips. "Does your

75

uncle know you've taken up smoking today?"

I leaned in a little. "No, and I'd appreciate it if you didn't tell him or anyone else. I'm not sure I'll continue with the habit. I can't seem to get the technique right." I inhaled and coughed again.

Mr. Hookly placed his cigarette between smiling lips. He blew out a smoke ring. "You'll get used to it. But perhaps giving up before you properly begin is a good idea. It's a terribly addictive habit."

"Tell me, what brings you to London—and The Mayfair in particular?" I asked, trying to sound as though I were merely attempting to make small talk.

"I've newly returned to English soil from Africa."

"Africa! How thrilling." He did not look as though he'd just come from a hot land. He wasn't tanned. I supposed he could have worn a wide-brimmed hat out of doors to protect his pale skin.

"Do you think so?" He seemed to like my enthusiastic response, his shoulders squaring ever so slightly.

"What were you doing there?"

"Mining. Trouble with the Boers was worsening, however, so I decided to return to England. I sold my mine near Cape Town just before war broke out and here I am." He spread his hands apart. "I came directly to London after my ship docked to purchase all necessaries for a brisk English winter. I don't recall it ever being this cold, however."

"Are you staying for the ball?"

"I think I will, yes. Sir Ronald has asked me to and issued me an invitation personally just today, as it happens. I suspect the personal touch was in response to the murder and not because he particularly desires my company for the evening. Nasty business, isn't it? I hope they find the killer soon."

"They arrested one of the footmen this afternoon."

"Good. Glad that's resolved. I feel better knowing there are no killers wandering the halls, looking for jewels to steal."

I didn't bother to correct him. It seemed like a good idea to let him think that I believed theft was the motivation and that the right culprit had been arrested.

A slim man with sleek black hair and a goatee beard entered with a beautiful woman on his arm. I found myself staring at her, unable to look away from her lovely face, the exquisite beaded cream silk gown and the diamonds at her throat.

The goateed gentleman offered her a cigarette from a gold case and lit it for her. She blew out her first breath of smoke in the direction of the two elderly gentlemen who'd not stopped muttering to themselves since her entry.

They promptly got up and walked out. Her languid gaze watched them go.

"She's striking, isn't she?" Mr. Hookly said quietly.

Good lord, I'd been staring too long. I cleared my throat. "Tell me more about yourself. You mentioned selling your mine at an opportune time just before the war, but what happens next for you?"

"I'll return home to Berkshire and find something to do, I suspect. I haven't decided what yet."

"And why did you choose The Mayfair for your stay in London?"

He flashed me a smile. "Spoken like a member of the Bainbridge family." He tossed the butt of his cigarette into the fire and pulled out the silver case again. "The hotel was recommended to me by a friend, Lord Addlington. Do you know him?"

"No."

"Excellent chap. Regular guest here. Sir Ronald knows him well, so he told me when he read his lordship's letter of recommendation." He suddenly glanced up and nodded at someone.

I followed his gaze and froze. Then my insides sank beneath Mr. Armitage's shocked stare.

He quickly recovered, however. "Good evening, Mr. Hookly, Miss Fox. May I say it's a surprise to see you in here. I didn't think you smoked."

"If you saw her attempt it, you'd realize she doesn't." Mr. Hookly chuckled. "Armitage, any word from that fellow I asked about?"

"As far as I'm aware, he's still coming to the ball."

"Excellent, excellent." Mr. Hookly threw his cigarette into the fire. "If you'll excuse me, I must go. I'm dining out tonight with a friend at his club."

"Enjoy your evening, sir."

Mr. Hookly took my hand and bowed over it. "A pleasure to meet you, Miss Fox. Perhaps I'll see you in here again tomorrow."

Not unless I could think of more questions to ask him.

Mr. Armitage checked the levels of the decanters on the sideboard. I ought to leave too, but I wanted to speak to him again. The air between us felt a little tense after he'd quite rightly accused me of doubting his father's ability as a detective. I was also very aware that he'd lied to his father about his whereabouts. I was considering how to discover the reason for the lie when he spoke.

"What are you doing in here, Miss Fox?" he asked idly.

"Smoking, of course." To prove my point, I inhaled on the cigarette. The resulting cough was unladylike. A sip of sherry helped a little.

Mr. Armitage plucked the cigarette from my fingers. He tossed it into the fire.

"I was smoking that," I said irritably.

"You were choking on it, not smoking it."

I abandoned the idea of trying to find out why he lied to his uncle. Not only could it put me in danger, if he were the murderer and guessed my motive for asking, but I simply didn't feel like talking to someone highhanded enough to take my cigarette and stub it out without my permission. He was not my uncle or cousin. Indeed, if Uncle Ronald or Floyd had done what Mr. Armitage had, I'd be just as vexed with them.

Unfortunately Mr. Armitage followed me out of the room. "You do realize that wasn't Count Ivanov's wife. She's his mistress."

Mistress! Good lord. What sort of man brought his mistress to a hotel like The Mayfair and treated her as if she were his wife? Russians, I supposed. Wealthy, titled Russians.

"I see I've shocked you," Mr. Armitage said.

I schooled my features. "Not at all. Anyway, I don't see that Count Ivanov's private arrangements are any of my affair, or yours, for that matter."

"On the contrary. As assistant manager to the hotel, the private arrangements of the guests are very much my affair. I need to know who is staying here, with whom, and why. Not that I expect Countess Ivanov to arrive from Russia out of the blue, but I must be prepared for the eventuality and act swiftly to divert a disaster."

"By disaster, you mean the wife meeting the mistress on the arm of her husband."

"You catch on quickly, Miss Fox."

I narrowed my gaze. He was mocking me. He must think me terribly naïve not to have realized she was the count's mistress. I even knew that only two types of women smoked and that lovely creature didn't strike me as a proponent for the female cause. But she didn't look like a prostitute, either. I'd only ever seen them slouched in tavern doorways, their clothing half-off and their faces painted. Admittedly, my experience was limited to a single accidental adventure into a Cambridge slum when I'd taken a wrong turn on my way to meet a friend after a lecture.

"Will you accept a friendly word of caution, Miss Fox?" he asked.

I didn't expect a friendly word. I expected a scolding, but I didn't want to get Mr. Armitage off-side. Not yet. Not until I knew whether he was involved in the murder or not. "Go on."

"The reason I told you about Count Ivanov's mistress is because the niece of the hotel owner shouldn't be seen smoking in public or people will think you're like her. If you must do it, reserve it for the privacy of your own rooms and swear your maid to secrecy. Sir Ronald would not approve of you doing it in the hotel's smoking room where anyone could see."

"Then perhaps you ought to put a sign on the door: women not allowed; mistresses excepting."

He took a small step back. "You're angry with me. I'm sorry. I was trying to help. I thought you might appreciate some advice from someone who knows what Sir Ronald is like." He gave me a curt bow. "I apologize."

I sighed as he stalked off. This wasn't going at all well. I was supposed to be obtaining information from him. I hurried after him. "Mr. Armitage, thank you for your advice. It *is* appreciated."

He stopped and eyed me carefully. He looked uncertain.

"I thought I would try something new," I went on. "I've never smoked before and Mr. Hookly was kind enough to give me a cigarette. Now that I've done it, I doubt I'll try again. I didn't enjoy it. How do you men like it so much?"

"I don't smoke."

"Does Mr. Hookly smoke every evening before dinner?"

"Before and after." He was still rather formal and stiff, and I wasn't sure how to make him relax and encourage him to talk. At least he didn't walk off again.

"He's an interesting fellow," I went on. "He recently returned from Africa."

"Near Cape Town, so he told me."

"Where he sold a mine, yes. What do you know about the man whose letter of recommendation he carries?"

"Lord Addlington? He's a regular guest when parliament sits. A very fine gentleman and well respected around here." He bid me a good evening, and went to walk off, but stopped suddenly. "Your uncle would have gladly introduced you to Mr. Hookly if you'd asked."

It was my turn to take a step back. I was about to ask him why I'd want my uncle to introduce me to Mr. Hookly when I suddenly realized that Mr. Armitage thought I was romantically interested in the African miner. Asking for an introduction would certainly have been a more respectable way to go about orchestrating an encounter instead of following him into the smoking room.

It was a rather horrifying notion that Mr. Armitage thought I was interested in Mr. Hookly and not in a way that required a respectable introduction. He must think I was hunting for a wealthy benefactor, someone who'd parade me in jewels at luxury hotels while his wife stayed home.

I watched Mr. Armitage leave, a storm of feelings brewing inside my chest. I wasn't sure whether to feel ashamed or annoyed. After all, he'd made his mind up about me after knowing almost nothing about me.

One thing I was sure of, however. I wouldn't get more answers out of Mr. Armitage. If he hadn't been inclined to trust me before, he certainly wasn't now.

CHAPTER 5

*I*t was Flossy who encouraged me to dine in the hotel dining room instead of in my suite alone. I sat with her as she prepared for her evening out. Three hours later, I could see why it took her so long to get ready. Her maid arranged Flossy's hair in three different styles, each more elaborate than the last, before Flossy settled on the first. She changed her clothes so often that I lost count, and when she discovered a loose thread in the dress she did decide to wear, her poor maid had to sit beside a lamp and quickly mend it.

I was rather glad when one of the footman knocked on the door and announced that her parents were waiting for her. I returned to my own suite and changed outfits and fixed my hair. It smelled a little smoky, but thankfully Flossy hadn't noticed. I sprinkled a few drops of perfume on it then slipped on my shoes.

Floyd hadn't invited me to join him for dinner so I assumed he'd gone out, as Flossy said he would. I took the lift downstairs, chatting to John all the way, and was about to turn from the foyer into the vestibule when I spotted one of my suspects. It was the man who'd been reading the newspaper in Mrs. Warrick's line of sight when she'd uttered words of surprised recognition.

"Excuse me," I said, stepping alongside him. "Are you Mr. Duffield?"

It was terribly unladylike of me to speak to a strange man, but this was an extraordinary circumstance that called for desperate measures. He stopped and gave me a polite, if strained, smile. "I am."

"I'm Miss Fox, the niece of Sir Ronald Bainbridge."

At the mention of my uncle's name, the strained smile vanished, replaced by a friendly one. He bowed over my extended hand. "Miss Fox! How lovely to finally meet you. I was just talking to your uncle about you. He said he wanted us to meet."

It rang utterly false, for some reason. Perhaps it was because he was a little too enthusiastic. "Oh dear, I hope he only said good things about me."

He laughed. "The best of things. Are you dining with him tonight?"

"He's dining out with my aunt and cousin, unfortunately. I find myself all alone on my second evening in London."

"Only your second! Well, we can't have you dining alone, can we? Would you care to join me? I find myself dining alone tonight too."

I graciously accepted and he thrust out his elbow for me to take. He gave his name and room number to Mr. Chapman the restaurant steward, but when Mr. Chapman recognized me, he made a point of closing his book without writing anything down.

"Enjoy your meal, Miss Fox, Mr. Duffield." If Mr. Chapman thought it odd that I was dining with a guest, he didn't show it. He was the epitome of formality as he signaled for a waiter.

I glanced over my shoulder as we followed the waiter to a table, but there was no sign of Mr. Armitage. I'd half expected to see him there, watching me with a scowl marring his too-handsome features.

Mr. Duffield pulled out the chair for me, and pushed it in as I sat, then took his own seat. He had a nice smile, which he freely bestowed on me, but that was where his good features began and ended. At first I'd thought him well over forty, but on closer inspection, he had the smoother skin of a man in his thirties. It was the lack of hair that made him seem older.

Aside from the clusters just above his ears, the rest of his head was bald. He didn't even have facial hair.

Mr. Duffield gave me his uninvited opinion of every dish on the menu and hailed a passing waiter without asking me if I was ready. He ordered a bottle of wine and our meals.

"You'll enjoy the duck, Miss Fox," he said as the waiter departed. "It's delicious."

"Fortunately I like duck," I said tightly.

Mr. Duffield's smile widened, pleased with my approval. "Tell me all about yourself, Miss Fox. Why have you come to live at this delightful hotel?"

I gave him the brief version, merely mentioning the recent death of my last remaining relative on my father's side, and my uncle and aunt's generous invitation to live with them until I married. His eyes lit up at the mention of marriage.

"And do you have a fiancé, Miss Fox?" he asked, oh-so-innocently.

"Not yet," I said, matching his tone. "Tell me all about yourself, Mr. Duffield. Where are you from?"

"I have an estate in Lincolnshire with several tenant farms. My family has lived there for generations."

Peter had said Mr. Duffield was the second son of a second son of an earl, so it shouldn't surprise me to hear that he was landed gentry. Still, I was a little taken aback. When he'd offered me his arm, I'd noticed the fabric at the elbow of his dinner jacket was thin. His shoes were well worn too, molded to fit hit foot to the point where I could see the outline of his smallest toe. My grandfather had kept his dinner suit and good shoes for only the most formal occasions. They were in the same condition as Mr. Duffield's.

It would seem Mr. Duffield wanted me to know he was landed gentry so that perhaps I'd overlook the evidence of his hardship.

"And what brings you to London and The Mayfair in particular?" I asked.

"Business matters bring me to the city. Always business." He leaned back in the chair, puffing out his chest. "As to The Mayfair, isn't it obvious?"

"Pardon?"

"The ball! I'm looking forward to attending. Are you going, Miss Fox?"

"I'm not sure. I'm in mourning and it doesn't feel appropriate."

He frowned and patted my hand. "I do hope you'll reconsider. You would be an ornament to the evening. Your uncle would be very proud, I'm sure."

"Oh, er, thank you." I'd hardly heard his compliment, if that's what it was. I was thinking about business during the quiet Christmas to New Year period. Surely the banks were closed and most men of business not in their offices. Perhaps Mr. Duffield's business was urgent and couldn't wait for the reopening of the banks in the new year. Or perhaps he'd come solely for the ball and lied about business.

Or perhaps there was another reason. A reason which Mrs. Warrick had confronted him about. If she knew he was too poor to afford to stay here, she could very well be surprised at seeing him. If she'd asked him about it, he might have worried that she would foil whatever plans he had.

"Awful matter, the murder, don't you think?" I asked as our meals arrived.

"Yes. Horrible. But let's not discuss such a thing."

"Oh, but I want to. Had you met poor Mrs. Warrick?"

"Who?"

"The victim."

"No, I don't think so. I might have exchanged words with her at some point, in the lift or the foyer. I don't know. How is the duck?"

Try as I might, Mr. Duffield refused to talk more about the murder or himself, unless it was to tell me how large his estate was, how many tenant farms were on it, and his long-deceased grandfather, the earl.

I was going to have a story to rival Flossy's for dullness by the end of the evening. I'd readily swap places with her and be forced to converse with an archaeological enthusiast over this self-important bore.

I was relieved when he excused himself after the meal. "I'll be back in a moment."

He left before I could tell him I had somewhere to be. A

few minutes later, he returned to the dining room. I made a study of the tablecloth and silverware while he stopped to speak to Mr. Chapman. Mr. Chapman's glance in my direction left me in no doubt that I was the subject of their conversation.

When he returned, Mr. Duffield did not sit down. "Thank you for your company tonight, Miss Fox."

"You're going?" I wasn't sorry to see him leave, but I was surprised the evening was ending so suddenly. I thought he'd enjoyed talking about himself.

"I have a headache." He touched his temple. "Goodnight."

"Goodnight," I said to his retreating back.

Mr. Duffield exchanged a look with Mr. Chapman as he passed.

I followed him out, smiled at Mr. Chapman, and made my way to the foyer. It was still early, but I was tired. It had been a long day. Even so, I wanted to look for a book in the library. The library was located through the sitting room, however, and the sitting room doors were closed.

I opened one and peeked in. It was dark. If I wanted to reach the library without knocking into tables and chairs, I'd need to turn on the light, and that would probably draw the attention of a staff member. Very well, so be it. I was doing nothing wrong.

I felt beside the door for the switch, but couldn't find it. It must be on the other side.

The lights suddenly went on. "Can I help you, Miss Fox?"

My stomach sank. Of all the ill luck, I'd caught the attention of Mr. Armitage. Going by the frostiness of his tone, he was still cross with me.

"I'm just going to the library," I said. "Thank you for turning on the light. I couldn't find it."

"The switch is beside the door, as it is in all the rooms."

I bristled. "I checked the wrong side first." I waited but he did not leave. "I'll turn it off when I'm finished."

"I'll wait."

"I could be a while. I like to browse."

"As I said, I'll wait." If his tone got any cooler, I'd need a coat.

"Afraid I'll steal a teacup on my way out?" I spun around and marched off towards the library.

The room wasn't large, but it was packed with books and periodicals of all kinds, even sensational novels. I skipped past those and scanned the non-fiction section. Very aware of the imposing figure of Mr. Armitage watching me from the sitting room, I read the spines without really taking them in, and had to read them a second time. Finally settling on two titles, I clutched them to my chest and rejoined him.

He stood with crossed arms, leaning against the doorframe. The casual pose was at odds with his usual straight-backed formality. The alert gaze was not.

"Found what you wanted?" he asked.

"Unfortunately you foiled my plan to steal the teacups, and I had to settle for books instead." I strolled past him and did not look back.

* * *

THE NEWS of Danny's release reached me mid-morning via Harmony. She was thrilled to report that he was back at work already.

"He's quite the sensation among the staff," she said as she tidied up my already tidy room. "He has some interesting tales to tell about his arrest and time in the holding cell, but he does like to embellish things, so I wouldn't trust a word he says."

"Did he say why the police released him?" I asked.

"Two reasons, apparently. The poison wasn't in the pot or cup of chocolate, and the time of death was estimated by the pathologist as occurring between three and six in the morning. Danny was with someone at that time."

I turned to face her. "He has a lover?" I wasn't sure why I was surprised. I might have led a sheltered life, but I wasn't so naïve to assume that people didn't have lovers. Perhaps it was because I suspected Harmony held a *tendre* for him, and that was why she'd advocated for his release so vehemently.

She didn't look upset to learn about his lover, however. She hummed a tune as she dusted a dust-free table.

"Why didn't he mention the lover to the detective at the time of his arrest?" I asked.

"He was probably protecting him."

"Him?" I blurted out. "Oh. I see." I turned back to the correspondence I'd been reading on my desk, my face hot.

"Only his closest friends know. Promise not to tell a soul," she said urgently. "Not even your family. You know what happened to Oscar Wilde, don't you?"

The homosexual playwright had been imprisoned for gross indecency a few years ago. The law was not on the side of men like him. "Why didn't the detective inspector arrest Danny for that once he revealed his alibi?"

She shrugged. "He must be a good man, like his brother, Mr. Hobart."

"Mr. Hobart knows about Danny?"

"Mr. Hobart knows everything about everyone in the hotel."

"Have the police returned this morning?" I asked.

"The detective inspector came and spoke with Sir Ronald, Mr. Hobart and Mr. Armitage first thing, then left again."

It was a relief that Danny was no longer a suspect; however, the sense of urgency to find the killer still ate at me. My uncle must be beside himself with worry. Having someone arrested had eased the minds of the guests, both those already here and those yet to check in. But once word got out that Danny had been released, fear would lead to cancellations. All it would take would be for the newspapers to report it, and the hotel's reputation would be in tatters.

Harmony joined me at the desk, her duster flicking back and forth over the lampshade. "Will you continue with the investigation now?"

"I feel as though I've come too far to stop."

"True. And there's always the danger that they'll arrest another innocent staff member."

"What makes you think they're all innocent? Perhaps one of them *is* the murderer."

She winced. "I don't want to consider that possibility. I don't even want Mrs. Kettering to be guilty of such a terrible crime. She's a dragon and a bully, but she has a moral compass as straight as an arrow. If she did it, it means my judgement of character is far off course."

I touched her hand. "You've proved to be an excellent judge of character so far. You were certainly right about Danny."

Harmony and I parted ways outside my suite. I headed downstairs while she went to clean Floyd's room. John the lift operator was in a good mood as he repeated what I already knew about Danny's release.

As I passed Goliath in the foyer, pushing a trolley laden with trunks towards the door, he whispered, "Did you hear? Danny's free."

I caught Peter's eye as he stood behind the counter, attending to a guest. He nodded and gave me a fleeting smile. The staff were certainly in a buoyant mood this morning. It didn't seem to cross any of their minds that one of them could be arrested next.

I wasn't sure who I hoped to find, only that I wanted to speak to someone more knowledgeable than Harmony. I'd considered talking to my uncle, but to be perfectly honest, I wished to avoid my uncle and aunt as much as possible. With him so busy, and her keeping to her room, it wouldn't be difficult.

Or so I thought. The last person I expected to bump into was Uncle Ronald as he emerged from Mr. Hobart's office.

"Cleo!" he said, sounding as surprised as I felt. "What are you doing here?"

"I wanted to ask Mr. Hobart something. Something about the hotel."

"What is it? I can probably answer. I do know quite a bit about my hotel."

"Er, yes. But this is about the ball."

He drew in a breath. "The ball," he muttered. "If it goes ahead, then you're right to ask Mr. Hobart. He's making all the arrangements."

"Do you think it will be canceled because of the murder?"

"I'm hoping not, but it will require many telephone calls to friends and invited guests, reassuring them it's quite safe." He sighed heavily. "The police released the footman. While I'm pleased we haven't hired a murderer, if the real culprit isn't arrested soon, the ball will be in jeopardy. Perhaps even the hotel itself."

Was the hotel so financially unstable that a shake of its reputation could bring it down?

"I'm sure the murderer will be found soon," I assured him.

"Does your interest in the ball mean you'll be attending if it goes ahead? Flossy will be pleased."

"I'm still undecided," I said. "I hoped Aunt Lilian could guide me."

His thick moustache settled into a frown. "It's best not to trouble your aunt today," he muttered. "If you'll excuse me, I have a lot of work to do."

He headed off through the foyer. I knocked on Mr. Hobart's door and entered upon his word.

"I hope I'm not disturbing you," I said.

"Not at all." He indicated a chair opposite his desk. "How may I help you?"

There was no subtle way of getting answers to my questions so I decided to be direct. "I have a terribly curious nature," I began. "I hoped you would satisfy my curiosity about Danny's release."

He removed his spectacles and folded the arms with slow, precise movements. "Murder is not the sort of subject that should interest a young lady," he said carefully.

"I am not an ordinary young lady."

That brought a smile to his face, one that seemed unguarded. It was the first time I'd seen a chink in his professional armor.

Still, he required more encouragement. "I'm used to having my mind engaged, you see. In Cambridge, I would attend lectures at the university, and I belonged to several societies where members would discuss the latest theories on all sorts of matters. Moving here has cut me off from all my former activities."

"You're bored. Is that what you're saying, Miss Fox?"

"I suppose I am." It wasn't far from the truth. Since arriving in London, my days had been occupied with learning about my new home and the murder. Once it was solved, I would need something else to do.

"There are societies in London that you can join. Harry will give you a list, if you like."

"He knows which societies accept women?"

There was that smile again. "He will find out for you."

"That's very kind, but I'm sure Mr. Armitage has a great deal of work at the moment, with preparing for the ball. Uncle Ronald says it's still going ahead."

Mr. Hobart picked up his spectacles. "We're proceeding as if it is."

"So, may I ask you some questions about the murder?"

"What makes you think I know anything?"

"I suspect your brother confides in you."

"Don't be so certain. At this point, I'm probably a suspect too." He smiled as he put on his glasses. "Very well. Go on, Miss Fox, I'll see if I can answer your questions. We can't have your brain shrinking from lack of use."

"Thank you, Mr. Hobart. All of my questions relate to poison. Since none was found in the chocolate pot or cup, does the inspector know how Mrs. Warrick ingested it? Did the police test the teacup delivered the following morning by the maid?"

"It was also negative for poison. Tests are also being undertaken on a bottle of tonic, tube of toothpaste, and a pot of face cream removed by the police from Mrs. Warrick's room."

"What type of poison was used?"

"Mercuric cyanide."

Mercury was commonly used in agriculture and industry, and wasn't difficult to obtain. That was the extent of my knowledge.

"Nothing else was delivered to Mrs. Warrick's room that night?" I asked.

He shook his head. "I checked with the staff myself. Mrs. Warrick received nothing else from the hotel kitchen between the time Danny delivered the hot chocolate and Edith brought Mrs. Warrick's tea at seven the following morning."

"She died between three and six, so the doctor said. Does your brother have faith that it's an accurate estimation?"

"He claims the science for estimating the time of death is

quite good. It means Danny's delivery was too early, and Edith was too late. I admit I'm relieved it's neither of them."

"Does your brother suspect anyone else on the staff?"

"He hasn't confided that to me, and nor would he. He knows I'll advocate for them. At least, he knows *now*, after arresting poor Danny."

If he advocated loudly for his staff, how loud would he be if he discovered his nephew were guilty? Then again, Mr. Armitage's own father wouldn't arrest him.

"So the poison must have been in the tonic, toothpaste or face cream," I said.

"The tests will prove which."

Someone must have added poison to the bottle, tube or pot, either when Mrs. Warrick wasn't there or directly under her nose. If she wasn't there, then someone must have let themselves in with a key, and that pointed to one of the staff. If Mrs. Warrick *was* present, but turned her back on the poisoner, then almost anyone could be guilty. They didn't need a key. They simply needed to know her so that she would allow them into her room.

"Did Mrs. Warrick have friends at the hotel?" I asked.

He frowned as he thought. "She dined alone and sat in the sitting room by herself. I don't recall her speaking to any of the other guests."

So the only person she did know was the man she'd recognized in the foyer on the day of her death. That narrowed the list to three suspects.

I rose. "Thank you, Mr. Hobart. You've given me some things to think about."

He put on his spectacles and peered over the top of them. "If you think of something that might be relevant, you will tell my brother, won't you?"

"Of course. If I learn something that would be of interest to him, I most certainly will." No doubt the inspector wouldn't be interested in learning something that would incriminate his own son, so I wasn't precisely lying.

"And Miss Fox? Don't ask anyone else questions about the murder. It's possible the killer has checked out of the hotel, but it's equally possible he has not. Trust only Sir Ronald, myself and Harry if you have anything else to ask."

"Thank you for your concern, Mr. Hobart. It's very kind of you." I closed the door behind me, and touched my tingling nose. His fatherly words had brought tears to my eyes. Clearly I was still feeling raw from Grandmama's death.

Peter signaled for me to approach as I passed his counter. "Harmony wants to speak to you," he said. "She's in the parlor with some of the others."

The "others" turned out to be Victor and Edith. Victor hadn't yet started his shift for the day, and Edith had just finished cleaning some of her allocated rooms and was waiting for more to be vacated before she returned to work. Harmony didn't explain her presence there. Either she was finished altogether and didn't want Edith to feel bad, or she shouldn't have been in the parlor at all.

"Did you discover anything further?" Harmony asked as she closed the door behind me.

I told them how the police found mercuric cyanide in Mrs. Warrick's body. "They've taken away a few items from her toilette for testing. The poison must be in one of those."

"What does mercuric cyanide taste like?" Victor asked.

"How would any of us know?" Harmony cried.

He drummed his fingers on his thigh and shrugged.

"Metallic, I imagine," I said.

"Probably not very pleasant," Edith added with a shudder.

Victor continued to drum his fingers, as if he needed to do something with his hands. He would probably like to be handling one of the knives housed in the belt slung around his waist, but it was likely Harmony had already scolded him for doing so before my entry. "It causes vomiting, that much we know," he said.

"Victor," Harmony hissed with a jerk of her head at Edith.

Edith had gone quite pale. "It was a horrible scene," she whispered through trembling lips. "I hope never to witness the like of Mrs. Warrick's face again."

Harmony took her hand and clasped it between both of hers. "We'll just have to wait for the results of the tests to know if poison was in her personal items."

"What else could it be in?" I asked.

"Her dinner?" Edith suggested.

I shook my head. "She ingested the poison between three and six AM."

Harmony perched on the edge of the table and her gaze met mine. "That would imply the poison was in the tonic. Nobody puts on face cream or cleans their teeth in the early hours of the morning."

"Unless they just returned to their room," Victor added.

Harmony frowned. "Did Mrs. Warrick seem like the type to have a midnight rendezvous?"

Victor shrugged.

"Mr. Hobart claims she knew nobody at the hotel," I said. "All we know is she recognized someone." I kept the information about Mr. Armitage being one of those men to myself. Until I knew if they would take his side or not, I wouldn't tell them.

"You say the latest she could have been poisoned is six AM," Edith said to me in her mousy voice.

"According to the medical expert, yes."

"And I was there at seven." She bit on her lower lip and looked down at her lap.

"What is it?" Harmony asked. "If you know something, Edith, you must tell us."

"I… I'm not sure if it's important."

"Tell us anyway."

Edith clasped her hands together in her lap. "I don't want to get her into unnecessary trouble. But if it might be important…" She drew in a deep breath and seemed to decide that telling us was the best course. "After I came out of Mrs. Warrick's room and spoke to the gentleman from the room opposite, I raced off to tell someone. I would have sought out Mr. Armitage, because I didn't think Mr. Hobart would be in that early, and Mrs. Kettering frightens me. But I found her in the corridor on the third floor."

Harmony gasped. "On Mrs. Warrick's floor."

Edith's gaze connected with Harmony's. "She usually checks the linen stock first thing in the morning."

Harmony nodded. "You're right. She shouldn't have been there."

No one said it out loud, but we were probably all thinking it. If Mrs. Kettering had poisoned Mrs. Warrick an hour beforehand, at six, she might have stayed in the vicinity to wait for the body to be discovered. It was a chilling thought, but not out of the realms of possibility. I'd read about murderers loitering near the scene of the crime to witness the response to their gruesome handiwork.

Edith shivered again, and this time I did too.

Victor checked the clock and pushed off from the wall where he'd been standing. He opened the door to see Mr. Armitage there.

"Sorry, sir," he said. "My shift's about to start."

Mr. Armitage moved aside to let him pass then looked in on us. "Are you lost, Miss Fox? Or are you having another adventure?"

I indicated the teacup beside Edith. "Harmony and Edith were kind enough to ask me in for a cup of tea."

"You do know you can get tea sent up to your room at any time. You simply have to talk into the speaking tube and someone in the kitchen will hear your order."

"Thank you, the device has been explained to me. But it's lonely drinking tea in my room by myself. I'd rather have company."

He opened his mouth to say something but must have thought better of it. He simply nodded and walked off.

Edith rose. "I'd best return to work."

I parted from the two maids outside the parlor and headed into the foyer, where I spotted Mr. Armitage striding towards the senior staff corridor. I raced after him, determined to have a word with him in Edith and Harmony's favor. While I didn't see anything wrong with having tea with them when they weren't working, I wasn't sure he saw it that way. He might be a stickler for societal rules and not want the staff mixing socially with the owner's family. I didn't want to get anyone into trouble, so if I could smooth down some ruffled feathers, I would.

I rounded the corner just as the door to one of the private chambers closed. It wasn't his, however. I was quite sure he'd pointed it out as belonging to Mrs. Kettering when he'd taken me on the tour. Why would he go into her room? Had he overheard us talking in the parlor and thought as we did—

that Mrs. Kettering shouldn't have been on the third floor on the morning Mrs. Warrick died?

I was considering whether to wait for him to come out and confront him when Mrs. Kettering herself suddenly entered the corridor from the foyer. She walked past her office and paused upon seeing me.

"Miss Fox," she said curtly. "What are you doing here?"

"I'm looking for you, as it happens."

"My office is there." She pointed behind her at the door labeled with her name.

"So it is."

She scowled. "Is something the matter with your room?"

"May we speak in your office?" I spoke loudly enough so that someone on the other side of her bedroom door could hear. If Mrs. Kettering were the killer then it was in both Mr. Armitage's interest and mine that he not be caught.

I followed Mrs. Kettering into her office and closed the door. She swept aside the keys and other tools of her trade attached to the chatelaine at her hip then sat.

"What is it you wanted to say to me, Miss Fox?"

I took my time. I hoped Mr. Armitage would leave immediately the coast was clear, but he might stay a few moments to look around. I scrambled to find a suitable topic to talk about.

"Miss Fox?" she barked. "Is there something wrong with your room?"

"No. It's very nice, thank you."

"Is Harmony doing a poor job?"

"No! Not at all. The room is very clean and tidy."

"Does she talk too much?"

"Pardon?"

"I asked if Harmony talks too much." She clicked her tongue. "The girl tends to prattle on uninvited. She's too clever for her own good, that's the problem."

"It doesn't sound like a problem to me."

She regarded me down her nose. "Cleverness in a maid is a curse, Miss Fox. It gives them airs and false expectations. You wouldn't understand."

I stiffened. I wasn't sure if I was more offended on Harmony's behalf or my own. "Considering you don't know anything about me, I don't know how you can make that assumption."

Her lips pinched as if she were holding in her retort.

"And I wouldn't think that being clever would give one either airs or false expectations," I went on. "A quick mind will make one very aware of the world and one's situation in it, for good or ill." I stood. If Mr. Armitage wasn't yet out of her room then it was his problem. I wasn't enduring Mrs. Kettering's company another moment.

I opened the door and strode out. Insufferable woman. A brisk walk in the fresh air outside might soothe my temper. My coat and gloves were upstairs so it would be a very brief and very cold walk. I headed for the front door but was intercepted by Mr. Armitage. It would seem he'd left Mrs. Kettering's room as soon as he could.

"A word please, Miss Fox."

"That is an excellent idea. You have some explaining to do. I've just endured a conversation with Mrs. Kettering on your behalf. Now I know why the maids call her a dragon."

He rubbed a hand over his jaw and indicated we should talk in the smoking room. It was empty, but I was very aware that someone could walk in at any moment.

"You diverted her away for me," he said.

"She was about to walk in on you."

"Why?"

"That's a good question. Why were you in her room?"

"That's none of your affair, and my question was why did you help me?"

I shrugged, not wanting to explain that I was investigating the murder. If he were the killer, it would alert him to the fact and put a target on my head. Indeed, if he were the killer, I ought not be alone with him.

"I have to meet my cousin," I said, edging closer to the door.

He followed. "I suppose I owe you thanks."

"It was nothing." I turned to go, but he caught my arm. Instinctively, I jerked free. My heart pounded in my chest and my skin prickled as I stared up at him.

He stared back. "There's a murderer in the hotel, Miss Fox.

I suggest you be careful and not sneak about." He opened the door and waited for me to leave.

I brushed past him, only to stop. We were mere inches apart. I was very aware of his superior height and those broad shoulders, the strong cheekbones and jaw. Despite our close proximity, I felt braver, most likely because we were now in full view of Peter, the guests and porters in the foyer.

"I wasn't the one sneaking, Mr. Armitage. Good day."

CHAPTER 6

$\mathcal{M}$y dramatic exit from the smoking room lost steam when I realized Mr. Armitage didn't follow me. My pace slowed, and I looked around the foyer for inspiration in how to proceed with the investigation. Peter stood alone at the front desk and I was about to approach him and ask if he'd learned anything about the addresses of Mr. Duffield and Mr. Hookly when an errand boy arrived carrying a rectangular box of considerable size.

"Delivery for Mr. Hookly," he told the post desk attendant named Terence.

"Another one?" Terence said. "Mr. Hookly must be your best customer."

"My master salivates when he sees Mr. Hookly coming through the door."

I waited for the errand boy to leave then I approached the counter.

"Good morning, Miss Fox," said Terence. "Have you more letters this morning?"

"Not today. I couldn't help but overhear. Is that package for Mr. Hookly?"

"It is."

"How fortuitous. I'm on my way to see him now, as it happens. May I deliver it for you?"

He looked as though he would protest but thought better

of it. I suspected he didn't want to tell me it was against hotel policy to give mail into the wrong hands. Being the owner's niece had some advantages. "It's very irregular, but I'm sure you can be trusted to deliver it safely."

He passed me the box and I hurried off with it, taking the stairs rather than the lift to avoid awkward questions from John. The parcel wasn't heavy but it was large, and by the time I reached my room, I was eager to set it down.

At my desk, I studied the return address. It was from Bentley and Sons on Saville Row. I untied the string then carefully opened the box, making sure not to damage it. Beneath the paper was a gray silk waistcoat with silver buttons and matching tie. Beneath those was a formal frock coat. The card accompanying the items stated the shirt and trousers would arrive soon, and that payment of the account was due at Mr. Hookly's earliest convenience. The figure was a staggering amount. It must be for more than this suit. Although well made from the finest fabrics, it wouldn't cost one tenth of the figure on the card.

I returned the items and card to the box, retied the string, and headed downstairs again. "He wasn't in his room, after all," I told Terence.

He gave me an uncertain look as he accepted the parcel.

I was about to return upstairs when Peter hailed me from the front desk. "I found the addresses for you, Miss Fox."

"Excellent. Thank you, Peter."

He handed me a piece of paper with three addresses written on it. He pointed to the first one. "This is the address Mrs. Warrick wrote in the reservation book. The next one is for Mr. Hookly. He lives in Berkshire."

"That matches what he told me."

"The last one is for Mr. Duffield, and look. It's also in Lincolnshire."

"The same as Mrs. Warrick." They could very well know each other if they were neighbors. I didn't know the county, however. The two addresses could be nowhere near one another. I said as much to Peter.

"That's what I wondered too, so I took the liberty of consulting with Terry." He nodded at Terence, sorting letters into the mail slots behind the post desk. "He has postal directories and maps from all over the country. It turns out that Mr. Duffield lives twenty-five miles from Mrs. Warrick, just outside of Grantham."

"Thank you, Peter. You've been most helpful."

"Let me know if there's anything else I can do for you."

"There is, as it happens. May I use your telephone?" I pointed to the brass device at the edge of the desk.

He looked uneasy. "It's supposed to be for receiving reservations only."

I spotted Mr. Hobart heading away from his office. "Never mind."

I intercepted the manager and asked if I could use the telephone in his office. "My friend in Cambridge is supposed to be sending my other trunk, but it hasn't arrived yet. I want to ask her if she dispatched it."

"Of course," he said. "My office door is unlocked. Help yourself."

I'd never used a telephone but I'd seen the staff at my local post office and some shops make and receive calls. Mr. Hobart's handsome brass candlestick shaped telephone sat on the corner of his desk. I plucked the receiver off the hook and asked the switchboard operator to connect me to the exchange in Grantham, Lincolnshire. The Grantham switchboard operator then informed me that Hambly Hall had a telephone and she proceeded to connect me.

The call was answered moments later. "I have a message for Mr. Duffield of this address," I said.

"The Duffields no longer live at Hambly Hall," came the voice down the line.

I moved closer to the mouthpiece. "The message is for Mr. *Maurice* Duffield, grandson of the earl of Hambly. I was informed that this was his address."

"The family sold the Hall two years ago. Mr. Maurice Duffield moved into a cottage in the village."

Mr. Duffield had lied. He no longer lived on the family estate. Indeed, the estate had been sold. It confirmed my suspicions that he was experiencing reduced circumstances. He'd not wanted the hotel to know, however.

Did Mrs. Warrick know, and that's why she noted that he ought not be here, because he couldn't afford the expense of The Mayfair? The more I thought about it, the more certain I was that it was him she recognized that day in the foyer. They were both members of Lincolnshire society, after all.

* * *

I ATE luncheon in the dining room with Flossy, Floyd and Aunt Lilian. My aunt looked a little pale, her eyes flat, as she waited for her food to arrive. Perhaps the previous night's dinner had taken its toll.

"He was as dull as I remembered," Flossy said when I asked her how it went.

I eyed her mother, but Aunt Lilian made no comment, and Flossy went on unchecked.

"All he wanted to talk about was a newly discovered Egyptian tomb." She pulled a face. "What sort of gentleman thinks mummified remains make suitable dinnertime conversation with a lady he's supposed to be courting?"

"The cad!" Floyd declared. "Want me to call him out for you?"

Flossy gave him a withering glare. "I don't see why I have to marry and you don't. You're older."

"I'm not a girl. I have plenty of time for my ideal wife to present herself."

Flossy sniffed. "Your ideal woman is a figment of your imagination. And if she did exist, she'd run a mile when she met you, if she knew what was good for her. Honestly, the way you behave these days, no respectable lady would want to be associated with you."

Floyd pinched her. She winced and rubbed her arm, then they both glanced at their mother. Aunt Lilian continued to stare out of the window, her gaze unfocused.

"So you *are* courting?" I asked Flossy.

"No. He's not for me."

Aunt Lilian turned to her daughter, proving she was listening after all. "He would be a very good match for you."

"Why? Because his family is rich?"

"Don't be vulgar."

"Well, we're rich, so I don't need to marry him." Flossy crossed her arms.

"The hotel could always use an injection of funds," Floyd said. "Particularly now."

Flossy lowered her arms and leaned in. "Are things very bad?" she asked quietly.

"I don't think it's dire, but the bad publicity surrounding the murder won't help."

"If it's not dire, then it will all work out. It always does."

"You could help by reining in your spending," Floyd said.

She screwed up her nose. "You first."

His gaze slid to his mother, but she seemed to have stopped listening again.

"And anyway," Flossy went on, "we have to look our best for the ball. Not only do we have to surpass last year's spectacle, but it's the last ball of the century. We can't ring in nineteen-hundred wearing last year's gowns or jewels. Everyone will notice, and the gossip will only lead to speculation that the hotel is in difficulty and we can't have that. It would be humiliating."

Floyd snorted. "Spoken like the Flossy I know."

"What is that supposed to mean?"

Aunt Lilian rubbed her temples. "Stop it, both of you. You know talk about financial matters gives me a headache."

Brother and sister called a ceasefire over luncheon, but not all discussion of the ball ended. Both Flossy and Floyd begged me to attend.

"We simply have to show off our cousin," Flossy declared.

"My friends are all dying to meet you," Floyd added.

I blinked at him. "You told them about me?"

"You seem surprised that my bachelor friends would be interested in hearing about my attractive cousin from Cambridge."

I laughed, despite myself. "Can I expect my dance card to be full or did you give a balanced picture and tell them my bad traits?"

"What bad traits?" he asked in mock seriousness.

"Floyd's friends are very shallow," Flossy said. "As long

as you're pretty and fun, they won't care that you're—" She stopped dead, her lips pursed to utter the P in poor. "That you're educated," she said quickly.

Floyd rolled his eyes.

Flossy tossed her red-gold curls. "Anyway, you have to go to the ball, Cleo. Mother thinks so too. Mother? Don't you think Cleo should come to the ball?"

Aunt Lilian roused and smiled at me. "Of course. You'll be most welcome." Her smile turned wistful. "Your mother would approve."

The sadness in her eyes brought a lump to my throat. It was easy to forget that I'd known my mother for only ten years, yet Aunt Lilian had known her much longer. The bond between sisters was strong, I'd been told, and it was natural she'd still think about her all these years later.

But if she'd been fond of my mother, why sever the connection? Had Uncle Ronald insisted? Or did Aunt Lilian come to regret their estrangement only after my mother's death?

"I'll think about it," was all I said.

"But it's in five days!" Flossy cried. "We'll need time to have one of my gowns adjusted."

"Surely it'll only take a maid an afternoon," Floyd said.

Flossy clicked her tongue. "Oh Floyd, *honestly*. You're so *male*."

He appealed to me. I shrugged. "It doesn't seem right for me to go," I told them both.

Flossy didn't respond as she picked up her sandwich. She studied it for some time, turning it this way and that, a small frown connecting her brows. Then she suddenly put it down again. She turned bright eyes onto her mother.

"May we go shopping this afternoon?"

"I have a headache," Aunt Lilian said. "In fact, I think I'll retire to my rooms for a rest." She rose, having hardly touched her sandwiches.

Flossy didn't seem surprised by her mother's response, or disappointed. "May I go if Cleo comes with me?"

"Very well," Aunt Lilian said, walking off.

Flossy clapped her hands. "We'll have such fun, Cleo."

Floyd watched his mother leave, both hands on the chair arms as if he would spring up at any moment if she looked as though she would fall. While her progress was slow, she wasn't unsteady.

"It's Hobart," he said as the manager appeared in the doorway to the dining room. He bowed to Aunt Lilian as she passed then scanned the room.

"He looks troubled," Flossy said.

Floyd signaled to Mr. Hobart. "Something wrong?" he asked when the manager joined us.

"I was looking for Sir Ronald," Mr. Hobart said. "Have you seen him?"

"I believe he went out for lunch. Why the grave face? Has something happened?"

Mr. Hobart swallowed and glanced at me.

"It's all right," Floyd said. "Cleo is family. If it's something that affects the hotel then you can say it in front of her."

Mr. Hobart moved closer. "I just received a telephone call from an acquaintance at *The Evening News*. He wanted to warn me of an article they're going to run about the hotel. I'm afraid it won't be a favorable article."

Flossy gasped. "Is it about poor Mrs. Warrick?"

"Yes, and the implications of her murder. My contact informed me that the front page article will mention the lengthy measures Sir Ronald is going to in order to ensure the ball goes ahead."

"What measures?" Flossy asked.

"Telephone calls to invited guests begging them to come, calling in favors, that sort of thing."

"Begging? Calling in favors?" Floyd spluttered a laugh. "Ridiculous. Father wouldn't stoop that low. Things aren't that desperate yet."

Mr. Hobart stood quite still.

Floyd's smile vanished. His face fell. "Why didn't he tell me it was that bad?"

"I suspect he didn't want to worry you, Mr. Bainbridge."

Floyd rubbed a hand over his jaw and mouth, shaking his head. Mr. Hobart looked sorry for telling him now.

"Can you ask your friend at the newspaper not to run the article?" I asked the manager.

"Unfortunately he does not have enough authority to stop it."

"Does Father have a friend with that power?" Flossy asked. "One who owes him a favor?"

Floyd looked up, hopeful. "Is that why you want to see him?"

Mr. Hobart seemed a little pained as he shook his head. "I simply came to warn him. He'll want to know so that he can be prepared with a response. Some of our guests will read *The Evening News*."

Floyd stood. "Come with me. We'll check his schedule in his office and see where he's having lunch."

"Thank you, Mr. Bainbridge."

Flossy sighed heavily as she watched them go. "This is terrible, Cleo. It's so cruel and so unfair. Who would go to the newspapers and spread rumors about us?" She picked up a napkin only to screw it up into a ball. "I'll wager it was one of the other hoteliers. They're always trying to be better than us, and it wouldn't surprise me if they'd stoop to talking to the newspapers."

I wasn't so sure it was a rival. Indeed, it could be worse. The information about begging invitations and calling in favors could only have come from one of the recipients of those invitations or calls—a guest.

Unless it was a senior staff member with knowledge of them.

* * *

FLOSSY PLACED a headpiece made of jet and set with several small diamonds against her hair. It was very becoming, but it wouldn't suit her ball gown. It must also be very expensive. "I thought your gown has seed pearls sewn into it," I said. "I don't think the jet is quite right."

She pursed her lips as she studied her reflection in the mirror held by the Harrods' jewelry counter attendant. "I'm not sure. Come closer, Cleo. I need to see how it looks on someone else."

She positioned the headpiece in my hair then stepped

back and studied the effect. She smiled. "You're right. Pearls are a better choice."

We spent some time choosing a headpiece for her and waited as the assistant packaged it up along with a matching necklace. It would seem Flossy wasn't going to heed her brother's advice and curb her spending. The two pieces would have cost a fortune.

"Would you like to take the items with you now, Miss Bainbridge?" the saleswoman asked.

"Have them sent to the hotel," Flossy said.

"Very good, Miss Bainbridge."

The staff at every counter we'd visited in Harrods' department store knew Flossy by name. Flossy hadn't paid for anything yet, so I assumed an account would be sent to the hotel along with the items she purchased.

"Now, gloves," Flossy declared, striding off.

I dutifully followed. I couldn't have left even if I wanted to. I didn't know which way was out. The lights were bright, the counters numerous, and there were smiling attendants dressed in black everywhere. Perhaps the intention was to trap shoppers inside for as long as possible, to encourage them to spend more.

"Are we going anywhere near Saville Row later?" I asked, stepping alongside her.

"It's not far from the hotel. Why?"

"My grandfather used to get his suits made at a tailor there. Bentley and Sons. I want to see it for nostalgic reasons." An idea had struck me as Flossy had gone from department to department in Harrods, sending her purchases back to the hotel. Now that we were coming to the end of our shopping expedition, it was time to act.

"Your grandfather had his suits made in London?" she asked. "I suppose Cambridge tailors aren't as good as ours. We'll look for gloves then head home via Saville Row."

She didn't buy gloves, in the end, despite trying on several pairs and having me do the same. We climbed into the hotel carriage that had waited for us outside Harrods and Flossy directed the coachman to take us to Bentley and Sons on Saville Row.

"There's no need for you to come in," I told her. "Stay warm and dry in here."

I dashed into the shop as the drizzling rain came down. The tailor looked up from the counter where he was writing something down in a ledger, and arched his brows. He seemed surprised to see a woman in his shop. At the moment, there were no customers so I had his full attention.

"I work for The Mayfair Hotel and have been charged with collecting Mr. Hookly's dinner suit. Is it ready?"

"There must be some mistake. The jacket was delivered this morning and the shirt and trousers are on the way there now." The tailor turned his ledger around and pointed at an entry. "Has it gone astray? Dear, dear me, this is a worry."

"Please, don't be concerned. Perhaps Mr. Hookly hadn't checked with the post desk when he sent me on this errand. I'm sure it's there waiting for him."

"Do check as soon as you return and let me know immediately if it has gone astray. I can't have one of Mr. Hookly's orders disappearing."

"One of?" I echoed. "Has he ordered several items from you? Should I be searching for other parcels too?"

He pointed at several entries in the ledger. "Two coats and two cloaks, four jackets, trousers and waistcoats." He flipped the page. "Two formal dinner suits—"

"Two!"

"Two formal dinner suits, seven shirts and ten ties. Could you check that Mr. Hookly received them all?"

Good lord, he had enough clothing for several men. "I suppose he requires new things for winter." I leaned in a little, hinting at a conspiratorial alliance between shopkeeper and hotel employee. "I believe he has just come from Africa."

"So he told me." The tailor spun the ledger back and closed it with a thud. It would seem he wasn't buying my attempt at friendliness.

"How odd that they don't dine in Africa."

"Pardon?"

I indicated the stiff shirt and formal jacket on the tailor's mannequin in the corner. "If they have dinners in Africa, he wouldn't need a suit, would he? He'd already have one."

The tailor regarded me down his nose. "Perhaps he

required a new one. It is neither my business nor yours as to the reasons for his purchases upon his return to home shores. I suggest you don't gossip about your hotel's guests, miss, particularly ones who are friends with Lord Addlington. His lordship would not approve."

"You know him?"

"He is a great customer of mine and a gentleman of the first order. Now, if you will check with Mr. Hookly that *all* packages have been received, I'll be most grateful."

"I'll be sure to ask him."

He studied the ledger and I turned to go. "One more thing, miss," he called out. "Do you know when Mr. Hookly is leaving London?"

"I'm not sure, but I believe he is staying for the ball." I recalled Mr. Hookly asking Mr. Armitage about an invited guest he wished to see that night so he must intend on staying until then.

The tailor looked relieved. I was considering whether to probe further when a customer entered. He held the door open for me and I left. The stop at the tailor's shop had been a waste of time. I'd learned nothing.

* * *

I LOITERED in the foyer again the following morning, pretending to study a tourist map of London which Peter had given me. I had coat, hat and gloves in hand, ready to follow out one of my suspects if they happened to leave the hotel.

My patience was rewarded when Mr. Duffield walked past. I hid behind the map then raced after him. He didn't stop to collect an umbrella from the luggage desk so I didn't either. Hopefully the rain would stay away for the duration of our walk. I tucked the map into my coat pocket then put the coat on. I was still pulling on my gloves when I exited the hotel.

"Heading out, Miss Fox?" Frank the doorman asked. "Do you require a conveyance?"

"No, thank you."

"A map?"

I peered after Mr. Duffield, not wanting to lose sight of him. "I have one."

"Would you like me to fetch you an umbrella from—"

"No, thank you," I called out as I headed off. Poor Frank was trying very hard to make up for his initial rudeness, but today was not the day for me to indulge him.

Mr. Duffield was a fast walker with a determined step. While Mr. Hookly seemed to be quite the shopper, Mr. Duffield was not. He did not venture into any of the shops, nor did he head to any parks for a leisurely stroll.

I was curious about where he was heading, and my curiosity piqued even further when he turned into Fleet Street. A boy selling newspapers outside *The Daily Telegraph* building tried to sell him a copy, but Mr. Duffield ignored him. He entered the office of *The Evening News*, two doors down. I put my map up to cover the lower part of my face and peered through the window. Mr. Duffield spoke to the clerk at the front desk. He then waited while the clerk sent a lad into an adjoining room.

A few minutes later, a middle-aged fellow emerged. He and Mr. Duffield greeted one another in what appeared to be a cordial manner, then they exchanged envelopes. Mr. Duffield tucked his into his coat pocket, while the other man opened his and read the enclosed letter. He smiled, nodding his approval, and extended his hand to Mr. Duffield.

For a long moment I thought Mr. Duffield wouldn't shake it. He eventually did, but not before the other man's smile turned cynical. Then Mr. Duffield hurried out of the office, his head bowed.

I lifted the map higher and didn't lower it until he'd passed me. Instead of following, I entered the newspaper office.

It wasn't difficult to draw a conclusion for Mr. Duffield's visit—*he* was the one passing on nasty gossip about the hotel and Uncle Ronald's desperate attempt to secure guests for the ball. I wasn't sure what else I could learn, but I'd regret not making inquiries.

"Good morning," I said cheerfully to the young man on the front desk.

The clerk had been slouching against the counter but

straightened upon my smile. He smiled back, revealing crooked teeth. "Can I help you, miss?"

"May I speak with the editor?"

The clerk's smile stretched further. "Which one? We have an editor in chief, managing editor, news editor, features editor, political editor—"

"The one who was talking to Mr. Duffield a moment ago."

His brows arched. "You know Mr. Duffield?"

"We're acquaintances and I want to warn your editor about using him as a source for gossip."

The clerk's smile vanished. He sent the same errand boy off to fetch a man named Collier. "He's the features editor," the clerk explained. "What do you mean you want to warn him about Mr. Duffield?"

I wasn't going to answer but changed my mind. There was as good a chance of learning information from him as from the features editor. "His information is malicious."

The clerk shrugged. "Most of what comes through our doors is told to us by someone with an axe to grind. It doesn't mean the information is worthless."

Mr. Collier shoved open the adjoining door, making it swing wide. "Yes?" he barked as the errand boy slipped past him into the foyer. He arched bushy brows at me.

I abandoned my usual tactic of being cheerful and charming. Most men fell for that manner in a young woman, but I could see this man would not.

"My name is Miss Smith," I said, meeting his gaze. "I was walking past when I saw you speaking to Mr. Duffield. I know him, you see, and I wanted to warn you about using his information without verifying it first."

Mr. Collier grunted. "I always check my sources."

Despite the glare he gave me, I felt a sense of triumph at having my suspicion confirmed by his lack of denial. It must have shown on my face because Mr. Collier's eyebrows moved apart from where they'd drawn together to form a hedge above his eyes.

"Do you have something for me, Miss *Smith*?" he asked, making sure I knew that he knew the name I'd given was false.

"I don't trade in gossip about my friends," I shot back.

"Perhaps not your friends, but what about acquaintances?"

I supposed Sir Ronald was not Mr. Duffield's friend. The extent of their acquaintance was limited to Mr. Duffield's stays at the hotel.

Mr. Collier grunted again when he realized I understood his point. "If you have something of interest to me, you know where to find me. I pay better than some of the other papers." He disappeared through the door, leaving me staring after him.

I blew out a shuddery breath. It was unnerving confronting such a gruff man. I was more familiar with meek academics.

"You all right, miss?" the clerk asked.

"Yes, thank you. Mr. Collier is very…direct."

The clerk glanced at the door through which the editor had left then leaned his elbows on the desk. "You don't have to come here in person."

I gave him a blank look.

"If you have some information you want to sell to Mr. Collier, you can send it. Mr. Collier will see that you get paid. No one need know what you're doing. I don't know why Mr. Duffield came. He usually sends a letter. I work in the mail room sometimes, and I see them."

"How often does Mr. Duffield send a letter containing gossip to Mr. Collier?"

"I couldn't say, miss."

Couldn't or wouldn't? "And is he paid well?"

"That's between him and Mr. Collier. If you write to him, he'll negotiate a fee that suits you both, so don't fret about that."

I wanted to tell him that I'd never betray a confidence, even for someone who was a mere acquaintance. My own financial circumstances had never been good. Indeed, I'd barely managed to keep a roof over our heads after Grandpapa died. It had never occurred to me to sell information about the people I knew. Not that a newspaper editor would be interested in the gossip I gathered. I wasn't acquainted with high society like Mr. Duffield. As the grandson of a nobleman, he probably heard all sorts of interesting tidbits.

Jealousy of their good fortune might also play a part in his motivation.

A thought occurred to me as I headed back to the hotel. If Mrs. Warrick and Mr. Duffield had mutual friends, and she learned that he sold gossip about them to the newspapers, she could have confronted him at the hotel.

And he could have killed her out of fear she'd expose him.

CHAPTER 7

*I*t served nobody to keep what I'd learned to myself. I went directly to Mr. Hobart's office to inform him. "I think he is responsible for that article in yesterday's edition of *The Evening News*. The source had to have been someone with knowledge of Sir Ronald's desperation."

Mr. Hobart clasped his hands on the desk in front him. Concern darkened his blue eyes. "That is a shame. Sir Ronald would be most upset to learn who it was."

"Is he close to Mr. Duffield?"

"No. Mr. Duffield has stayed here before, but not for some time. I'd guessed his circumstances were reduced, but I hadn't realized how far. Poor man."

"Poor man! He has betrayed the hotel."

"Not out of maliciousness. He was desperate and desperation can make a man do things he wouldn't usually do."

"Aren't you concerned that he won't be able to pay for his room here?" I asked.

"I'm quite sure he'll see his account settled. He wouldn't want his name blacklisted altogether."

"But why stay here at all? If he must be in London at this time, why not stay somewhere more affordable?"

"I suspect he wants to attend the ball. Mr. Duffield is unmarried, you see, and the New Year's Eve ball at The Mayfair attracts a particular caliber of guest. He could find himself a wife amongst them."

"You mean a wealthy wife."

He gave me a knowing smile.

That was why he accepted my impromptu invitation to dinner, and also why he abandoned me just as readily. He must have asked Mr. Chapman about me, and the steward informed him that I was a poor relation. Although I wasn't quite sure how Mr. Chapman knew.

"May I ask why you followed Mr. Duffield into the office of *The Evening News*?" Mr. Hobart asked.

"I know my uncle doesn't want the police to question the guests about the murder, and I felt that directive too limiting, so I decided to follow Mr. Duffield when I saw him leave this morning."

His lips twitched. It would seem my attempts at investigation amused him. "If my brother thinks the guests ought to be questioned, he will do it, directive or no directive."

"Oh. Well, that is a relief."

"But why Mr. Duffield? Why not one of the other guests?"

"He struck me as suspicious. He wears old clothes yet he stays at a luxury hotel. I found it odd."

"Your investigative skills are excellent," he said. "My brother would be impressed."

"Will you inform him of what I told you about Mr. Duffield?"

"If it becomes relevant, but I don't see how Mr. Duffield's tendency to gossip could be linked to Mrs. Warrick's murder. For now, I will tell only Sir Ronald."

"I do think you ought to tell the detective inspector. Let him decide if it's important enough to question Mr. Duffield about the murder. Perhaps he can find a link between him and Mrs. Warrick. Perhaps she knew him."

"Perhaps she did." He gave me a wan smile. I suspected he was still thinking about informing my uncle of Mr. Duffield's betrayal, and wasn't looking forward to it.

"Would you mind if I told Uncle Ronald about the source of the information for that nasty article?" I asked. "It is my information to pass on, after all. I can't let you have all the accolades."

"I'll tell him it came from you."

I winked and he chuckled at his misunderstanding my

intention. "I would be grateful if you informed him. Perhaps he won't be so eager to berate the messenger if the message is delivered by his favorite niece."

"Considering I'm his only niece, there is no contest. Does he have a temper?"

He hesitated and was saved from answering by the arrival of Mrs. Kettering.

I headed upstairs and knocked on my uncle's office door. He bade me to enter, but did not look up from his desk. "What is it?" he asked.

"I wanted to tell you something that I learned about one of the guests," I said.

"Cleo! I am sorry, I thought it was Hobart. Please, sit. Would you like some tea?" He pointed at a teapot and cups on a tray on the sideboard next to the decanter.

He looked harried, his eyes tired. A stack of newspapers made a tower on the corner of his desk. Beside the stack was a folded copy of *The Evening News*.

"That would be lovely," I said. "Don't get up. I'll pour." I was parched after my brisk walks to and from Fleet Street. I handed Uncle Ronald a cup and sat with my own.

"You look as though you needed that," he said after I took a large gulp.

"I've been out and about." I took another sip then put the cup on the desk. "Indeed, that's why I wanted to talk to you. I paid a visit to the office of *The Evening News*."

"Filthy rag," he muttered into his cup.

"It bothered me greatly to learn that they'd published such awful things about the hotel."

"So you visited their office and gave them what for?"

"Not quite. I can't blame them for writing something that will sell the most copies. The real culprit here is the one who passed on the information about your, er, strident measures to ensure guests come to the ball. I wanted to find out who could have done such a thing."

"Since it could only be someone with very particular knowledge." He was about to take another sip but suddenly lowered the cup to the desk. "Do you mean to tell me you asked them point blank who it was?"

"Not quite. I watched the office from across the street and

my patience was rewarded when Mr. Duffield entered the building."

"Duffield! You know him?"

"He and I dined together the other night. It was…not an entirely pleasant experience."

He frowned. "Why would you dine with Duffield?"

I dismissed his question with a small wave. That produced an even deeper frown, and I suspected my uncle wasn't used to being dismissed. "I thought Mr. Duffield's presence at the newspaper office too coincidental, so I waited until he left then went inside and spoke to the editor I'd seen him speak to. He claimed Mr. Duffield passes on gossip about people in his circle in exchange for money."

Uncle Ronald's moustache twitched with the movement of his mouth as he thought. "Thank you for informing me," he said after a moment.

"What will you do about it?"

"Nothing." He picked up his teacup.

"Why not?"

"Duffield is a guest here. I don't want to embarrass him by confronting him. If it got out, it would affect our reputation."

"But what if he provides the newspaper with further gossip about the hotel?"

He smiled over the rim of the cup. "He won't have that opportunity again. Not about The Mayfair."

Silence was one way of solving the problem, I supposed. Indeed, it was probably the best way for the hotel. Mr. Duffield might not be wealthy, but he did have friends in society who were. I was rather glad I hadn't confronted Mr. Duffield myself as he left the newspaper's office.

"There's one more thing," I said. "It's regarding the murder. Have the police informed you of any developments today?"

"None."

"What about the results of their tests for poison in the items they took away from Mrs. Warrick's room?"

He shook his head. "They are keeping the results close to their chest." He sighed heavily and looked as though he was about to tell me something, but thought better of it.

"Uncle? Is there something you wish to say? Perhaps if you share it, the burden will lighten."

"That's kind of you, Cleo." He squeezed the bridge of his nose. "I'm merely concerned that one of the staff may be found guilty after all."

"I understand. You don't want to think that you could have hired a murderer."

"We're like a family here. It would be a betrayal." He leaned back in his chair and rubbed his jaw. "I've never had any trouble from them, so why now?"

"It could be one of the guests."

His gaze snapped to mine. "I don't want you to worry, Cleo. The Mayfair Hotel is a London icon. It'll take more than this to shake us."

I smiled, although I hadn't been terribly worried about the hotel's future until now. He didn't sound very convincing. "I'm sure the ball will be a sensation."

His gaze softened. "Thank you, Cleo."

I rose and headed for the door.

"And Cleo?" I turned around to see my uncle looking small and insignificant beside the stack of newspapers. "I appreciate what you did today in Fleet Street. I know I ought to tell you not to spy, but I find I can't. You were very brave, and very loyal. Thank you."

"I'm glad I could help. Let me know if there's anything else I can do." I left, feeling pleased with my efforts. Now that he'd seen what I could do, perhaps he'd consider me for a more permanent role within the hotel.

* * *

FLOSSY WANTED to go shopping again, but I declined, claiming tiredness. I had no plans to rest, however. I wanted to think about the investigation so far, and how to proceed. While I'd learned some interesting things about my suspects, I needed to know more, particularly how they were connected to Mrs. Warrick, if at all. I would have liked to discuss it with Harmony, but one of the footmen said the maids had all finished. Some would return later to assist ladies who hadn't brought their own maid, but he didn't know if Harmony was one of them.

I had a good collection of notes beside both Mr. Hookly and Mr. Duffield's names, but very little against Mr. Armitage. All I knew was that he was adopted as a teen. I considered asking Mr. Hobart about his nephew but discarded the idea. It would be too obvious.

I also considered telling Mr. Armitage about my own parents' deaths as a way of getting him to open up about becoming an orphan, but discarded that idea just as quickly. Not only would it dredge up my painful memories, it was also a low act to use my misfortune as a tool to encourage him to trust me. I'd rather rummage through his office for clues. His bedchamber might reveal evidence of a more personal nature, but I couldn't bring myself to break into it. Not only was it also a low act, but I'd have no excuse if I was caught. At least if I was discovered in his office I could claim I was looking for some hotel stationery.

I ventured downstairs in the hope of seeing Mr. Armitage leave his office. I was rewarded after only a few minutes. But instead of speaking to a guest or staff member as he usually did, he left the hotel altogether.

After a quick word with Frank and Goliath at the front door, he strode off along Piccadilly. I made up my mind in an instant. Despite having no coat, hat or gloves, I decided to follow. I'd been rewarded with answers when I followed Mr. Duffield; hopefully I'd have equal good fortune by following Mr. Armitage.

"Miss Fox, you have no coat!" Frank cried as I passed him.

"It's not too cold and I won't be gone long," I assured him without stopping.

I kept Mr. Armitage in sight but did not get too close. He walked at a steady, unhurried pace into the chaotic throng of Piccadilly Circus. I dodged pedestrians, carts and conveyances of all shapes and sizes, and despite being almost run down, I managed to spot him heading along Shaftsbury Avenue. If he hadn't been so tall, I might have lost him altogether.

From there he entered Dean Street and stopped outside a handsome building. He entered without knocking.

According to the bronze plaque beside the door, it was St Andrew's Home and Club for Working Boys, and its patron was a lord. Could Mr. Armitage have lived at this institution when he was younger? Had it given him a roof over his head when he'd needed it most? If so, it could provide me with answers about my suspect.

I continued on until I reached a lamp post where I waited and watched. The walk had been brisk enough to keep me warm, but now that I'd stopped, the cold seeped through my clothing to my skin. I blew into my hands but it did little to thaw them.

I had no watch and lost track of the time. Mr. Armitage could have been inside for fifteen minutes or forty-five. I was immeasurably glad when he emerged and walked off in the other direction to me, back the way we'd come. I was also very glad to enter the building. There was no fireplace or heating grate in the hall but at least it was warmer than outside.

I'd had between fifteen and forty-five minutes to think of something to say, but even so, I found myself hesitating when a vicar greeted me. I hadn't expected to lie to a man of God. I wasn't sure I could go through with it.

"May I help you?" he asked.

He had a friendly face with small round spectacles that drew attention to his kind eyes. I cringed just thinking about what I was about to do.

But do it I must. A murder had been committed and Mr. Armitage was a suspect.

"I couldn't help but notice Mr. Armitage leave here," I said.

"You know Harry?" The wrinkles at the corners of his eyes deepened with his smile.

"I work with him at the hotel."

"Ah."

"Is this where he grew up?"

The vicar's eyes shuttered. "You'd have to ask him that."

If Mr. Armitage hadn't lived at the orphanage, wouldn't the vicar have said as much? It was a flimsy clue to latch onto, but latch on I did.

"It's just that he's very proud and I do so want to donate

to the institution that took care of my friend. My *very* good friend."

The vicar's brows rose. "A donation? Come with me, and we'll discuss the particulars."

He took me through to a large office with a wide desk and filing cabinets lining one wall. The cabinet drawers were labeled with letters of the alphabet. The vicar asked me to take a seat as he cleared away two teacups. Mr. Armitage had probably sat in this very room a few minutes ago and shared a cup of tea with the vicar. I wondered what they'd talked about.

Somewhere in the building a bell clanged and feet trampled over floorboards.

The vicar cringed. "My apologies, Miss…"

"Miss Smith."

"My apologies for the noise, Miss Smith. The boys are moving between classes." He extended his hand. "The Reverend Collin Belfour, at your service. I'm the vicar at St Andrew's, and I work here most days to give the boys an ecclesiastical education. Teachers give them a more practical one, arming them with the skills they'll need in service or industry."

"That's very commendable."

He sat and I took the moment to quickly scan the contents of his desk to glean a clue as to what he and Mr. Armitage had been discussing. The desk was neat with a Bible opened to the book of Genesis. Beside it was a page of written notes. Beside that was a small pouch. The vicar picked up the pouch and dropped it into the top drawer of his desk. Coins jangled.

"Tell me about the donation," the vicar said.

"Mr. Armitage recently did a good turn for some of the staff at the hotel and we want to thank him. He's too proud to accept money, so we thought we could make a donation to a charity close to his heart. What could be closer than the orphanage that took care of him?"

The vicar clasped his hands and rubbed his thumbs together, frowning. Clearly he wanted the donation, but he didn't want to break a confidence. "A donation would be very welcome," he said. "Would you like to look around and see the good work we do here?"

"Only if Mr. Armitage was here as a boy."

"Have you considered asking him?"

"You know how proud he is. He doesn't like talking about his past."

He chewed on the inside of his lip.

"Perhaps if you left the room for several minutes, I could look through the cabinet drawer labeled A, and if I happened to find Mr. Armitage's details, I could discover what I need to know. You wouldn't be breaking any rules yourself."

"Miss Smith! I am shocked!"

I stumbled through an apology and rose quickly. My face heated beneath his scowl as I backed towards the door. "I feel awful for misreading the situation," I said. I truly did feel awful, but I wasn't sorry for making the suggestion. It had to be done while there was a slim chance that it would work.

I almost ran out of the office, however, unable to face the vicar's scowl.

"I'll still welcome your donation," he called out when I reached the front door.

I fled into the street only to find it was raining. With no umbrella or coat, I got thoroughly wet as I hurried back to the hotel.

Frank gasped when he saw me. "Miss Fox! You're half drowned."

"It's just a little water."

"You really should have taken an umbrella."

"Thank you," I said wryly. "I'll do so next time."

He signaled to Goliath. The porter hurried over, frowning at me. "You went out without a coat?" He clicked his tongue.

I gave them both tight smiles. "Yes, I went out without a coat and umbrella."

"And gloves," Frank said.

"And hat," Goliath added.

I glared at them. I wasn't in the mood for their scowls and lectures. I just wanted to get inside and dry off.

"You should have a nice warm bath," Frank said as I passed him. "Have one of the footmen bring up a cup of tea for you from the kitchen while it's filling. There's nothing quite as soothing as drinking tea while soaking in a warm bath."

Goliath screwed his face up. "When've you done that? Our bathrooms are communal in the men's staff quarters," he told me. "No one's going to bring this idiot a cup of tea while he takes a bath."

Frank bristled. I thought it was because Goliath called him an idiot, but it turned out he was offended for other reasons. "I've worked places other than here. Places where I can sneak off for a long bath when the master and mistress aren't home."

I headed inside before I froze to death. I planned to race up the stairs before anyone saw me, but unfortunately I had to pass Mr. Armitage and he missed nothing.

He eyed me up and down.

"I left in a hurry and the rain caught me unawares," I said before he could lecture me too. "If you'll excuse me, I don't want to drip on the floor any more than necessary."

"I'm on my way to the kitchen now. Shall I send up a cup of tea and cake?"

I blinked at him. I'd expected censure or mocking not kindness. "Thank you, that's very thoughtful."

"And a maid to fix your hair." He walked off.

Well! I must look bedraggled and my hair frightful, but there was no need to point it out. Just when I began to like Mr. Armitage again, he did or said something to remind me why that was a mistake.

* * *

I SPENT my bath time thinking about the filing cabinets in the vicar's office at the orphanage. While I was quite sure Mr. Armitage had lived there as a youth, I wanted to know more. What had he been like? Had he shown a tendency for violence? It might point to signs of guilt if he had. All of that information would be kept in his file, and that would be kept in the cabinet. The only way I could read it was to sneak in.

Harmony helped fix my hair after my bath. She asked me how the investigation was going but I gave her little information. "It's too early to know," I told her. "I do need some help, however. I need to unlock a locked door without a key. Do you know how?"

She regarded me, one hand on hip. "I'm not a burglar, Miss Fox."

"I wasn't suggesting that you were." I sighed. "I'm sorry, Harmony. I can see how you misconstrued my meaning."

She lowered her hand and continued to pin my hair in place. "Ask Victor."

I gasped. "Was he a burglar before he became a cook?"

She shrugged. "I don't know, but he's a suspicious character."

"Tell him to meet me outside the hotel at midnight but don't let the doorman see him."

I dined alone with Flossy at eight. Floyd dined at a club, Uncle Ronald ate at his desk, and Aunt Lilian didn't want to leave her room. Flossy was pleased to have company and we played cards after dinner until eleven.

Just before midnight, I donned coat, hat and gloves in my room, and collected an umbrella from the night porter. Frank and Goliath were not on duty, so I was able to slip away and meet Victor without anyone asking where I was going. He waited for me in the shadows, well away from the hotel's lights.

"Harmony says you want me to unlock a door for you," Victor said as we trudged along the pavement. "Want to tell me what building that door belongs to?"

"A home for boys on Dean Street."

"I know it. Why there?"

"All I can tell you is that it might give us a clue about one of our suspects."

Victor hunched into his coat, the collar flipped up to protect his neck from the icy breeze. With his hat pulled low, the light from the streetlamps didn't reach his face and I couldn't even make out the scar. Even so, if I'd been walking towards him at this hour alone, I would have crossed the street to avoid him.

To be fair, he didn't exude menace. I would have crossed the street to avoid any man if I walked London's streets alone on a winter's night. But there was a nefariousness about Victor that I couldn't quite put my finger on. Harmony was right; he was a suspicious character.

Perhaps it was his affinity for knives. He didn't wear them

on a belt around his waist tonight. He'd changed out of his chef's whites too. He must have been home and returned to meet me.

"How long have you worked at The Mayfair?" I asked.

"Two years."

"And where were you before that?"

"You ask a lot of questions."

"I'm hearing that often lately."

The collar hid his mouth, but the creases around his eyes drew together as if he smiled. "Be careful, Miss Fox. Some people don't like it when you ask questions."

"Is that a threat, Victor?"

"A warning. If I were threatening you, you wouldn't need to ask. You'd just know."

"Understood."

We passed through Piccadilly Circus, notably quieter compared to that afternoon but not altogether without life. Hackneys and private carriages still drove past, though there were no pedestrians. The shops were closed, the nearby theaters shut for the break between Christmas and New Year, and few people had a reason to be out in mid-winter at midnight.

The blurred lights of the streetlamps tried valiantly to pierce the descending fog, but it was a hopeless cause. It seemed to thicken with every step we took, and by the time we reached Dean Street, our footsteps echoed in the cold, dense air.

"Why do you trust me?" Victor suddenly asked. "It's not usual to walk with a man you hardly know in the middle of the night."

"Harmony trusted you enough to recommend you, and I trust Harmony."

He made no comment, just kept up the pace until we reached the orphanage. "Cover me," he said, crouching.

I put up my umbrella which I'd brought to use as a weapon in case we were set upon by thieves, and used it and my body to shield him. "Can you see?" I asked.

"I don't need to see. It's done by feel and sound."

"How interesting. Perhaps one day you can teach me."

He looked up at me. "I said feel *and sound*."

"Sorry," I whispered.

I watched as he inserted two long pin-like instruments into the lock.

Then he suddenly glanced up at me again. "Keep watch."

I scanned the street, but there was no one about. After one or two minutes, Victor stood and turned the doorknob. The door opened.

I lowered my umbrella and followed him in only to bump into his back. I gave him the umbrella then pulled out a small candlestick and holder from the pack slung over my shoulder, and a box of matches. I lit the candle and tiptoed to the office door. It was also locked.

Victor crouched again and had it unlocked quickly. Inside the office, the cabinet drawer marked A was not locked. The files were sorted alphabetically by surname, as I'd expected when I'd seen the drawer labels earlier. For common surnames, like Adams, the files were then sub-sorted by first name. Each child had only a single page dedicated to them. It was somewhat sad to think that a life could be summed up by a page of notes. Indeed, many were not even a full page.

There was only one Harry Armitage. A quick calculation in my head confirmed that the date of birth written on the file matched the age I assumed Mr. Armitage to be. I folded up the piece of paper and pocketed it before returning to Victor, keeping watch at the office door.

I closed the door softly behind me, turned and froze. A boy of about twelve stood in the doorway to an adjoining room, a large piece of pie halfway to his mouth. He stood just as frozen as he stared wide-eyed back at us.

Victor put his finger to his lips to shush the lad then blew out my candle. He led the way back outside, closed the front door, then grabbed my elbow and hustled me down Dean Street.

I didn't dare look back until we reached the corner. "No one seems to be following us," I said. "But if that boy raises the alarm, we could still be caught."

"He won't," Victor said.

"How can you be certain?"

"Thieves don't snitch on each other."

I was about to protest about being called a thief when I

remembered the piece of paper in my pocket. "Let's hurry back to the hotel. He might change his mind."

"And explain why he was raiding the kitchen? Unlikely."

Even so, we walked quickly. Once we reached the hotel, Victor remained in the shadows until I was safely within the arc cast by The Mayfair's welcoming lights. The doorman greeted me by name and opened the door for me. I'd wager gossip about my nocturnal outing would be all over the hotel by morning, but hopefully only among the staff. I didn't have to answer to them. I did have to answer to my uncle, however.

I raced up to my suite and flattened the piece of paper on the desk. I quickly read it then re-read it, hardly believing the words. This couldn't be possible. The Harry Armitage I knew couldn't be the same one as the boy in this file. My uncle would not have employed him.

Unless he didn't know that Mr. Armitage had been arrested as a thief.

According to the file, Harry Armitage had been placed at the orphanage aged eleven when his parents died. My gut twisted in pain for that boy. It was very close to the age I'd been when my parents died, and I clearly remembered how awful it had been. I'd had loving grandparents to take care of me, however. Harry Armitage had no one. He'd gone to live with strangers.

The file noted that he was clever, particularly with numbers, and well behaved. He'd been taken aside and given a rudimentary education in bookkeeping. After a year, he was considered well-equipped for a life of work and a factory owner hired him to assist the bookkeeper at his factory.

The rest was written in a different colored ink but by the same hand. It was dated another year later. At aged thirteen, Harry Armitage had been arrested for theft and served a three-month sentence. The arresting police sergeant and his wife had subsequently taken Harry in upon his release.

My first thought was that it was a very light sentence. My second was, why? Why had the thirteen-year-old boy gone from promising bookkeeper in good employment to thief?

And if he were a thief, could he also be capable of murder, particularly if he wanted to keep that part of his life a secret?

CHAPTER 8

J could tell by the way Harmony brushed my hair that something bothered her. She raked the brush through with vigorous strokes then thumped it down on the dressing table.

"You don't have to do my hair if you don't want to," I said. "I'm capable of doing it myself."

"I want to."

"Then can you be a little gentler? I'd like some hair left when you've finished."

Hand on hip, she regarded me in the mirror's reflection. "When I told you to ask Victor to open a locked door for you, I wasn't expecting you to leave the hotel in the middle of the night."

"Ah. So you heard about that."

"The whole hotel heard!"

I spun around in the chair. "My uncle?"

"I don't think anyone would have told the Bainbridges. We don't talk to them as freely as we do each other."

I turned back to the mirror. "Does anyone know that I went out with Victor?"

"No, but you probably should have let on that you met him. Everyone thinks you went out alone. A lady can't do that without everyone thinking the worst of her."

"I don't care what the staff think. I know what I was doing, and it wasn't what you're implying. Just as long as my uncle doesn't hear of it. I'd rather not incur his wrath this early in our acquaintance."

Harmony twisted a section of my hair and checked the effect in the mirror. Satisfied, she proceeded to stick pins into it. Fortunately her temper had cooled and she didn't stab my scalp. "Next time you have to go out at night alone, wear a disguise so the doorman doesn't recognize you."

"He wouldn't let me back in if I didn't show my face. Or if he did, the night porter would accost me in the foyer."

"Then just don't go out. You can't have nasty gossip attached to you."

I sighed. I wasn't going to win, even if I reminded her that a murderer needed to be caught.

"So where did you go?" she asked.

"I'd rather not tell you until I have more answers. I don't want to implicate an innocent person."

"I can just ask Victor."

I hadn't sworn Victor to silence, but I hoped he would also be discreet. I suspected Harmony could be quite determined when she wanted to be, however.

"I'm not sure if we discovered anything important anyway," I went on. "It was probably nothing."

She finished my hair and left to begin her cleaning duties while I ate breakfast, delivered by one of the footmen. He eyed me with a narrowed gaze as he passed me the tray and did not wish me a good morning as he had done the day before. It would seem my reputation was thoroughly ruined, at least as far as the staff were concerned.

I nibbled the toast but left the boiled eggs untouched. I was still reeling from the news that Mr. Armitage had been arrested for theft as a boy. If Mrs. Warrick knew him back then, and knew of the arrest, she would certainly be surprised to see him at a luxury hotel in a position of responsibility, surrounded by wealthy guests. If she told my uncle, Mr. Armitage would lose his job and reputation. Stopping her seemed like a very strong motive for murder to me.

What I needed to do now was find that connection between Mrs. Warrick and a young Harry Armitage. Perhaps she knew the factory where he had worked before running away. Perhaps she was a patroness of the orphanage, or she could even have been the victim of his thieving. I could check none of those things easily, however. I was at a loss for what to do next.

I ventured downstairs since I was unlikely to find answers to my questions on my breakfast tray. I greeted Peter with a smile. He responded stiffly without meeting my gaze.

First Harmony and now Peter thought poorly of me. Despite my earlier statement that I didn't care, I found I did care what they thought of me. I cared very much.

"I was following up a clue," I told Peter. "That's why I was out late last night. And Victor went with me. If you don't believe me, ask him. I wasn't doing anything of the nature you are all thinking. Is that understood?"

"Yes, Miss Fox."

"Kindly inform the rest of the staff. Only leave out the part about me investigating the murder and meeting Victor. I don't want to get him into trouble."

"I knew it," came Goliath's voice.

I jumped. I hadn't seen him approach. For a big man, he had a light step.

"I knew it was something innocent," he went on. "I'll be sure everyone is made aware that you had a good reason for going out."

"What good reason?" Peter asked.

Goliath tapped the side of his nose. "I'll think of something."

A porter emerged from the manager's corridor and approached. "Mr. Hobart wishes to see you, Miss Fox."

"Oh dear." He'd heard too and wanted to lecture me about fragile female reputations. Given what I'd learned about Mr. Armitage, I wasn't keen to see either man, but I doubted I was in any physical danger from them this morning. They didn't know that I'd been investigating the murder.

I entered the manager's corridor and approached Mr. Hobart's door when movement in Mr. Chapman's office caught my eye. It was Mr. Armitage searching through the pockets of a coat hanging on the stand. He'd angled himself so he could see the door and he quickly withdrew his hand from the pocket and brushed down the jacket sleeve. He didn't fool me, however.

"What are you doing?" I asked.

"Looking for Mr. Chapman," he said, joining me. "There was some dust on his jacket so I brushed it off. We're very particular about presentation here."

It was the most ridiculous excuse I'd ever heard, but I wouldn't let him think I didn't believe him. If he were the murderer, I must not let him know I suspected him.

It took all of my resolve to feign innocence, however. Now that I strongly suspected Mr. Armitage of the murder, I couldn't help seeing him in a different light. The charm was all a façade. It was a very convincing façade, and one that he knew how to employ with maximum effect, but I'd seen it slip occasionally. When he thought I doubted his father's ability as a detective, for one, and when he thought me a woman of ill repute when he caught me in the smoking room.

And now.

"I'm glad you're here," he said. "I'd like a word. Please step into my office."

"No!"

He blinked at my outburst.

"I mean, not right now," I said quickly.

"If you won't step into my office, then I'll say what I have to say out here." He placed his hands at his back. "It's about Sir Ronald, as it happens, and the fact that he doesn't yet know what you got up to last night."

I wasn't sure whether to groan or roll my eyes. What I did, however, was blush which only made it worse. I wasn't guilty. Well, I was guilty of leaving the hotel in the middle of the night, but I had not been alone.

"If you have a secret paramour, that's your affair," he went on. "But meet him in the open. Don't sneak away. The staff see everything and they talk, and I doubt you want your secret exposed to your family by one of the staff."

It galled that he was accusing me of secret liaisons when I'd just caught him rummaging through another man's coat. Not to mention the secret of his arrest. I suspected my uncle would care more about that than my supposed illicit love affair.

"I think I've heard enough," I said through clenched teeth. "Good day, Mr. Armitage."

I went to walk off but he grabbed my elbow. He relaxed his grip instantly and I pulled free, but I rounded on him and gave him what I hoped was a glare of defiance.

He glared right back, not in the least concerned that I was the niece of his employer. "How could you do something so foolish?" he went on. The charming façade had slipped away altogether, revealing someone more formidable and earnest beneath. "If he was worthy, he would court you properly. Is there something wrong with him? Is he beneath the Bainbridges?"

I barked a harsh laugh. "Good lord, this has gone too far. Let me make myself clear, Mr. Armitage. I do not have a secret lover. I went out for reasons which I don't have to divulge to you or anyone else. If my uncle discovers it, so be it. I will deal with the consequences."

The glare vanished, but his frown remained. "Are you in trouble?"

"I don't even know what sort of trouble you could be referring to that would require me to leave in the middle of the night. The truth is quite dull, I'm afraid. I couldn't sleep and I was feeling a little melancholy. I decided to go for a walk to clear my head. I was gone less than thirty minutes. Satisfied?"

A muscle in his jaw bunched. "It was just some friendly advice, Miss Fox. London is dangerous at night. I wouldn't want anything bad to happen to you."

"Please don't concern yourself on my account," I bit off.

He drew in a deep breath and looked to the ceiling, no doubt searching it for some patience. I was well aware how trying the conversation must be from his point of view, but I couldn't tell him anything that would ease his mind, and I did not like to be patronized.

I turned and walked off, but the heat of his glare on my back remained with me as I passed into the foyer. I hadn't forgotten that Mr. Hobart wanted to speak to me, but I was in no mood for his lecture. It could wait.

Goliath must have already spoken to the other porters and the staff manning each of the desks because they no longer looked at me like I'd committed a sin. They greeted me as they had done since my arrival, with a friendly "good morning" and a nod or smile.

It occurred to me, as I headed into the vestibule behind the foyer, that Mr. Armitage could have been trying to distract me from what he'd been doing in Mr. Chapman's office. If so, the deflection hadn't worked. While I couldn't think of a reason why the murderer of Mrs. Warrick needed to search the pockets of one of the other staff, that didn't mean there wasn't a connection. I just hadn't found it yet. But find it I must. The police, headed by Mr. Armitage's own father, wouldn't arrest him without solid proof.

As I hoped, I found Mr. Chapman in the dining room, addressing the waiters. I waited until he dismissed them and they dispersed around the dining room to set the tables for luncheon.

"Is there something I can do for you, Miss Fox?" He peered down his nose at me, as if I were one of his waiters who'd been found somewhere he ought not to be. It would seem he'd also heard the gossip about by nocturnal adventure, but had not yet been told whatever reason Goliath had made up to explain it.

"I wanted to talk to you about Mr. Armitage."

His superior demeanor shattered with his surprise. "What about him?"

I didn't want to be specific, but I did want answers. I needed to tell him something that would get him confiding in me. I leaned forward and lowered my voice. "I've seen him acting suspiciously."

"In what way?" he asked, voice also lowered.

"I'd rather not say at this point. It might be nothing, and I don't want to get him into trouble. But I do want to talk to someone who knows him. Someone from the senior staff. Naturally, I can't go to Mr. Hobart, and I prefer to speak to you rather than Mrs. Kettering."

Although his mouth didn't move, this last comment seemed to please him. He was a handsome man, tall and slim, with dark-hair and a cleanly shaved jaw and upper lip. His snobbish superiority did him no favors, however. It instantly put me off.

"What do you know about Mr. Armitage's past?" I asked. "Before he came to work here."

A small crease appeared between his eyebrows. "Very little. He was taken in by Mr. Hobart's brother, and Mr. Hobart found him a position here. He was promoted to assistant manager over some more eligible candidates." He sniffed. "No doubt Mr. Hobart wants to keep the line of succession in his family."

His jealousy took me by surprise. While it was interesting, it wasn't relevant to the investigation. Except that it might give Mr. Chapman a reason to divulge more than he ought about his rival.

"Has Mr. Armitage ever used his position here to his advantage?"

"I'm not sure what you mean," he said. "I have to admit he's very good at what he does. He takes a great load off Mr. Hobart's shoulders." So much for jealousy.

I needed to be even more direct if I was going to establish a connection between Mr. Armitage's past and Mrs. Warrick. "Has Mr. Armitage ever been seen somewhere he shouldn't be? In the office of one of the other senior staff without them being present, or in a guest's room, perhaps?"

He glanced past me towards the door then bent his head to mine. "What do you think he has done?"

"Nothing."

"Then why the questions?"

"So he has never abused his authority?"

He gasped. "Is this about Mrs. Warrick's murder? Do you suspect him?"

"Everyone is a suspect at this point in time." I'd gone too far to back away now. Mr. Chapman wasn't a fool and wouldn't believe me if I pretended my questions weren't related to the murder.

"Do you know, it did occur to me that he might have done it," Mr. Chapman said. "But I dismissed the notion. He's not the type to poison someone."

The detective inspector's words about all types being capable of murder rang in my head like a bell.

"And I didn't think it a strong enough reason," Mr. Chapman went on.

"What reason?"

He glanced behind me at the door again. "I overheard Mrs. Warrick having words with Mr. Hobart in his office. The door was closed but she spoke loudly and I could clearly hear her mention Mr. Armitage's name."

I knew from experience that one had to press one's ear to the door to overhear conversations coming from within. Accidentally overhearing something was impossible. "In what context?" I asked.

"I don't know. All I heard her say was that Mr. Armitage should be spoken to severely, that she expected better from The Mayfair."

If she had recognized Mr. Armitage and remembered his past as a thief, the first person she'd tell would be his immediate superior. Not knowing Mr. Hobart was his uncle, she would have told him everything. She expected better from The Mayfair because she did not expect a thief to be employed at a luxury hotel.

It fit neatly. Very neatly. Perhaps Mr. Hobart had tried to deny it or brush it off, and she had then threatened to speak to my uncle. That would have worried Mr. Hobart and Mr. Armitage greatly. With Mr. Hobart knowing Mr. Armitage's past, he should never have hired him at the hotel. Their subterfuge would be exposed and they would both be ordered to leave the hotel immediately.

That night, before she had a chance to speak to my uncle, one or both of them had silenced her.

I wasn't sure what bothered me more. That Mr. Hobart was complicit in the crime, or that Mr. Armitage had murdered someone. I'd liked them upon first meeting them. Not to mention that my uncle trusted them implicitly. To think them capable of poisoning Mrs. Warrick to ensure her silence was sickening.

Mr. Armitage had proved to be someone other than what he pretended, however. His coldness towards me could be indicative of something even colder, darker, within him.

"I see I've done the right thing in telling you," Mr. Chapman said, straightening.

My mind reeled and my stomach rolled. The implications

of this were enormous. I needed to be very careful and very sure before proceeding.

"Thank you," I said, my voice thin. "You will be discreet about this, won't you?"

"Of course."

I left the dining room and caught the lift to the fourth floor. I hardly heard John as he chatted about the weather. There was just too much to think about. Too much at stake. I needed to be absolutely certain of my theory.

But how?

I stepped out of the lift and saw my uncle about to enter his office. He greeted me warmly.

"How have you settled into the hotel so far, Cleo?"

"Very well, thank you."

"Flossy and Floyd treating you well?"

"Like a sibling," I said, meaning it.

"God, I hope not." He chuckled, but it vanished suddenly. "The death of Mrs. Warrick has dampened the mood here, somewhat. Usually at this time of year everyone's excited about the New Year's Eve ball." He sighed heavily. "Nasty business, and the police aren't being helpful. The detective refuses to tell me what he's uncovered so far. Wish he was more like his brother, our Hobart. Good fellow, Hobart."

I bit my lower lip.

"At least the newspapers haven't reported any vicious rumors today. Hobart sent Armitage down to the office of that rag, *The Evening News*, and he threatened legal action on behalf of the hotel. Seems to have done the trick. Can't have The Mayfair's good name dragged through the mud, and the Bainbridge name along with it."

He opened his office door and stepped over the threshold. I stood there, wanting very much to confide in him and yet not wanting to at the same time.

"Is there something else, Cleo? Is it about your allowance?"

"No, it's not that." I bit my lip again.

"You'd better tell me or you'll do yourself some damage." He smiled as he indicated my lip.

Perhaps there was a compromise, a way of finding out

more but not naming names. If he didn't know about Mr. Armitage's past, then my theory was viable. If he *did* know then there was no reason for Mr. Armitage to kill Mrs. Warrick.

"I do have a question for you, as it happens. Would you ever hire someone who'd been arrested in the past?"

"Arrested! Who has been arrested?"

"Nobody. At least, not at the moment. I was simply asking if you'd ever hire someone who had a criminal record. For example, someone who was arrested as a child for theft."

"Of course not. Can't have thieves roaming about the hotel with guests' valuables lying about. Even if they were a reformed character, can you imagine the damage it would do to our reputation if the press got wind of it? I'm sorry, Cleo, if you have a friend in mind for a position here, but I simply can't take them on."

"A friend? Oh."

"Not a friend?" He frowned. "Cleo, what are you trying to tell me?"

I put my hands up and backed away. "Nothing. It was just a silly question." So much for thinking I could be discreet. "I'm sorry to bother you."

"Cleo!" Flossy called out.

I was so relieved to be rescued that I almost ran to her. She stood beside her door, arms crossed. "What were you talking to Father about? He looks troubled."

"Nothing. It was nothing. Are you heading out for a walk?"

"Yes, and then luncheon. Care to join me?"

"Gladly."

* * *

FLOYD JOINED us for luncheon in the dining room. I studiously avoided Mr. Chapman's gaze the entire time, and that of as many staff as possible. With the turn the investigation had taken, I was glad for some frivolous conversation for a change.

"There's only three more days to go until the ball, not counting today," Flossy said after the waiter deposited a bowl of soup in front of her. "You must have made a decision about attending by now, Cleo."

"I haven't had time to think," I said.

"Haven't had time?" Floyd echoed. "What do you ladies do all day that takes your mind off important things like balls?"

His tone was teasing, but Flossy gave me a serious look. "Yes, Cleo, what else could you possibly have to think about? You don't know anyone in London except us, so you haven't got any gossip to mull over. You don't like to shop, so I know you're not reading fashion periodicals from the library. What do you do when you're not with me?"

"Perhaps she likes to improve her mind with books," Floyd said as he scooped up a spoonful of soup. "Our cousin is a bit of a scholar, you know."

"Don't be absurd. She attended lectures and read books in Cambridge because there's nothing else to do in a university city. Now that she's in London, there's so many other, more exciting things available to her."

"Like shopping?"

"Yes, and the theater, the opera, dances. She could even go to museums and galleries if she wishes to continue to improve her mind."

"I'm quite sure they have all of those things in Cambridge too, Sis."

"But inferior, surely."

Mr. Armitage entered the dining room and I found my gaze following him as he passed Mr. Chapman and surveyed the room. Mr. Chapman watched him too, then his gaze met mine.

I looked away, but not before Floyd and Flossy noticed. "Why are you watching Armitage?" Floyd asked.

"I'm curious about him," I said. "What do you know of him? His past, I mean."

"Hobart's brother the detective took him in when he became an orphan," Floyd said with a shrug. "He came to work here a few years later. That's the extent of my knowledge. Why the interest in Armitage?"

Flossy dropped her spoon in her bowl and gasped. "Cleo," she scolded.

I stared at her. Oh God, she'd guessed. Of all people, Flossy had worked out that I suspected him of the murder.

"You're not interested in Mr. Armitage in *that* way, I hope."

Floyd set down his spoon too and regarded me from beneath a frown. "Cleo? Are you?"

I wasn't sure whether to be relieved or worried that I'd opened up another Pandora's box. "No, of course not."

"Good." Flossy patted my arm.

"Why?" I pressed. "Is there something wrong with him?"

Flossy dabbed at the corners of her mouth with her napkin. "Dearest Cleo, you are so terribly provincial. There's nothing wrong with Mr. Armitage. He's a perfectly fine fellow. But you can do better."

I blew out a measured breath. She didn't know about his previous conviction then. I glanced at Floyd, who was nodding along with his sister's judgement. Neither of them knew. I wasn't sure why I thought they might, when their father didn't.

Mr. Hobart entered the dining room and had a quiet word in his nephew's ear. He looked worried. No, not worried. Terrified. Both men left.

I waited a few moments before making my excuses and leaving too. I caught sight of both men stepping into the lift and giving John instructions to stop at the fourth floor. I picked up my skirts and raced up the stairs, pausing on the fourth-floor landing to catch my breath. I peeked around the corner and spotted them entering Uncle Ronald's office. I could not see their faces, but a sense of dread washed over me.

My uncle was going to confront them about Mr. Armitage's prior conviction, the very thing they'd killed Mrs. Warrick for. He could be in grave danger.

The door closed and I tiptoed closer, placing my ear to it. I had no trouble discerning what my uncle was saying. His booming voice could have blasted a hole in the door.

"I trusted you, Hobart! How could you do this to me?"

"Do what?" came Mr. Armitage's voice, loud but not shouting.

"Lie to me!"

"Mr. Hobart would never lie to you, sir. He's an honest man."

"He is *not* honest! He has been lying to me for years. Years!"

"Perhaps if you tell me—"

"Stop! Enough! Get out, both of you. You are both dismissed."

My stomach plunged. I'd expected it but hoped it wouldn't happen. Not yet. Not until we knew for certain whether they were murderers. I rested my hand on the door-knob but didn't open it. I was a coward. To walk in now and tell them my theory would draw their ire to me, and that could prove very dangerous indeed. But my uncle was alone with them.

"Dismissed?" Mr. Armitage said. "From the hotel?"

"You will receive what you're owed and not a penny more. Get your things and get out of my sight. Both of you."

I could hear a quieter voice which I guessed to be that of Mr. Hobart, but I couldn't discern what he was saying.

"Cleo?"

I jumped at Floyd's voice, directly behind me. I hadn't heard him approach.

"What are you doing?"

I put a finger to my lips as Mr. Armitage asked why they were being dismissed.

"Dismissed?" Floyd asked, having heard it too. "What the devil?" He pushed open the door and I stumbled forward into the room. "Father, what's going on?"

"That's what I want to know," Mr. Armitage said with a scowl for Uncle Ronald. "What are we being dismissed for? What have we done wrong?"

My uncle pointed a finger at Mr. Hobart. The manager shrank back. He wasn't a big man, but now he seemed even smaller as he cowered beneath my uncle's wrath. He knew what this was about, and he knew he'd done the wrong thing.

"Your uncle lied to me when he employed you," Uncle Ronald said darkly. "Don't try to deny it. He already admitted it to me."

He must have confronted Mr. Hobart immediately after I told him.

"I don't understand," Floyd said, shaking his head.

"Quiet!" Uncle Ronald snapped without taking his gaze off Mr. Hobart. "Tell him, Hobart. Tell him that I would never have employed him if I'd known he was a thief."

Mr. Armitage dragged a hand down his face, muttering something into it. When his hand came away, he looked stricken. "I'll leave immediately and quietly as long as my uncle is allowed to stay."

"No. He is disloyal."

"He has given his life to this hotel! He made one mistake in employing me, many years ago. Have some sympathy for your old friend, sir."

"He is not my friend. He is my employee. Now he is nobody to me."

"Please, sir, don't act hastily. I will go, if that's what you want, but let him stay."

"Get. Out."

Mr. Armitage put up his hands. "I've given years of loyal, honest service to this hotel. Despite that unfortunate situation when I was arrested, I've done nothing criminal before or since. My father the detective inspector will vouch—"

"I said get out of my sight!" If I'd ever doubted my uncle had a temper, I knew it to be true now. His face had gone a deep red, ridged with purple veins. He was fierce, and we all cowered before him.

Everyone except Mr. Armitage. "Have some sympathy. I was just a boy then."

"Once a thief, always a thief!"

"Thief?" Floyd echoed. "I don't understand. What's going on?"

My uncle stabbed a finger at Mr. Hobart. "This man appointed his nephew to a position here knowing he was a convicted thief."

"He was just a child," Mr. Hobart said, voice trembling. "The situation he found himself in was very difficult."

There was that familiar twist in my gut again, for the boy who'd been orphaned about the same age as me. I felt an affinity with him, and knew partly how lonely he must have felt.

But I had to remember that he was most likely also a murderer.

I remained near the door, not moving, hardly daring to breathe, hoping everyone had forgotten I was there.

"I don't care if he had to beg on the street for food," Uncle Ronald snarled. "His very presence here could have destroyed this hotel. Our reputation hangs by a thread after the murder, and if this got out too, it would bury us beneath a pile of cancelled reservations."

"You've made your point," Mr. Armitage said. "I'll leave. But tell me, how did you find out?"

"A loyal member of the family with a nose for ferreting out the truth made me suspicious that I'd hired a criminal. I asked Hobart if it was true, and which staff member it could be, and he admitted everything."

Mr. Armitage's hard gaze settled on Floyd. Floyd quickly put up his hands in surrender. "It wasn't me!"

Uncle Ronald signaled to me to step forward. "It was Cleo."

I wanted the floor to swallow me up. I wanted to disappear and hide from their shocked and severe glares. But I found myself stepping closer as if a noose were tied around my neck and my uncle pulled the rope.

Mr. Armitage huffed out an ominous, humorless laugh and shook his head.

Mr. Hobart pressed a hand to his stomach. "Miss Fox? How…?"

"It doesn't matter how she discovered it," Uncle Ronald growled. "Thank God she did. She's got a brain, this one." He looked directly at Floyd as he said it.

Floyd crossed his arms and studied the floor at his feet.

I wanted to put my arm around him and tell him I was sorry. I hadn't intended for him to get hurt by this.

I hadn't expected anyone to get hurt. I'd expected to feel glad that murderers had been brought to justice, and wrongs had been righted. But Mr. Hobart looked so sad, so vulnerable and very old all of a sudden, that I doubted he could have harmed Mrs. Warrick.

Mr. Armitage, on the other hand, looked ferocious. "Why?" he barked at me. "We've done nothing to you."

"She told me because she's loyal to me." Uncle Ronald stabbed his thumb into his chest. "Somebody around here is."

Mr. Armitage didn't take his gaze off me. It was as fierce as my uncle's but where Uncle Ronald's was filled with hot anger, Mr. Armitage's eyes were filled with cold censure.

"Why?" Mr. Armitage demanded.

I lifted my chin. I had both Floyd and my uncle on my side now. They could protect me if necessary and capture Mr. Armitage if he tried to flee. It was now or never. "Because I believe you murdered Mrs. Warrick."

"What!" all four men blurted out at once.

"No, he didn't!" Mr. Hobart cried.

"Are you sure?" my uncle asked, all the bluster gone now.

"Bloody hell," Floyd murmured, eyeing Mr. Armitage carefully.

Mr. Armitage merely laughed another of those bitter, humorless laughs. He did not try to flee or stop me from elaborating. Indeed, he said, "I want to hear this. Go on, Miss Fox. Why do you think I'm a murderer?"

I cleared my throat. "Mrs. Warrick knew about your past as a thief and was going to expose you."

Mr. Hobart suddenly sat on the chair. He covered his mouth with a shaking hand.

"Is that so?" Mr. Armitage's voice might be calm, but it was edged with the sharpest steel. "And your proof?" He was every inch the policeman's son at that moment. He might not share Detective Inspector Hobart's blood, but his manner was as authoritative and direct.

"First of all, she recognized you," I said, keeping my chin raised. I would not let this man intimidate me. It was much easier to be brave with Floyd beside me, although Mr. Armitage was taller and broader. "I overheard her saying as much in the foyer the day of her murder. She said she knew you when you were younger and that you shouldn't be here at the hotel."

"The foyer is busy during the day. She could have been referring to any number of people."

I didn't tell them there were two other men in her line of sight when she'd said it. I didn't want to dilute my argument.

"Secondly, you've been sneaking about." At his raised

brows, I added, "I saw you checking Mr. Chapman's coat pocket in his office this morning. I've also seen you coming out of Mrs. Kettering's private chambers. You later lied about that to your own father when he inquired as to everyone's whereabouts on the day of the murder."

Uncle Ronald shook his head sadly. "Once a thief, always a thief."

"He's not a thief!" Mr. Hobart cried. "Not anymore," he added in a mumble.

Mr. Armitage didn't take his gaze off me. "What does that have to do with Mrs. Warrick's murder?"

"It proves you aren't an upstanding fellow," Floyd shot back.

Mr. Armitage ignored him. His entire attention focused on me. I felt the icy blast of it through to my bones.

I swallowed again. It was becoming increasingly difficult to forge ahead with him looking at me like that. But I had to. There was a lot at stake. "Mrs. Warrick was also overheard having a heated conversation with Mr. Hobart about you on the day of her death. It's not unreasonable to conclude she'd told him she recognized you and knew you'd been arrested years ago. Not knowing the family connection between you, she probably assumed he would act accordingly, but when he brushed aside the matter, she became cross."

"In which case she would raise it with Sir Ronald." Mr. Armitage looked to my uncle.

Uncle Ronald glared back. "I did speak to her that afternoon, but she didn't mention your background. She only spoke about the footman who'd spilled her hot chocolate and the reparation she expected for the damage he'd caused to her fur coat."

"That's what she spoke to me about too," Mr. Hobart said. "She told me she'd brought it up with Harry but he'd refused to dismiss Danny. She came to me demanding I do it, and I also refused. I suspect that's when she went to Sir Ronald."

My heart sank to my stomach.

Mr. Armitage arched his brows higher at me. "That is the sum of your proof, Miss Fox?"

"It may not be enough to convict you of murder," Floyd

said, "but it seems you've been thieving from the other senior staff."

"Harry wasn't thieving," Mr. Hobart said on a sigh. "He was trying to uncover a thief. Someone has been stealing the silverware. When one of the waiters brought it to my attention, I asked Harry to investigate." He appealed to my uncle. "You know this, sir. I brought it to your attention a week ago and told you Harry would find out who was responsible."

Uncle Ronald gave a single nod.

My heart plunged further, all the way to my toes. I felt sick. I'd accused an innocent man of murder. But it got worse. I'd exposed the lie of a good man who'd simply wanted to give an orphan a second chance. And now they were going to pay for it.

"Oh," Floyd murmured. "Sorry, Armitage."

I wanted to say I was sorry too, but my throat ached as I tried to hold back my tears.

"It doesn't excuse the fact you lied, Hobart," Uncle Ronald said, taking his seat. "You both did. I would never have hired him if I'd known he was a convicted thief."

"But he's reformed!" Mr. Hobart cried.

"You're both dismissed. I want you gone before dinnertime."

"No!" I cried. "Please, don't dismiss them."

"I have to, Cleo. I know it seems cruel to you, but I can't have people taking advantage of me." He waved at the door. "Get out."

"But—"

He slammed his fist on the desk. "That's enough!"

Floyd placed his hand at my back, either to comfort me or to warn me to keep quiet. It was not comforting enough, but I did keep my mouth shut. My uncle was too angry to listen to reason.

Mr. Armitage was not prepared to remain quiet, however. He pressed his knuckles on the desk and leaned forward. "Let my uncle stay, and I won't create a scene."

Mr. Hobart touched his nephew's arm. "It's all right, Harry."

"It's not all right!"

"Harry, please. I'm begging you."

Mr. Armitage straightened and squared his shoulders. He shot a blood-chilling glare at me then stormed out of the office. Mr. Hobart followed.

Floyd signaled to me that we ought to leave too.

I walked steadily to my suite, but the moment I shut the door, my legs turned to jelly. I slid onto the floor and cried into my hands.

CHAPTER 9

 allowing in my own misery would not solve anything, but I did indulge long enough to get the tears of self-loathing out of my system. Some would call crying a weakness, but to me, it was a reminder that I was human. In this instance, my wretchedness over what I'd set in motion was a reminder that I had a habit of overstepping. I'd been too eager to prove myself here at the hotel and to my new family. Finding the murderer was a way of demonstrating that I could be useful.

That eagerness to prove myself had blinded me to the fact that my evidence against Mr. Armitage was flimsy. I should never have gone to my uncle with my concerns about Mr. Armitage's past. Even though I hadn't mentioned him by name, I should have known he'd follow up with Mr. Hobart. The manager had crumbled when confronted with Uncle Ronald's wrath.

Once I'd got the tears out of my system, I washed my face and ventured out of my suite. I had to set everything right before it was too late.

My uncle was not in his office, however. Very well, I would go downstairs and enter the lion's den. It had to be done, and it served me right if I was shouted at.

It was clear the moment I entered the lift that all the staff knew Mr. Hobart and Mr. Armitage had been dismissed. John couldn't stop telling me what a tragedy it was, and speculating on the reason behind it. He didn't know any of the particulars, and going by the way he spoke to me, he didn't know of my involvement.

Goliath's reaction was the same. "Can you believe it, Miss Fox?" he asked with a shake of his head. "What do you suppose they did?"

"Yes, what do you know?" Peter asked. He'd even come out from behind the front desk to speak to me.

"I need to see them," was all I said. "Excuse me."

Both Mr. Armitage and Mr. Hobart's office doors were closed. Being the coward that I am, I chose to knock on Mr. Hobart's. He bade me enter and I opened the door. My heart skipped a beat at the sight of Mr. Armitage standing behind his seated uncle, a hand on his shoulder.

"Come to gloat at your success?" Mr. Armitage sneered.

"Harry," Mr. Hobart scolded. His eyes looked as red as mine, his face just as drawn.

I swallowed the lump in my throat and entered the office. I closed the door and drew in a steadying breath. "I'm so sorry for what I've done," I began.

Mr. Armitage grunted. "Go away. We have things to do."

His anger was horrible enough, but it was Mr. Hobart's reaction that brought tears to my eyes again. He diverted his gaze. He couldn't even look at me.

"I'm going to speak on your behalves to my uncle just as soon as I find him," I went on. "I'll tell him I was mistaken. Or that I made it up."

"You're forgetting that my uncle already confessed," Mr. Armitage said. "The truth of the matter is, I am a convicted felon, and Uncle Alfred knew it and still hired me. Sir Ronald won't forgive that."

"He might."

"You haven't been here long enough to know, but you'll learn he never backs down from a decision. Not for anyone. Not even when his own family begs him."

"Harry," Mr. Hobart said, sharper this time. "Don't take your anger out on her. She was only doing what she thought was best."

Mr. Armitage's nostrils flared and his chest rose and fell with his deep breaths.

"I have to try anyway," I said. "I have to fix this."

Mr. Hobart nodded.

"I truly am very sorry," I went on. "I let my imagination run away with me and..." I did not go on. My excuses were pathetic and could not adequately account for my actions.

"Since you enjoy playing detective, you can take over where I left off in the case of the missing silverware," Mr. Armitage said through a hard smile. "But forgive me if I don't hand over the evidence I've already gathered. I don't feel inclined to help you."

Mr. Hobart shook his head. "I will leave everything we've learned about the thefts thus far in the top drawer."

I nodded and thanked him. "I hope this is not goodbye," I said, not knowing what else to say.

I left only to find Mr. Armitage following me out. I stopped, not because he blocked my path or held me back, but because I deserved whatever angry words he wanted to fling at me away from his uncle. I steeled myself.

"I thought you were different to them," he said, voice low and harsh. "But I see you're the same."

I shook my head, not quite following. "I'm sorry you think this was a result of whatever prejudice you assume I have against you, but I can assure you, this is purely a result of me thinking you were a murderer. You might not believe it, but I had everyone's best interests at heart."

His jaw hardened. "I don't care for myself. I'll find other work. But this hotel is my uncle's whole life. He has given decades of devoted service to Sir Ronald, and yet he is being thrown away like a piece of rubbish for making one mistake years ago. The worst of it is that everyone will think he was dismissed for something heinous; his reputation will be ruined. But I challenge you to find anyone who thinks giving a boy a second chance is a crime worthy of dismissal after decades of loyalty."

Every word was like a twist of the knife in my gut. It took all of my willpower not to let the tears burning my eyes to fall.

"Harry," Mr. Hobart said from the doorway. "Don't say something you'll later regret."

Mr. Armitage marched off to his own office and slammed the door.

"He doesn't mean what he says," Mr. Hobart told me.

I blinked back tears. "Yes, he does."

I took several moments to compose myself before returning to the foyer. There were few guests about and none seemed to be aware of the turmoil that had befallen the hotel. The front of house staff, however, looked worried.

"Harmony's in the parlor," Goliath told me as I passed him. "She wants to speak to you."

I wanted to retire to my room to avoid them all, but I had to face everyone at some point. Goliath followed me to the staff parlor where Harmony, Edith and Victor sat. The women nursed cups of tea while Victor tossed his knife up and caught it. They turned forlorn and troubled gazes upon me.

"Edith and I came back to the hotel early," Harmony said. "We're not supposed to return for a few more hours yet, but we can't stay away after something like this. We can't believe it. Both Mr. Armitage and Mr. Hobart both dismissed and no one is saying why."

"Do you know?" Edith asked in her small voice.

I didn't dare look at Victor. If I did, he might realize it was linked to our midnight visit to the boys' home. No matter how many times they asked, I would not tell them about Mr. Armitage's past. I didn't want to be responsible for changing their opinions of him on top of everything else.

I shook my head.

"It must have been something real bad," Goliath said. "Sir Ronald wouldn't dismiss both of them without a good reason. He knows how it'll look, and when the guests find out, they won't like it."

"Why will the guests care?" I asked.

"Because they love Mr. Hobart, especially the regulars."

"Many of them return because of him and his personal service," Harmony went on. "The Mayfair is one of a handful of luxury hotels in London, and some have more modern amenities, but none have a manager like Mr. Hobart. He's attuned to their every need and whim."

Edith nodded. "He might ask us to put a particular flower in a guest's room because he knows that's her favorite, or we'll have to put out different soap because she doesn't like the scent of lavender."

"He'll tell the kitchen in advance of a guest's arrival what their favorite dishes are so we make sure we have it in stock, even if it's not on the menu," Victor added.

"He can get tickets to a sold-out opera or for the best seats at the theater," Goliath said. "I don't know how he does it."

"He knows everyone there is to know," Harmony told him. "They do favors for one another. He also keeps notes on every guest and only shares those notes with Mr. Armitage."

"Mr. Armitage was going to take over from him," Goliath said.

"Who will be our manager and assistant manager now?" Edith asked.

"Mrs. Kettering and Mr. Chapman will have to do more until someone is appointed," Harmony said. She and Edith pulled faces at the prospect.

Victor resumed his knife tossing. "There are going to be ramifications."

Harmony frowned. "What sort of ramifications?"

"Bad ones."

She rolled her eyes.

Edith looked up from her teacup which she'd been studying intensely. "Could their dismissal be related to the murder?"

"They're not murderers!" Goliath cried.

She looked down at her teacup again. "It was just a thought."

Harmony placed her teacup on the table and put her arm around my shoulders. "You look like you've taken this very hard, Miss Fox."

I tried to smile but I suspected it was not very convincing. "Have you seen my uncle?"

"He went out," Goliath said. "He told Frank he'll be gone the rest of the day—tonight too."

I heaved a deep sigh. I wouldn't get the opportunity to speak to him before Mr. Hobart and Mr. Armitage left.

* * *

BY THE FOLLOWING MORNING, everyone had heard about the dismissals of the manager and his assistant. A number of guests demanded to know why, but the staff could give them no answers. Poor Peter looked as though he'd explode if someone asked him again. He was usually so unflustered, but his tight smile and curt responses spoke of his frustration.

"Will I still be able to swap rooms?" asked a gentleman of Goliath.

"I don't know, sir."

"Mr. Armitage was going to take care of it today. What happens now?"

"I don't know, sir," Goliath said. "You could ask Mr. Chapman."

"The restaurant steward?"

"He is taking over the role of manager for now."

"Where is Mr. Chapman?"

"I don't know, sir."

The gentleman sighed and turned instead to Peter when the guest he'd been speaking to moved off. Peter shot Goliath a harried glance, as if blaming him for not resolving the issue.

By late morning, the journalists had returned, demanding to know whether the dismissals of the manager and assistant manager had anything to do with the murder. Two of them got past Frank, but after they were thrown out by Goliath and the other porters, the doorman was more prepared and the rest were not allowed in. Fortunately they didn't create a scene, but they lurked outside and accosted the guests as they left. Some brushed them aside, but others stopped to speak to them.

"I wouldn't go out there if I were you," Flossy said as she and Floyd joined me in the foyer. "A thunderstorm would be more inviting than walking through that lot."

"They're persistent," I said.

"They smell blood," Floyd added. "They can see we're in trouble and want to beat us into submission while we're down."

Flossy made a small squeak. "Floyd, don't be so ghastly."

"They think the murder and dismissals are connected. Can you imagine if they get someone to say they are? It'll be all their dreams come true."

I pressed my lips together.

"Someone ought to go out there and disabuse them of the notion." Floyd tugged on his jacket hem. "It should be me."

Flossy grabbed his arm. "Don't you dare! Father will tan your hide, particularly now, given his dreadful mood."

"Why?" I asked. "Wouldn't he be pleased that Floyd sets the press straight?"

Floyd and Flossy exchanged knowing glances. "He wouldn't like me to do it without his knowledge," Floyd said. He glanced at the front door but made no attempt to go outside.

"Mr. Hobart and Mr. Armitage used to take care of the newspapermen," Flossy said. "They were very good at handling them." She sniffed and I realized she was crying. "I can't believe they're gone. Mr. Hobart has been here forever. He's part of the hotel. Oh, Floyd, this is dreadful. Just dreadful. Why would Father do such a thing?"

Floyd peered at me. There was no anger or censure in his eyes, just disappointment.

"And so close to the ball too," Flossy went on. "It will be canceled now."

"It must go on," Floyd said.

"How can it? Mr. Hobart was in charge of most of the arrangements, and Mr. Armitage responsible for the rest."

"There are only two days to go, so I'd wager most of it is done. It'll be too late to cancel now."

Flossy wiped her tears. "Tell Father that."

Floyd frowned. "Do you think he's considering canceling it?"

"Who knows what he's considering?" She pushed his arm. "Go and tell him."

"No. You do it."

Flossy looked as though she wanted to speak to her father about as much as she wanted to face the herd of journalists.

"I'll do it," I said. I'd been meaning to speak to my uncle all morning, but when I'd checked his office, he hadn't been there. "Is he upstairs now?"

Floyd nodded.

I took the lift to give myself time to calm my nerves. I thought John's easy chatter would help, but he couldn't stop talking about the dismissals in worried tones. I was glad to get out, but my anxiety returned as I knocked on my uncle's office door.

He heaved a sigh as I entered. "I've never been more glad to see a friendly face," he said, indicating the chair for me to sit. "The only people who've come to see me today are ones asking me where things are, what they should be doing, and how to do this or that. They seem to think I ought to know every little thing Hobart and Armitage did on a daily basis."

"There's a way to stop all those questions." At his inquiring look, I added, "Reconsider your decision."

His brow plunged. "No."

"Please, sir, hire them back so life here can return to normal."

"I never go back on my word." He waved his hand, dismissing me.

But I would not be dismissed. Not with something so important at stake. "Could you not this time? For the sake of two very good, loyal employees with an exemplary record for all the years they've worked here."

He wagged a finger at me. "I didn't expect this from you, Cleo. Not after it was you who brought Armitage's crime to my attention."

I closed my eyes and winced. "I wish I hadn't. I thought I was exposing a murderer, and I feel foolish now for ever considering Mr. Armitage the poisoner."

He gave a harsh laugh. "Ironic, isn't it? If Armitage's father had done his job more efficiently, his son's theft would never have been uncovered."

"The blame for this is all mine."

"Nonsense. You are the only blameless one in this entire debacle."

I shook my head. "It's kind of you to try to make me feel better, but I will always feel guilty. Please, sir, overturn your decision and give them their positions back."

He stabbed a finger into his chest. "And make it look as though *I* was in the wrong?"

"You *are* in the wrong," I snapped.

He went very still. "I beg your pardon?"

I drew in a breath and gathered my nerves. If I was going

to make amends, then I had to be prepared to suffer the consequences that Mr. Hobart and Mr. Armitage had suffered because of me—dismissal. Dismissal from the hotel, the family… From what I knew of my uncle, it was a very real possibility. "Neither man deserved to—"

"They lied to me."

"Listen to me!" I clasped my hands in my lap, twining my fingers together. "Please, just let me finish. Mr. Armitage was an orphan."

"I know that."

"Yes, but you don't know what it was like to be orphaned at such a young age. I do, and I can assure you, it's a lonely position to find yourself in. But I was fortunate, compared to him. I had my grandparents, and your generosity in providing me with an allowance. He had no one."

"Your sympathy for his plight is understandable, considering your circumstances. I can see that Mr. Armitage's story upsets you. You're a woman, and I would expect you to feel sorry for him. But I'm a businessman, Cleo. If word reaches those vipers waiting outside, I hate to think what will happen to The Mayfair's reputation. Reputation is everything in this business. Hobart knew that. He built his career with that at its core. But it was all built on a lie, a rotten core, and I can't condone that. I'm sorry you're upset."

"Spare me your lecture," I spat.

His lips parted and his gaze lifted as I stood.

"I may be a woman, and you a man, but which of us acted rashly, emotionally?" I pointed at him. "You did. And which of us has more common sense?" I pointed at myself. "Me, because I can see that your business is going to suffer with them gone. Mr. Chapman and Mrs. Kettering are not up to the task of performing the manager and assistant manager's duties in addition to their own. And have you forgotten that one of them might be stealing your silverware? I also doubt you'll find suitable replacements for Mr. Hobart and Mr. Armitage soon—perhaps not for a very long time. And when —if—you do find replacements, it will be months before their knowledge of the hotel matches Mr. Hobart's and Mr. Armitage's. Perhaps even years. Can The Mayfair survive that long?" I turned to go but thought of something else, something which might get through to him more than anything else I'd said. "Added to which, if they return, they have every incentive to keep Mr. Armitage's childhood arrest quiet. Right now, what's stopping them from telling the newspapers? It will only hurt you. It can't hurt them any more than it already has."

"They wouldn't dare."

"If I were in their position, revenge would be a very tempting carrot."

My uncle stared at me like he'd only just begun to see me.

I felt no satisfaction as I marched out of his office. It was a relief to have spoken to him finally, but the weight that had been pressing down on my chest ever since he'd dismissed Mr. Hobart and Mr. Armitage was still there, as leaden as ever.

* * *

I HAD no inclination to continue with the investigation. I threw away the notes I'd made on my suspects and decided to send back Mr. Armitage's file to the boy's home on Dean Street. I'd go to the post desk directly after breakfast.

Harmony didn't arrive to do my hair at eight as she usually did, and I was glad for the sleep-in. I'd hardly slept a wink. I kept replaying my confrontation with Uncle Ronald over and over, and how I could have done it differently, in a less heated way that did not jeopardize my stay at The Mayfair.

I expected to be told to leave the hotel by the end of the day, just as he'd ordered Mr. Hobart and Mr. Armitage to leave. At least if I expected it, it would not come as a surprise when it happened. I should have heeded Grandmama's warnings to keep my opinions to myself.

Harmony arrived at nine, a bundle of enthusiasm and big smiles. "He's back, Cleo! Isn't it wonderful! Mr. Hobart is back. We've just had a staff meeting in the dining room with him, and he says he can't wait to finalize arrangements for tomorrow night's ball."

I pressed a hand to my rapidly beating heart and broke into a grin. If Uncle Ronald had relented then perhaps he wouldn't throw me out. "That is a relief. And Mr. Armitage?"

Her smile slipped. "Mr. Hobart said he won't be returning."

I lowered myself onto the chair at my dressing table. "Oh."

"The position of assistant manager is now vacant and Mr. Hobart said he'll be hiring a replacement in the new year." She indicated I should face the mirror. "How would you like me to do your hair today?"

"I don't care."

She tilted her head to the side. "Don't be so sad. Mr. Hobart's back."

"But not Mr. Armitage."

"True, but he's young enough and clever enough to find other work. He'll be fine, and the hotel can manage with just Mr. Hobart at the helm for a while." She laid her hands on my shoulders and smiled at my reflection. "I think he's more upset that he can't retire knowing the position of manager is staying in his family."

I subjected my hair to her ministrations and was pleased with the result. She'd arranged it in a very modern swept-up style that flattered my features nicely.

"You've outdone yourself, Harmony."

"Just getting in some practice."

"For what?"

"If you change your mind and decide to go to the ball after all. That style could be the basis for something more elaborate if I just add a few curls."

"I don't think I'll be going."

"There's time to change your mind."

"It's tomorrow."

She merely smiled. "So now that the hotel is returning to normal, will you continue with the investigation today?"

"I've lost my appetite for it."

"Lost your appetite for finding the truth? Miss Fox, I'm surprised to hear you say it."

If she knew where my truth-seeking had got me, she'd encourage me to stop. "It's impossible to continue without knowing how the poison was delivered and as far as I'm aware, the police haven't shared the results of their tests with anyone. I don't know whether it was in the toothpaste, cream or tonic, or none of them. Besides, I'm sure Detective Inspector Hobart will solve it."

Now that his son wasn't a suspect, I had no reason to believe he wouldn't.

She sighed. "I suppose. But I'll continue to keep an eye out for suspicious activity."

I left her to clean my suite while I went downstairs to post Mr. Armitage's file to the boys' home, but changed my mind before I reached the post desk. A hotel mark would make it obvious that someone from here had stolen it. I would slip it under the orphanage's door myself.

I spotted Mr. Chapman and Mrs. Kettering leaving the manager's corridor, their steps purposeful and brisk. It was likely they'd just come from a meeting with Mr. Hobart. I drew in a deep breath and went in search of him. We would see one another around the hotel so I might as well speak to him now and get it over with.

He did not look surprised to see me, nor did he look anything like the troubled, vulnerable man I'd last seen in this same office. The hotel manager was once again the master of his emotions with a calm manner that pervaded everything he did, from the sweep of his hand to indicate the chair opposite his desk, to the sympathetic smile he bestowed on me.

"How are you?" he asked.

"Better now that you're back." I tightened my grip on the chair arm. "I want to say again how sorry I am for causing so much trouble."

"It wasn't your intention."

"But it happened, and I can't forgive myself."

"Please, don't blame yourself. The fact is, I hired Harry knowing his past and knowing Sir Ronald wouldn't allow him to work here if he was aware. It was bound to come out eventually. The truth always does."

"But it wasn't my place to tell him."

"Why not? You're his family. Your loyalty should always be with family."

"I hardly know them. I'm not even sure I like them, yet."

He sat forward a little. "Family is family. You can't change that. Now stop blaming yourself. A young woman shouldn't be burdened by guilt over something that isn't of her making."

"I wish you wouldn't be so forgiving since Mr. Armitage is not back yet."

"There is no 'yet', Miss Fox. He won't be coming back."

"Perhaps my uncle will give in," I said, desperately hoping it to be true. "He changed his mind about you."

He shook his head. "He reversed his decision about me because it was in the best interests of the hotel, but it would have been difficult for him. He's very proud."

"And it would be doubly hard for him to swallow that pride a second time?"

He merely smiled, always the diplomat. "Harry wouldn't return anyway. He is just as proud." He clasped his hands on the desk and regarded me levelly. "I want you to know a little of Harry's past. It will explain why he was arrested."

"You don't have to tell me anything. His past is none of my affair, and I'm sure he had good reasons for stealing."

"Even so, I want to tell you what I told Sir Ronald. But I would appreciate it if it didn't go any further."

"It won't," I said on a breath, eager to hear more, despite what I'd just told him.

"You know that Harry found himself in a boys' home after his parents died?"

I nodded.

"After a year there, he was sent to be apprenticed to a bookkeeper at a button factory. The bookkeeper was not kind to him and would tell the factory owner that Harry made mistakes. He made things up to put Harry in a bad light. I suspect he was jealous of Harry's quick mind, but it's impossible to know why he was so cruel. The upshot is, the owner sent Harry to work on the factory floor as punishment."

"But he was a child!"

"He was tall for his age, and none of the other workers dared go against their employer. Harry had no one to turn to for advice. When you're a child with no family, no adult friends, then you're very much alone." He shifted in his chair, the story making him as uncomfortable as it made me. "The conditions were hard for a boy, the hours long. He endured it for several months until one day he was beaten by the factory owner for something as trifling as dropping a box of buttons."

"My God," I murmured.

"Harry ran away. He didn't return to the orphanage. He thought they'd send him back to the factory. Years later, he discovered that he would have been taken in there again if he'd only told them what happened, but as a thirteen-year-old, he assumed the adult world was against him."

"So where did he go?"

"He lived on the streets with other children. They were quite wild, but they liked their freedom, so he told me. Unfortunately, they had to steal to survive. He was caught by my brother and arrested."

"He only served three months."

"You are well informed," he said with a hint of irony. "It was his first offense, and his age was taken into consideration. My brother also put in a good word for him. He saw something in Harry immediately. He was quick-witted and intelligent, but generous and kind-hearted too." Mr. Hobart smiled to himself. "He'd stolen a ribbon to give to a girl he liked and a basket of apples which he handed out to the younger children."

If he'd told me the story to make me understand Mr. Armitage better, it worked. But it also made me feel so much worse.

"My brother and his wife had no children of their own, so perhaps that explains why he took an interest in Harry's welfare. He and his wife visited Harry in prison every day and asked him to live with them when he got out. He moved out of their home only when he was given a position here and moved in with the other hotel staff at the residence hall."

"He calls the detective inspector his father and you his uncle."

"We're his family."

I blinked back tears. "It's good to have family."

His gaze softened. "It is."

"You jeopardized your own position here by hiring him."

"Family must take care of one another. Harry needed work or he would have gone mad. He wanted to join the police force and follow in my brother's footsteps. He would have made a good policeman, but unfortunately they don't accept felons, even reformed ones."

My fingers ached and I realized I'd been gripping the chair arm too tightly. I released it. "You must be very busy," I said, rising. "I just wanted to tell you how very glad I am that you're back."

He smiled. "So am I. I don't know what you said to Sir Ronald but it worked."

"Why do you think it was me?"

"Because you have the right amount of courage and persistence."

"Actually, I'm a terrible coward. I didn't want to face you and Mr. Armitage after you were dismissed."

"But you did it anyway. Thank you."

Perhaps it was his forgiveness that bolstered my confidence, or his thanks, but I had a sudden thought that I couldn't shake. I wanted to see Mr. Armitage. I *needed* to see him. "Can you tell me where I can find your nephew now?"

He sat back and did not answer for some time. I thought he would tell me it was a terrible idea, but instead, he drew a piece of paper towards him and scribbled down an address. "I should warn you, he's still very angry with you."

"All the more reason to apologize to him again."

"He won't be kind. In fact, I expect him to say things he wouldn't usually say to a lady—or to anyone."

"It can't be worse than the things he's already said."

He handed me the piece of paper. "You really are quite courageous, Miss Fox."

"No, Mr. Hobart. I just don't like living with guilt."

CHAPTER 10

he address Mr. Hobart had given me belonged to a semi-detached house in Ealing, a short walk from the station. It would have been a more pleasant walk if not for the incessant rain and my anxiety at seeing Mr. Armitage again. That anxiety grew worse when I saw the family sized house. Mr. Armitage must have moved back in with his parents.

Not only had he lost his job yesterday, he'd also lost his home.

I huddled beneath my umbrella on the small porch as I knocked, but the near-horizontal angle of the rain meant I still got thoroughly wet. The door was answered by a woman with gray hair and slightly protruding teeth with smiling eyes. This must be Mrs. Hobart, the detective inspector's wife and Mr. Armitage's mother.

"Good morning," I said. "My name is Cleopatra Fox. Is Mr. Armitage—?"

"Miss Fox!" Her features hardened. "What do you want with my son?"

I swallowed. "I want to talk to him."

"Did Alfred Hobart give you this address?"

I nodded.

She clicked her tongue. "He shouldn't have. Harry doesn't want to talk to you."

"Please don't close the door!"

She slammed it in my face.

I supposed I deserved that. I knocked again. "You can't make me feel worse than I already do," I called out through the door. With the rain starting to come down harder, she could certainly make me feel colder and wetter, however. "I'll keep knocking until you open up! Your neighbors are already peering out of their windows, Mrs. Hobart."

The door suddenly opened and I almost knocked her on the nose. She scowled at me, arms crossed.

"Haven't you done enough damage, Miss Fox?"

"You're right, I have done quite a lot of damage to your family, and I'm very sorry for it. I know nothing I can say will make it up to Mr. Armitage, but perhaps there's something he can say to me that will help."

She frowned. "I don't follow."

"Let him get some things off his chest. If there's a small chance that it will help, I'd like to try." She seemed to consider this, so I pressed on. "If nothing else, you'll get to listen to him cut me down to size."

"You're stubborn, I'll give you that."

"Mr. Hobart calls me persistent."

Her lips flattened. "My brother-in-law has always been too kind for his own good." She retreated inside. She did not invite me across the threshold.

A few moments later, Mr. Armitage appeared at the door. He opened it wider, but also didn't invite me in. He wore no jacket and his shirtsleeves were rolled up to the elbows. He held a spanner in a grease-stained hand and his hair looked as though it hadn't been combed. He leaned a shoulder against the doorframe, crossed his arms and glared at me.

"Let me begin by saying again how sorry I am for costing you your position at the hotel," I said.

"You've already apologized."

"I wasn't sure you heard me yesterday."

"I heard you."

I cleared my throat. "What I did to you and your uncle was horrid, but I want you to know that I did it because I truly did think you were the murderer."

His glare hardened. "I feel so much better knowing you think I'm capable of poisoning people."

I adjusted my grip on the umbrella. Despite wearing gloves my fingers were going numb from the cold. "I've been told my imagination is too vivid sometimes. My grandmother warned me it would get me into trouble one day."

"It's not your imagination that's the problem, it's your eagerness to insert your nose into other people's business."

"Yes, you're right."

"Is there anything else, Miss Fox? I'm very busy."

I nodded at the spanner. "So I see."

His eyes narrowed. "I was about to go out to look for work."

I swallowed and lowered my gaze. "Oh. Yes, of course. If I hear of any opportunities, I'll be sure to let you know."

"I don't want your help."

I bit my lower lip and the silence stretched. I ought to walk away, but I hated leaving with him still angry. "I could try speaking to my uncle again on your behalf."

He barked a harsh laugh. "He could have re-hired me yesterday when he visited Uncle Alfred." He pointed the spanner at the house next door. "Don't worry about me. I'll find something, even if I have to muck out stalls or join the army."

"But there's a war on!"

"I hear the weather's pleasant in Africa at this time of year."

I stared at him. "Don't join the army. I'll find you a position somewhere you won't get shot at."

He crossed his arms again. "Your concern for my well-being is a little late, Miss Fox. But don't worry. It seems the army don't like convicted felons either."

"Oh. You were being sarcastic about joining." I scrambled for something more to say, something to dissolve his anger, even just a little bit. But I could think of nothing. His glare was leaving me discombobulated.

A strong wind hit me from the side, almost ripping the umbrella out of my hand. Mr. Armitage grabbed it and helped me hold it until the wind died down again.

He blew out a breath as if resigning himself. "If you're not going to leave, you should come in. You're getting wet."

"I'll stay here, thanks. It's colder inside."

"Now who's being sarcastic?"

I smiled, and for a very brief moment I thought he returned it. But the moment was so fleeting that I instantly doubted myself when his scowl returned with extra ferocity.

"I won't keep you any longer," I said. "Goodbye, Mr. Armitage."

I descended the front steps, tears once again burning my eyes. This meeting had achieved nothing. He was still angry with me, and I was still feeling guilty. Even worse, I could think of nothing to say or do to make the situation better.

"Miss Fox?" he called out.

I spun around. "Yes?"

He leaned a forearm against the doorframe and tapped the spanner with his finger. After a moment, he simply said, "Goodbye," and closed the door.

At least he didn't slam it. That was one positive thing to take away from the meeting.

There were no others, however, and I spent the journey back to the hotel feeling more miserable than I had on the journey there.

* * *

"DETECTIVE INSPECTOR HOBART was here again while you were out," Harmony said as she entered my suite behind me. I had the distinct feeling she'd been lurking on the fourth floor waiting for my return. "He spoke with Sir Ronald."

I pulled a face as I removed my damp coat and flung it over the back of the armchair in the corner. "Do you know how that went?"

"I wasn't listening in, if that's what you mean," she said, snippy.

I smiled, despite myself. "It's not. Was Floyd in the meeting? Perhaps he can tell me how it went."

"I believe Mr. Bainbridge was out. He's back now, playing billiards downstairs with some gentlemen."

I removed my gloves and set them down on the dressing table in the bedroom. "Did the inspector speak to anyone else?"

"Some guests on the third floor nearest Mrs. Warrick's room."

"He must have wanted to know if any of them heard noises coming from her room during the night."

"Or saw anyone lurking about who shouldn't be there." Harmony picked up a pillow from the bed and fluffed it. "I wonder if he learned anything important."

I unpinned my hat and touched my hair to see if it had gotten wet. Then I suddenly straightened and turned to her. "Do you think he was asking those questions because there was no poison found in the tonic, toothpaste or face cream?"

"And he wants to find out if someone delivered the poison in something else during the night?" Harmony shrugged. "After he spoke to the guests, he sought out the footmen who were working that night so you are probably right." She frowned. "But he already asked the footman a few days ago and no one delivered anything further to Mrs. Warrick's room that night between Danny taking her the hot chocolate and Edith taking her the tea the following morning."

"But what if they delivered something to another guest's room and the guest added the poison there before taking it to Mrs. Warrick? If he or she was known to Mrs. Warrick, she might have invited them in. The poisoner then offered her the poisoned drink or food, waited for her to die after she ate or drank it, then took the leftovers away with them."

Harmony continued to fluff the pillow although I suspected she'd forgotten she was holding it. Her clear gaze met mine. "Which is why the police can't find any traces of poison in anything that was left in the room. Miss Fox, I think you might be right. It explains why the inspector is continuing to interview guests now."

"My uncle would not like that. He was against the guests being questioned." It seemed the inspector had overruled him, and quite rightly, too.

"I'm glad he thinks it's a guest and not a staff member," she said. "I've been so worried that he'd arrest someone else, ever since he released Danny."

"You can't know all of the staff that well, Harmony. Perhaps one of them *is* the poisoner. You should prepare yourself for that possibility."

She sighed. "So what will you do next? Do you want me to ask the footmen questions too? Or would you rather do it?"

I returned to the sitting room and picked up one of the books I'd borrowed from the hotel library. "I'm not doing anything next. I've given up."

She followed me, my damp coat slung over her arm. "If you've given up, why did you just ask all these questions about the inspector's visit?"

I paused then said, "Habit."

She regarded me with her one eyebrow raised. "I know you have suspects."

I sat and opened the book. As curious as I was to know if either Mr. Hookly or Mr. Duffield had asked for something from the kitchen during the night, I wasn't prepared to step on the inspector's toes. With Mr. Armitage no longer a suspect, I was quite sure Detective Inspector Hobart would discover the poisoner. Everyone would be better off if I stayed out of his way.

"Fine," she said, snippy again. "If that's how you want to be, I won't bother you until later."

"Later?"

"I'll return to do your hair for dinner."

"I'm having dinner in my room tonight. I don't feel like seeing anyone."

She sighed again and left, taking my coat with her.

"Harmony!" came the shrill voice of Mrs. Kettering. "What are you doing in Miss Fox's room at this hour?"

"I was cleaning it, ma'am."

"Without your linen cart, cleaning products, sponges, or duster?"

"I, um…"

"Put that coat back this instance then come with me to my office."

"I'm not stealing it! Miss Fox asked me to dry it for her by the fire."

"Miss Fox is not here. I saw her leave."

I hurried to the door, book in hand. "I am here."

The housekeeper stiffened. "My apologies, Miss Fox. I thought Harmony was in your room uninvited. She claims to be cleaning it, when clearly she is not."

"She was in my room because I asked her to come in," I snapped. "Her other duties are finished and we were simply talking."

"Talking?" Mrs. Kettering's nostrils flared. "Be careful, Miss Fox. She has always been strange, this one, with a busy tongue which she doesn't know when to hold still."

A well of emotions within me surged, fierce and hot. They were not all the result of Mrs. Kettering's nastiness, but she was going to bear the brunt of them. "You had better hold *your* tongue, Mrs. Kettering, or my uncle will hear of this."

She huffed a breath through her nose and her lips stretched into a thin gash with her defiant smile. "I have been here years, Miss Fox. You have been here five minutes. Which of us do you think he will listen to?"

"The reasonable one who also happens to be his niece. Good day, Mrs. Kettering. I have no need of your services at this moment."

The housekeeper looked very much like a bull about to charge with her flaring nostrils and heavy breathing. "Get back to work," she snapped at Harmony. Then she marched off, back ramrod straight, the keys at her hip jangling with every stride.

Harmony blew out a breath. "Thank you. But don't think this means I've forgiven you for giving up on the investigation." She winked at me.

I watched her go, glad to have done one good deed since my arrival at the hotel.

* * *

FLOSSY FLOUNCED onto the sofa in my sitting room, picked up the book I'd been reading and put it down again, screwing up her nose. "You simply must dine with me tonight, Cleo. I'm so *bored*."

"I don't feel like dining out," I said.

"It's not out. It's just downstairs."

If it required the effort of dressing elegantly, doing my hair, and smiling at the other guests and the waiters, then it was out. "I'd rather stay in my room."

She flopped back into the corner of the sofa. "I'm so restless tonight. I need a distraction. I think it's because the ball is tomorrow night and I simply cannot wait." She sat up again and clapped her hands lightly. "It's going to be wonderful, Cleo. There'll be over a hundred glamorous ladies and handsome gentlemen. Father said there'll be *two* famous actresses in attendance, and one opera soprano, but he won't tell me which ones, the devil. Floyd is thrilled, of course. He hopes one of them is Marie Lloyd."

"Speaking of Floyd, can't you dine with him tonight?"

"He's going out."

"He dines out a lot."

"Yes, but this time it's on Father's orders. He wants Floyd to make sure his friend the duke's son is coming."

"Floyd is friends with the son of a duke?"

"They're not terribly close, but they do move in the same circles. The duke's son's set is very fast. Father doesn't always like Floyd going out, but he makes an exception for him. Sometimes Floyd tells Father he's meeting him when he's actually not." She put a finger to her lips. "Don't tell Father."

"What about your parents? Are they dining out tonight?"

She sighed. "They are, also in a last ditch effort to secure attendees for tomorrow night."

"I don't understand. Haven't people said whether or not they're coming?"

"The hotel guests have. That's why they're still here. It's the invitees who aren't staying here who are more difficult to pin down, particularly this year, given the murder. Those people don't need to stay in hotels as they own townhouses in the city."

"They must be very wealthy."

"Extremely. Father needs to court them, so he accepted an invitation to a dinner where he expects many of them to be."

"Aunt Lilian is also going?"

Flossy's face fell. "I wish she wouldn't. She'll be out late tonight and late again tomorrow night. It might be too much for her."

"I'm sure your father will take care of her and return home if she feels unwell."

She picked at the sofa cushion seam with her fingernail.

"Flossy, what's wrong with her? Is she ill?"

"She has suffered from melancholia for years. Her doctor prescribed a new medicine which lifts her spirits greatly, albeit temporarily." She waved a hand. "Let's not worry about Mother. I've got an idea. You don't want to dine in the dining room, but you have to eat, so let's dine in my room, just the two of us."

"That would be lovely."

"We'll order something expensive. Oh, and let's have champagne too."

"I don't feel like celebrating."

"We're not celebrating. We're indulging."

* * *

WE SENT our order down to the kitchen via the speaking tube in Flossy's room. "Luckily the room delivery orders are only sent to Mr. Hobart at the end of the day and not Father," she told me as she settled on the sofa again. "Father wouldn't like me having champagne, but Mr. Hobart will overlook it." She giggled. "I hope he doesn't think I'm having the entire bottle myself."

"He'll see the rest of the order is for two meals," I said. "I'm sure Mr. Hobart will realize I dined with you."

I sat bolt upright and stared at the brass speaking tube. Two meals, but only one delivery to one room… Mrs. Warrick did not dine in the dining room on the night of her death, nor can the doormen remember her leaving the hotel. I had assumed she'd not eaten at all, but what if she dined in another guest's room?

What if that guest was her killer?

She had recognized either Mr. Hookly or Mr. Duffield that afternoon. Perhaps she'd confronted one of them and he'd subsequently invited her to dinner to discuss whatever it was that bothered her. While it was scandalous to think of her meeting a gentleman in private in his room, Mrs. Warrick was hardly an innocent debutante. Perhaps she'd even accepted the invitation in the hope something more than a discussion would eventuate.

It seemed to take a long time for our meals to arrive, but according to the clock on Flossy's desk, it was only forty-five minutes. I ate quickly, consumed only one glass of champagne, and made my excuses, much to Flossy's disappointment. I convinced her that she needed to have an early night so that she would be fresh for the ball.

I headed downstairs, where Goliath pushed off the front desk where he'd been leaning as he chatted to Peter. He intercepted me as I passed.

"Harmony says you're no longer investigating the murder." He glanced around. There was no one in the foyer, although I could hear voices coming from the billiards room.

"I wasn't, but I think I have a clue. I just need to verify it before I pass it on to Detective Inspector Hobart."

That lifted his spirits. He'd been looking rather glum. "Can I help?"

"Shouldn't you be outside waiting for guests with luggage?"

"There are no guests arriving at this time, and the doorman's in a bad mood."

"Then you can come with me to Mr. Hobart's office."

"He's gone home."

I had expected as much. "Does he lock his office door at night?"

He shrugged. "Peter will know."

The hard-working Peter looked just as bored as Goliath. He yawned before leaning both elbows on the front desk. "Only two more hours before the night porter takes over," he said. "I'm that tired. Mr. Hobart's had me going over the guest register for tomorrow, seeing as Mr. Armitage no longer works here. There's going to be a lot of new arrivals in the afternoon."

"Speaking of Mr. Hobart," I said, "does he lock his office door when he goes home?"

"Yes. Why?"

"I need to look at the records of the room deliveries for the night of Mrs. Warrick's murder. I want to see if one of my suspects ordered enough food for two people at dinner time."

"You think she dined with her killer?"

"I'm not sure. It might amount to nothing, but I want to check before I pass on what I know to the inspector."

"I know where you can find a key to Mr. Hobart's office," Peter said.

He ducked behind the counter. Goliath leaned over to see what he was doing, but Peter stood again, a set of keys on his palm.

"One of them is for Mr. Hobart's office. Another is for Mr. Armitage's office and his private chamber, and I'm not sure what the fourth one unlocks. They both handed in their keys to me when they left. I gave Mr. Hobart's set to Mr. Chapman, who gave them back to Mr. Hobart when he returned. He told me to hold onto Mr. Armitage's." He held them up by the ring.

"Why didn't he want you to give them to Mr. Chapman or Mrs. Kettering?" Goliath asked. "They're more senior than you."

"If we hold onto them here, then anyone can ask for them if they need something from Mr. Armitage's office. This desk is always manned."

I took the keys and promised to return them.

"I'd better come and keep watch for you," Goliath said, following me into the senior staff corridor. "I'll whistle if someone comes."

I lowered my voice to a whisper. "If I close the door, it will be as it was before. Nobody will know I'm inside."

"You have to turn the light on. Or can you see in the dark?"

"Very amusing. But you do have a point. Very well, whistle if someone approaches, and I'll quickly switch off the light."

Goliath positioned himself where he could see the foyer as well as along the corridor in both directions. Mr. Chapman should be in the dining room all evening, and as far as I was aware, Mrs. Kettering was in her private chambers or her office. If she happened to come out while I was inside Mr. Hobart's office, I hoped I'd have enough time to turn off the light upon Goliath's whistle before she noticed it.

As quietly as possible, I tried the keys until I found which of the three opened Mr. Hobart's door and I slipped inside and turned on the light. His desk was neat; all the day's paperwork had been safely stowed away. I searched the bookshelf of ledgers but found nothing relating to the kitchen except for some old renovation plans. I expected to see ledgers listing the supplies, but there were none. Perhaps they were in Mr. Armitage's office or the head chef kept that information himself.

Nor could I find a ledger listing the room service orders taken through the speaking tubes. I checked the books again, pulling them off the shelf and checking inside, in case their spines had been mislabeled. They hadn't. Perhaps it was kept in the kitchen.

But surely Mr. Hobart would need that information so he could add it to the guests' expenses. He would also require it each day, to account for guests checking out. Either he took down notes for the guests, then handed the ledger back to the kitchen, or they simply used loose paper, starting afresh the next day.

I searched the stack of papers in Mr. Hobart's tray then turned to the filing cabinet. I clicked my tongue in frustration as I tried to open some of the drawers only to find them locked. Thankfully, the bottom two weren't. I pulled out the leather document wallets and rifled through the contents.

Success! One of them contained loose sheets of paper with neat columns ruled in ink. Each entry was written in pencil, and included the date, time, room number, guest name and their order. A tick had been placed in ink beside each entry, probably by Mr. Hobart after he'd transcribed the details over to the guest's account.

There was one piece of paper for each day. The name of the staff member who'd taken the order was written beside it. Victor had been responsible for taking the room service orders on several occasions.

I flicked back through the papers until I found the one dated Christmas Eve and traced my finger down the entries. There it was, one of the names I'd been hoping to find. Now that I'd found it, I couldn't quite believe it. I felt a little giddy as I read through what he'd ordered. It was two of everything.

Mr. Hookly was either a hungry man or he'd entertained a guest in his room.

I returned the sheet to the wallet and placed it back in the drawer and hurried for the door, only to suddenly stop.

Goliath whistled the Pirate King's song, from *The Pirates of Penzance*, loudly and clearly. I switched off the light, hoping it hadn't been visible beneath the door.

"Mr. Hobart asked me to check on Mr. Armitage's office from time to time," I heard Goliath say. "I've just come from there."

There was a pause in which I could just make out Mrs. Kettering's shrill tone, if not her words.

"Yes, I'll move on. Goodnight, Mrs. Kettering."

I waited a moment before opening the door a crack. The coast was clear. I slipped out of the office and quickly locked the door behind me, racing into the foyer.

I didn't draw breath until I reached the front desk. "Thank you, Goliath," I said to the porter as I handed the keys back to Peter.

"So?" Goliath asked. "What did you find?"

I could hardly contain my excitement. The stalemate in the case had finally been broken. "Mr. Hookly ordered enough for two on Christmas Eve, yet he's here alone."

"Hookly?" Peter echoed. "The gentleman just back from Africa? The one who gave his address as Berkshire?"

"I think Mrs. Warrick recognized him. I overheard her say as much that afternoon and comment that he shouldn't be here."

Goliath leaned against the counter, arms crossed. "So she confronted him, he got worried and decided he had to kill her to stop her telling someone that he shouldn't be in the hotel. He invited her up to his room for dinner, poisoned her food, and she returned to her room where she died."

It didn't quite make sense. Apparently she was poisoned between three and six AM. Either the pathologist was wrong about the time of death or she took some food back to her room with her and consumed it later. But where was the evidence? There were no plates or cups that shouldn't have been in her room, and no leftovers.

"*Why* did she think he shouldn't be here?" Peter asked.

Goliath rubbed his jaw. "What if she thought he should still be in Africa? Perhaps that's why she was surprised to see

173

him here." He clicked his fingers. "What if he got into trouble there, maybe murdered someone, and came back to England to escape justice, and Mrs. Warrick knew it."

And I thought *my* imagination was vivid. "I like your theory, Goliath. It makes sense."

Peter shook his head. "It's a mad theory. You're both mad." He suddenly stopped and bit his lower lip. "Forgive me, Miss Fox, I don't mean it."

I leaned forward a little. "It's quite all right, Peter. I'm not going to get you into trouble with my uncle when you're simply being honest."

He looked relieved. "In that case, I don't think you're right. It can't be Hookly. He's got a letter of recommendation from Lord Addlington."

"It could be falsified."

"It's on our hotel stationery. How could he falsify it on our stationery if he hadn't checked in yet?"

I didn't think it was a watertight argument. Blank hotel stationery wouldn't be easy to obtain outside the hotel, but it wasn't impossible. "Pass me the keys to Mr. Hobart's office again."

"Why?" Peter asked.

"I want to make a telephone call to Mr. Hookly's address. We can ask someone there when Mr. Hookly is expected to return home and if they know why he came back from Africa."

"How will you discover that?"

"Lie, of course. I'll pretend I'm working for the police on the murder case and am just following up on all the guests' addresses. " I put out my palm but Peter shook his head.

"No one will believe a woman works for the police. Let me make the call from here. There's no one about now."

There were a handful of people leaving the vestibule and heading to the lift, smoking room or billiards room, but none approached. Peter flipped the pages of his register until he came to Mr. Hookly's entry.

After a few brief conversations as he was passed from one exchange to the next, he finally had a longer conversation with the person on the other end. His frown deepened. He thanked the other speaker then hung the receiver on the cradle.

"You look like you've seen a ghost," Goliath said.

"That's because I have." Peter swallowed. "Mr. Hookly is dead."

CHAPTER 11

"*I* got through to the police station nearest Mr. Hookly's address." Peter looked down at the reservation book, open to Mr. Hookly's entry. "They said he died two months ago."

"Bloody hell," Goliath murmured. "So who's our Mr. Hookly?"

"And how did he get Lord Addlington's letter?"

"Did the policeman say if the real Mr. Hookly died in suspicious circumstances?" I asked.

"Natural causes. His heart gave out."

So our Mr. Hookly was not Mr. Hookly at all. "If he's used a false name to check in here, it's reasonable to assume his real name is associated with wrongdoing, and Mrs. Warrick knew it."

"So we need to find out his real name and what he did," Goliath said. "The maid who cleans his room can look through his things in the morning."

I shook my head. I wasn't prepared to put the maids in danger. If Mr. Hookly found out, we could have another murder on our hands. "I'll inform the detective inspector in the morning. No one is to confront Mr. Hookly in the meantime. Is that understood? We'll let Scotland Yard know and they can decide what to do next."

"I'll call the Yard now and ask for the inspector to come

first thing tomorrow," Peter said, reaching for the telephone again.

I didn't sleep well that night. The turn of events had made me quite sure the poisoner was Mr. Hookly. Innocent people didn't use a dead man's name for good reasons. But two things didn't make sense. First of all, Mrs. Warrick had been poisoned in the early hours, and there was no evidence of food or drink in her room. If Mr. Hookly had added the poison to her meal, she would have died earlier. If she'd returned with extra food or drink to her room and consumed it in the small hours, where was the cup or plate or leftovers?

Had the police made a mistake in determining the time of death? How accurate was their estimate?

Or had Mr. Hookly given her the face cream as a gift and she'd got up in the middle of the night and used it? It was an odd gift, but it was a little more feasible than him giving her a tube of toothpaste or a bottle of tonic.

Something else troubled me even more. Mrs. Warrick had not been frightened or outraged when she saw Mr. Hookly in the foyer that afternoon. She'd simply been confused and surprised to see him. So he was probably not a murderer or criminal. If so, wouldn't she have alerted Mr. Hobart immediately? She'd spoken to him about Danny that afternoon, and she had not mentioned Mr. Hookly at all.

I fell asleep sometime during the night with a series of questions swirling around my head and no answers.

* * *

I FOUND a message from Harmony slipped under my door the following morning to say she couldn't do my hair, and she was having a short break at ten-thirty in the parlor if I wanted to talk. I got the feeling either Goliath or Peter had hinted that something was afoot but not given her more details and she hoped I would.

I waited in my room for detective inspector Hobart, but he didn't come. At ten-thirty, I went downstairs to find the hotel undergoing a transformation. Floral garlands were being hung and four men carefully wheeled a flatbed trolley across the tiles, its large load hidden beneath a sheet of canvas. It was New Year's Eve, the day of the ball, and every staff member seemed to have a task. No guests were allowed to dine in the dining room for breakfast or luncheon as the room was turned into a ballroom, and the adjoining vestibule was off-limits too. Mr. Hobart stood by the Christmas tree, clipboard in hand, directing staff. He looked exhausted as he spoke sternly to a delivery man for not using the rear entrance. He was doing the work of two men, thanks to me.

"May I offer some assistance, Mr. Hobart?" I asked.

"No, thank you," he said without looking up from his clipboard.

"I could deliver messages to the staff for you."

"Thank you, but there's no need. We can manage." He spotted some newly arrived guests and went to greet them, smiling all the way.

I sighed and headed to the parlor where I found Harmony and Edith sitting with four other maids, drinking tea. They separated from the group and joined me in the corner.

"Shouldn't you be helping with preparations?" I asked.

"We've been scrubbing the dining room and foyer since dawn," Harmony said. "We're just having a quick fifteen minutes to ourselves before we clean rooms."

Edith pressed a hand to her lower back and winced. "I'll be glad when this is all over."

"Sorry about your hair," Harmony said to me.

I touched my hair. "It's not as elegant as one of your arrangements, but I have been doing it for many years now."

She smiled. "I'll fix it later for tonight."

"I'm not going to the ball."

"Don't tell me it's because you have nothing to wear. If you'd made your mind up days ago, you would have something by now."

"I was going to say that I don't feel like joining in the revelries," I said defensively. "I'm still in mourning."

Her lips flattened but her eyes were sympathetic.

Edith poured a cup of tea and handed it to me. "Harmony says Goliath is acting strange this morning. He says there's been a development in the murder case but he can't say more until you've spoken to the police."

"He's got a nerve not telling me," Harmony said into her

teacup. "I'm the one who got you involved in the investigation in the first place."

Victor pushed open the door and entered with two other young cooks. Harmony straightened, as did several of the other maids. Where they smiled flirtatiously, however, Harmony pursed her lips and pretended not to see them.

"Good morning, ladies," Victor said, joining us. "So what's this I hear about Peter calling the police?" he asked me.

It would seem I wasn't going to get away with keeping silent any longer. I told them about Mr. Hookly dining with a second person on the night of the murder, and then Peter's telephone call to the police station nearest Mr. Hookly's address.

"According to them, Mr. Hookly is dead," I said.

Harmony gasped. "Then who's our Mr. Hookly?"

"Maybe he killed the real Mr. Hookly," Victor said, sitting on the edge of the table.

Edith put a hand to her throat. Her eyes were huge as they stared back at me, full of worry.

"Don't be afraid," I told her gently. "He died of natural causes. But the man we know as Mr. Hookly is impersonating him, for some unknown reason."

"To kill people," Victor said.

Harmony scowled at him. "Do stop it, Victor. You're frightening Edith and not making any sense whatsoever."

"Or I'm the only sensible one here."

She rolled her eyes. "It was a good idea to contact the police, Miss Fox. Why haven't they come yet? Did Peter stress how important it was?"

I hadn't heard Peter's call so I couldn't be sure.

"There must be a mistake," Edith said, frowning into her teacup. "If Mr. Hookly were dead, why does he have a letter of recommendation from that lord?"

"You know about the letter?" I asked.

"Doesn't everyone?"

"Not me," Victor said.

"I heard it from Peter," Harmony said.

Edith searched my gaze. "Miss Fox? What do you think? Can Lord Addlington's word be trusted?"

I patted her arm. "I'm sure it can. He's very well known here, after all." I didn't want to tell her the letter could have been falsified. I didn't want to upset her more.

Victor stretched out his legs, his heels trapping the edge of Harmony's skirt. She didn't notice. "You can't assume it was Mrs. Warrick dining in his room that night either. For starters, she's much older than him."

"So?" Harmony said. "What's wrong with a middle-aged woman having a liaison with a younger man?"

"She's past middle age."

"So?" she asked again.

He turned to me and she rolled her eyes again. "It's more likely he entertained a...different kind of woman in his room," the cook said.

"Victor!" Harmony's voice drew the attention of the other maids and cooks. "Don't be so vulgar in front of Miss Fox."

Victor adjusted his crossed arms, pushing his hands into his armpits. "Sorry, Miss Fox, but I didn't want to say whore in front of you."

Harmony rubbed her forehead and sighed.

I tried to suppress my smile. "I didn't think those sort of women came into the hotel."

Victor merely shrugged and the women didn't comment, but the moment I said it, I remembered the Russian count and his mistress in the smoking room. It would seem the hotel's staff looked the other way if the whore looked sophisticated enough.

"Hopefully the police will arrive soon," Harmony said with a glance at the clock. "If they don't, make sure Peter calls them again."

"Of course," I said, thinking the same thing. The message he left last night must not have reached the detective inspector.

"I have to return to work," Edith said, rising.

Harmony rose too, only to find her skirt trapped beneath Victor's shoes. Instead of pulling it free, she glared at him until he drew his legs back, releasing the skirt. He put his hands up in surrender but didn't offer an apology. Harmony marched out of the parlor behind Edith and the other maids. Victor watched her go, a small smile on his lips.

I left the cooks and returned to the foyer where I asked Peter if the police had arrived yet.

"Mr. Hobart just informed me they're on their way," he said through a smile as a guest approached his counter.

The foyer was even busier than before, with several guests milling about or arriving. I was surprised to see Aunt Lilian greeting many of them personally. She smiled brightly as she flitted between groups like a mauve butterfly, but a closer inspection revealed the dark circles under her eyes.

Flossy broke away from the women she was talking to and joined me. "There you are! I've been looking for you."

"Your mother looks well this morning."

Flossy pulled a face. "She's cross with me. She just learned that the man she wanted me to marry isn't coming to tonight's ball."

"The one with the interest in Egyptian archeology?"

She nodded. "Apparently her friend, his mother, said I'm not the right girl for him. Mother is blaming me for not putting more effort into capturing his interest. But honestly, I tried, Cleo. I truly did. I even asked questions about the temples in Egypt."

"Do you mean pyramids?" I said, trying to keep a straight face.

"Perhaps *you* should try. He seems more your type, and you're closer in age to him than I am."

"I don't intend to marry," I told her.

She laughed, but when I didn't join in, she blinked at me. "You're serious."

"Yes."

"But…" She frowned and seemed to be grappling with the concept. To be fair, it must be an idea she'd never entertained. Perhaps she didn't even know she *could* entertain it. "But there's nothing wrong with you, Cleo. You might not come with a dowry, but a man with his own fortune will overlook that."

I pressed my lips together to stop my smile from breaking free.

She patted my arm. "I'll introduce you to some gentlemen tonight. Floyd has some friends who are in line to inherit. One or two are even good company."

"I'm not going to the ball."

Her pout returned. "Oh, Cleo, do change your mind. It's not too late."

I didn't want to argue with her so I remained quiet.

"Isn't that Mr. Hobart's brother, the detective?" she asked.

I followed her gaze to see the detective inspector and another man arrive. The two Hobart brothers exchanged words, which left the hotel manager frowning. They approached me together. I excused myself from Flossy and met them halfway.

"Good morning, Miss Fox." There was nothing friendly about the inspector's businesslike manner. "The message that was left for me said you have information regarding the murder."

"I think so," I said. "Thank you for coming."

"You can't talk about that out here." Mr. Hobart glanced around. "Go into my office. Quickly now, before Lady Bainbridge sees you. I can't have her informing Sir Ronald."

The inspector regarded his brother. "You don't want me here solving your murder?"

"It is not *my* murder. And no, I don't want you here. Not on the day of the ball. There's too much to do, and if the guests find out the police are here, it'll remind them of the incident."

"Perhaps they ought to be reminded. There is a murderer here, after all."

"We don't know that. He could have been one of the guests who checked out."

"I doubt that."

Did he mean he doubted the murderer had left, or that it was a guest at all? If not a guest, then he must suspect a staff member. Even more reason to present him with my evidence against Mr. Hookly.

Mr. Hobart stiffened. "You may speak with Miss Fox in my office."

"Can you join us?" I wasn't quite sure whether I was asking because I wanted him to hear what I had to say about Mr. Hookly, or whether I wanted someone capable of deflecting the inspector's ire.

"Of course, but only for five minutes. I have a lot of work to do."

"If only you had an assistant," the inspector muttered.

The barb stung, just as he'd intended. It would seem neither of Mr. Armitage's parents would forgive me for what I'd done. I was glad I wouldn't be seeing them again after this investigation was over.

"Stephen," Mr. Hobart chided.

The inspector indicated that his brother should lead the way.

The second policeman followed and closed the door behind us. He stood in front of it while the inspector sat in his brother's chair. Mr. Hobart remained standing while I sat on the guest chair.

"What do you want to tell me, Miss Fox?" the inspector asked.

"First of all, I wish to apologize for being responsible for Mr. Armitage losing his position here. I plan to make it up to him by pressing my uncle to give him back his position."

"Harry won't accept it."

"Then if I hear of other employment opportunities, I'll put his name forward."

"That's a nice sentiment, Miss Fox, but you have no friends here in London, as I understand it. You won't hear of other suitable opportunities."

"Stephen," Mr. Hobart snapped.

I looked down at my clasped hands. This wasn't going at all well. "May we discuss the murder instead?" I asked, looking up again. "I find the topic more palatable."

The inspector grunted. "Go on."

"There's a guest staying here by the name of Hookly." I told the inspector how I'd overheard Mrs. Warrick say she recognized someone, and explained how it had led me to first believe she was talking about Mr. Armitage, but then my suspicions had shifted to Mr. Duffield and Mr. Hookly.

"I discovered that he entertained a guest in his room on the night of the murder," I went on. "He ordered two meals and wine to be brought up to his room. Mrs. Warrick didn't dine in the hotel dining room that evening, nor did she leave the hotel, so I suspect *she* was his guest."

"How do you know about the meals and her not leaving the hotel?"

"I asked the staff."

"Is that all of your evidence?"

"There's more. I thought it best to find out more about Mr. Hookly, so I telephoned the police station closest to where he lives." I thought it best to leave Peter's name out of it, particularly in the presence of his superior. "I discovered that Mr. Hookly is dead."

"Dead?" Mr. Hobart cried. "No, he's not. I saw him this morning."

"He died two months ago," I told him. "The Mr. Hookly here is not the real Mr. Hookly."

Mr. Hobart slowly lowered himself onto a chair. "My god. He must be the murderer."

The inspector put up his hand for silence. "How did you get the local police to tell you that, Miss Fox?" He leaned forward, his gaze on me the entire time. When he looked at me like that, with those piercing blue eyes, I felt like blurting everything out.

"I'd rather not say."

"Hmmm."

"So what do you think of that?" I asked. "It's worth interviewing him now, isn't it?"

"Very much," Mr. Hobart agreed. "Don't worry about Sir Ronald. I'll smooth his feathers."

"I can handle Bainbridge," the inspector said.

Mr. Hobart gave his brother an arched look. "You don't seem to be at your most diplomatic right now, Stephen."

The inspector sat back and clasped his hands over his stomach. "I won't be interviewing anyone yet anyway. Hookly isn't the murderer."

"Why not?" I asked. When the inspector didn't answer, I pushed on. "Is it the time of death? I was wondering the same thing. How could Mr. Hookly have poisoned Mrs. Warrick in his room at dinnertime when she didn't die until much later?"

He regarded me with narrowed eyes. I couldn't determine if that meant he was annoyed at my impertinent question or impressed I'd thought of it.

"Was a slow acting poison used?" I asked when he didn't immediately answer.

"There was enough mercuric cyanide in her body to kill her instantly."

"Could the time of death be wrong?"

"No."

"Not even by a little?"

"The temperature of the body means death occurred between the hours of three and six. We can't be more accurate than that." He was definitely annoyed. If he had been impressed before, he wasn't anymore. Not with lips pursed as severely as that.

"Could he have given her the jar of face cream as a gift and she put it on later?" I asked.

He twiddled his thumbs. Well, not so much twiddled as fought a battle.

"Was poison found in the jar?" I pressed.

The twiddling stopped and he stood. "Leave the police work to the police, Miss Fox."

I flinched at his harsh tone and lowered my head. He was right. I'd wasted his time with an incorrect theory. I wished he'd tell me why he'd dismissed it, but the police didn't share such details with the public.

He must have felt sorry for me, or regretted his tone, because his next words turned my assumption about the police not sharing information on its head. "There was no poison found in the jar of face cream, or the tube of toothpaste, or the bottle of tonic. There was no poison found anywhere in Mrs. Warrick's room. Since she died in her nightclothes in bed, it's very unlikely that she consumed the poison elsewhere, and as I already told you, there was enough mercuric cyanide in her body to kill her quickly."

"Meaning she couldn't have consumed it elsewhere then returned to her room and gone about her usual nighttime routine. She would have been in great pain, wouldn't she?"

"Absolute agony."

Mr. Hobart made a small sound of horror in his throat. "Poor Mrs. Warrick."

"So the poisoned substance was removed from her room,"

I said. "The poisoner took it away with them when they left. And since the door was locked…" *Oh God. No.*

"The poisoner is a member of staff," Mr. Hobart muttered, his face draining of color. "Stephen, why haven't you told me this?"

"The test results only came back yesterday. Since then, I've been sifting through the staff statements again. There are a lot of them."

"There aren't many with a key to Mrs. Warrick's room."

"Can other staff members get access to the keys easily?"

"It's possible." Mr. Hobart sighed. "Unfortunately it wouldn't be all that difficult. I don't think Mrs. Kettering would pass her key out, and I have spare keys to each room locked in the bottom drawer of my desk. The maids also have keys to the rooms they clean and are under strict instructions not to give them to anyone else."

"That doesn't mean they don't," the inspector said.

"Or that someone didn't steal Mrs. Warrick's key," I added.

Mr. Hobart rubbed his forehead. "This is dreadful."

"Nothing can be done about it today," the inspector assured him. "I'm still reading through interviews and gathering other evidence."

"Is that wise?" I asked. "Shouldn't you act as quickly as possible? Perhaps you could round up all of the suspects and keep them at Scotland Yard while you interview them."

"I can't keep them there unless I arrest them, and I won't arrest anyone until I have evidence. That's not *my* way. At the moment, what I do have is more than a hundred statements to re-read as well as men out making inquiries to local suppliers of mercuric cyanide. Is there something else you'd like me to do, Miss Fox?"

"That sounds like enough to me," I said, sheepish.

"I can't believe it's a staff member," Mr. Hobart muttered. "They have to be exceptional to work here, the best of the best. I check all their references thoroughly, and Harry interviewed every one of them personally."

"They duped him and forged their references," the inspector said, matter-of-factly. "Harry might be a good judge of character but if one of them set out to be deceitful, he wouldn't know, particularly if he's not on the lookout for duplicity."

"Speaking of forgeries," I said. "Mr. Hookly must have falsified the letter from Lord Addlington. Are you going to confront him about that, Mr. Hobart?"

"No one will confront anyone about anything," the inspector said.

"Not today," Mr. Hobart said, gentler. "But I don't see how the letter can be forged. I checked it against another from Lord Addlington that we have on file and the handwriting matched."

I frowned. "Why do that when you didn't suspect Mr. Hookly of wrongdoing?"

"A jeweler came to me asking about him. He'd become worried that Mr. Hookly was going to leave London and not settle his very substantial account. The jeweler had extended credit to Mr. Hookly based on Lord Addlington's letter, you see. The jeweler knew Lord Addlington well too. He's a good customer, apparently, so the jeweler had no difficulty extending credit. But as time wore on and more items were ordered, he became concerned. Since the items were sent here, he came to me and asked if I could vouch for Mr. Hookly's character. I couldn't, of course. Not personally, but I mentioned Lord Addlington's letter. I came to the same conclusion as you, Miss Fox, that perhaps Mr. Hookly wrote a message on our stationery and signed it with Lord Addlington's signature. I asked Mr. Hookly for the letter again, checked it against the letter I had on file, and saw that the handwriting and signature matched. I was relieved, to be honest. A measure of doubt crept in after the jeweler's visit. Mr. Hookly has ordered a lot from some very expensive shops. It's unusual."

"What excuse did you give Hookly for borrowing the letter?" the inspector asked.

"I told him I needed to write down Lord Addlington's address again as our copy was badly smudged and we like to send him a small gift for his birthday."

The inspector grunted his approval. "Well done, Alfred. We'll make a detective of you yet."

"I doubt it. I didn't know he's not the real Mr. Hookly.

Miss Fox is the better detective of the two of us. How do you think he managed to forge Lord Addlington's letter?"

"Or steal that one from the dead Mr. Hookly?" I added.

"You can ask him after this is over." The inspector rested his hand on the doorknob. "But not yet. I don't want to rattle cages and frighten the killer into leaving before we learn who it is."

Mr. Hobart clasped his brother's shoulder. "Thank you for your discretion, Stephen. Sir Ronald will appreciate it."

"I'm not doing it for him."

"Then *I* appreciate it."

The inspector's gaze softened as he nodded at his brother. They were so alike in appearances, yet I was discovering how different they were in character. Mr. Hobart was definitely the kind-hearted, diplomatic one, whereas the detective inspector was crustier. Or perhaps he was simply that way with me because he was still annoyed with me over my role in his son's dismissal.

The detective and his colleague left as discreetly as they'd arrived. Flossy and Aunt Lilian were still in the foyer, chatting to friends, and didn't seem to notice. I followed Mr. Hobart to the front desk where he briefly discussed new arrivals with Peter.

When he saw me still standing nearby, he frowned. "Is there something I can do for you, Miss Fox?"

"I'd like to offer my services again. Let me assist you."

He sighed. "I appreciate the offer. I do. And don't take this the wrong way, but you don't know enough about how the hotel works to be helpful to me and I don't have the time to teach you, nor can I spare anyone else to teach you. Not today. Perhaps you should start getting ready for the ball."

"It's the middle of the day. Anyway, I'm not going."

"And deprive the gentlemen of your good company? That is a shame."

I huffed out a laugh. "Nicely done, Mr. Hobart."

Flossy spotted me and signaled for me to join her and Aunt Lilian.

"I suppose I must," I said with reluctance dripping from every syllable.

"You *can* help, as it happens," Mr. Hobart said brightly.

"You can talk to the guests on behalf of the family. Your aunt will tire soon and Miss Bainbridge tries hard but she lacks… how shall I put it?"

"Sophisticated conversation?"

"She's very young."

She was nineteen, which wasn't all that young, but I didn't correct him.

I did as he suggested and found myself invited to luncheon in Flossy's room with two of the young women. She introduced them as her friends, and while their mother joined Aunt Lilian for a light luncheon in her own suite, we four retired to Flossy's.

We ordered sandwiches through the speaking tube and chatted for the next hour. Flossy's friends were nice, but they only wanted to talk about the ball, what they were going to wear, who was going to be there, and which gentlemen they wanted to dance with. They were sweet and entertaining but only to a point.

Instead of being rude and excusing myself, I tuned out of the conversation. My mind naturally wandered to the meeting I'd had with Detective Inspector Hobart in Mr. Hobart's office. I'd thought my theory about Mr. Hookly was quite solid, and to learn that it was not was disconcerting. Thank goodness I hadn't accused him last night. He might be guilty of impersonating the real Mr. Hookly, and stealing Lord Addlington's letter in order to get away with not paying his creditors, but he was not a murderer.

One of the staff was, however. It was a troubling turn of events. I felt as though I'd made friends with some. They'd even helped me in the investigation. It couldn't be them or they'd not have been so encouraging and helpful. There were a lot of *other* members of staff, however. Almost a hundred.

And I knew someone who could help narrow down the suspects. Someone who knew every single staff member well and who didn't have to prepare the hotel for the biggest event of the year.

I made my excuses to Flossy and her friends, telling her I needed to go out for a while. "I'll be back well before the ball," I told her. "I want to help you with your preparations."

"Or get ready yourself," she said, grinning.

I left without correcting her again. My mind was no longer on the ball. It was focused on murder and seeing Mr. Armitage. I found the prospect far more thrilling than a young lady should. Indeed, for the first time in months, I was looking forward to something.

CHAPTER 12

*I*f I had to speak to Mr. Armitage on the doorstep again, so be it. At least it wasn't raining this time. I had to first get an interview with him, however, and that meant getting past his mother. After my last visit, I wasn't so sure she'd agree to a second meeting.

"You've got courage coming here again," she said when she opened the door to me.

"Some would say I had a nerve."

Her frown deepened. "Why are you here? You've already apologized."

"It's hotel business. It's very busy there today with preparations for the ball, and I needed to talk to someone about the staff. I can't think of anyone better to ask than Mr. Armitage."

She crossed her arms. "He just arrived home. He's been out all morning looking for work and is having lunch now."

"I can wait for him to finish. Will you tell him I'm here, please?"

She looked torn between her desire to send me away and the need to be polite. When the lines around her mouth relaxed, I knew long-ingrained habit had won over maternal retribution.

She disappeared and a few moments later Mr. Armitage stood in the doorway, wiping his hands on a towel. He wore no jacket, but this time his shirt sleeves were firmly fastened at the cuffs.

"I'm surprised to see you here again, Miss Fox," he said, leaning a shoulder against the doorframe. It was impossible to tell if he'd worked the anger out of his system or if I was going to endure more sarcasm.

I decided it was best to steel myself for a few barbs directed my way. It was better to be armed than caught unawares. "A situation has arisen and I need your help."

"I can't help you."

"You don't know what it is yet."

He merely smiled. It was not one of his charming ones. He was definitely still angry with me.

"It's about the staff," I went on. "Your father believes one of them is the murderer."

He straightened. "He does?"

"He doesn't know which one yet. He's still investigating."

His frown deepened. "You still don't trust him, do you? Miss Fox, why are you trying to insult my family further?"

"I'm not! There's no insult intended. Your father is very thorough. I have absolute faith in his abilities and that of Scotland Yard." I swallowed. His glare was unnerving. "It's just that he is perhaps too thorough. I spoke to him this morning and he told me he suspects the murderer is a staff member."

"Then I'm sure he'll interview the relevant staff again."

"That's the problem. He hasn't narrowed down the list of suspects. He's going through their statements again as well as checking with suppliers of mercuric cyanide."

He slung the towel over his shoulder. He did not try to the shut the door or tell me to leave. It was a positive sign.

"The thing is," I went on, "what if the murderer leaves the hotel before the inspector returns to question the staff again? If it were my investigation, I'd be speaking to the staff members with keys to Mrs. Warrick's room."

"Why isn't he?" he said, more to himself than me.

"He claims he needs to be thorough before he accuses anyone. I think that's my fault since I leapt to the wrong conclusion based on flimsy evidence."

"There are some things that are you fault, Miss Fox, but my father's thoroughness is not one of them." He stepped aside. "You might as well come in. This isn't going to be over in a few minutes."

I peered into the hallway beyond. "Are you sure?"

"She won't bite."

"It's her bark that worries me more."

He led me through to a cozy parlor at the front of the house and added coal from the scuttle to the fire. I sat on the sofa and he occupied one of the armchairs. It was a pleasant room that reminded me of my grandparents' house with its heavy drapery and embroidered cushions. The small space was filled to bursting with knickknacks, furniture and family photographs, which made it seem even smaller.

"Is this you as a boy?" I asked, picking up a framed photograph of a younger Inspector and Mrs. Hobart with a lanky youth standing behind them. It was clearly Mr. Armitage but with longer hair and a softer jaw. He was already quite tall, although I'd guess him to be no more than fourteen or so.

He plucked the frame out of my hand and set it down on the table. "Don't change the subject. You were telling me that my father believes a staff member is the murderer but he's not re-interviewing any of them until he has further proof."

"I also wondered if he's holding back until after tonight's ball as a favor to your uncle."

"My uncle wouldn't ask him to do that."

"Would your father do it anyway? Particularly knowing that Mr. Hobart is under pressure because he no longer has an assistant?"

"Not to mention he knows that my uncle feels as though he owes Sir Ronald for giving him his job back," Mr. Armitage added.

I hadn't thought about that. It was possible Mr. Hobart felt guilty and wanted to repay Uncle Ronald by being extra dutiful and efficient. It was understandable that his brother the detective would want to make it easier for him at the moment.

Mr. Armitage drummed his fingers on the chair arm only to stop when his mother walked in. Mrs. Hobart ignored me and strode up to her son. She snatched the hand towel off him and finally turned to me.

"I would offer you tea, but we've run out." She marched out of the parlor, the towel balled up in her hand.

"At least she didn't throw me out," I said on a sigh.

Mr. Armitage seemed not to notice the exchange. He looked lost in thought. "Why does my father think one of the staff is the murderer?"

I told him how poison had not been found in Mrs. Warrick's room, and that she couldn't have consumed it elsewhere then come back, changed into her night clothes and climbed into bed as if nothing were amiss.

"Her door was locked," I finished. "Edith had to open it with her key."

"So only someone with a key could have done it."

"Between the hours of three and six, according to the temperature of the body," I added.

"My uncle and I had access to his set of spare keys," Mr. Armitage went on. "He would have noticed if they went missing. Mrs. Kettering also has a set, and the maid cleaning the room for the day does too. It's possible either that one or Mrs. Kettering's was stolen and they never reported it, or didn't notice it missing before it was returned."

"Considering Mrs. Warrick was poisoned when they would have been asleep, that's likely. I've met Edith," I added. "She seems nice but has a nervous constitution. I can't see her killing anyone."

"Nor can I. I don't have much to do with the maids, but I remember interviewing her along with Mrs. Kettering. I found her to be timid. Not the sort capable of murder."

"And Mrs. Kettering?"

"The opposite of Edith. She likes to lord it over the maids. She's very unpopular. She's a hard worker, however, and has been at the hotel for years. I can't see why she would kill Mrs. Warrick."

"That could be said about all of the staff," I pointed out. "But not about all of the guests."

His gaze sharpened and focused on me. It was intense and unexpected. "You said Mrs. Warrick could have been referring to one of two other guests that afternoon. Aside from me, that is."

"The inspector doesn't think a guest did it. It had to be someone with access to Mrs. Warrick's key."

"Unless one of *them* stole a key."

"Oh, yes, I suppose." I'd been assuming another staff

member stole a key, but there was no reason why a guest couldn't.

He gave me a smug look. "You hadn't considered that possibility, had you?"

I was quite sure he was being irritating on purpose. "I don't think your father has, either."

"I'd wager he has and decided not to tell you. He won't share everything he knows with members of the public."

"Members of the public or just me?" I asked, recalling the inspector's cool reception earlier.

He ignored the comment. "We need to find out which one of those two guests has a motive for killing Mrs. Warrick."

"I already have." It was my turn to give him a smug look.

"This isn't a competition, Miss Fox."

"Then stop acting as if it is, Mr. Armitage."

"Just tell me about the two guests."

I settled back into the sofa. This could take some time. "Mr. Duffield lives near Mrs. Warrick, so it's a natural assumption that they would know one another. Further investigation proved that he is experiencing reduced circumstances."

"Very reduced, if he had to resort to selling gossip about the hotel to the gutter press."

"I thought he might have also sold gossip about his friends, perhaps even about her, but that would give *her* motive to kill *him*, not the other way around. I suspected she'd simply known about his reduced circumstances and wondered how he could stay at an expensive hotel, if she was referring to him at all."

"He's probably hunting for a wealthy wife at the ball," he said.

"Mr. Hobart thinks so too. It makes sense, since Mr. Duffield didn't stay for dessert after he spoke to Mr. Chapman about me."

"You dined with Mr. Duffield? Why?"

"To learn more about him, of course."

"By flirting with him," he said flatly.

"I didn't need to flirt. He feigned interest only until he learned from Mr. Chapman that I was living at the hotel because I, too, am experiencing reduced circumstances."

"Reduced?" He grunted.

I ignored him and pressed on. "I discovered that Mr. Duffield's family had sold off his family estate and he moved into a cottage. As humiliating as that must be for him, I didn't think it enough of a reason to kill someone to keep them quiet about it."

"Agreed. And what about the second guest you think Mrs. Warrick could have recognized that afternoon?"

"My Hookly."

"Hookly?" He chuckled. "Do you mean to tell me you were flirting with him in the smoking room to get information from him?"

"Again, I was *not* flirting," I said tightly.

"I'm sure he'd see it differently."

I bristled. "I was only in the smoking room for one reason —so I could talk to him."

"So you weren't attempting a rebellion against your uncle?"

"No! I'm twenty-three, Mr. Armitage, not fifteen. Anyway, through subtle questioning—not flirting—I discovered that Mr. Hookly has recently returned from southern Africa after he'd sold his mine."

"I know all that."

"But you don't know that Mr. Hookly is dead. The real Hookly, that is."

It was immensely satisfying to see the shock on his face. "How did you discover that?"

"Through clever deduction."

"You telephoned the address in the reservations register, didn't you? Remind me to have a chat to Peter about—" He cut himself short. He'd forgotten that he no longer worked at the hotel. "It doesn't matter if Mrs. Warrick knew the real Mr. Hookly was dead," he went on. "She would have been surprised to see him if his ghost had shown up, but she couldn't have recognized his imposter."

"Unless she did. Perhaps she knew he wasn't the type to stay at luxury hotels. Or perhaps she knew he should still be in Africa, not here in London. He might be telling the truth about his mine there, but lying about some other aspect of his life."

He rubbed his forehead. "It doesn't quite add up. It almost does, but there are holes."

I sighed. "I know. I do think he's not at all as well off as he claims and he's using Lord Addlington's letter to order expensive clothes and jewelry on credit."

"He does have a lot of parcels delivered."

"Lord Addlington's letter is real, however. Your uncle checked the handwriting against a letter from his lordship on file."

Mr. Armitage nodded slowly. "The imposter could have stolen it off the dead Mr. Hookly. I do know the fake Mr. Hookly wants to attend the ball to speak to another guest who will also be attending. He asked me about him a number of times, making sure he was still coming."

"Who?"

"A banker known for giving loans to his friends, at generous rates, for their business ventures."

"Is he a friend of Lord Addlington's?"

Mr. Armitage's lips curved with his triumphant smile. "I think you've just found your motive. Lord Addlington is friends with everyone who matters. It's conceivable the fake Mr. Hookly will show the banker the letter tonight at the ball and ask for a loan."

"A loan which he wouldn't have to pay back because the banker would never be able to find him again, seeing as Mr. Hookly is deceased."

He shot to his feet and put out his hand to me. "We have to return to the hotel."

I hesitated, surprised at the offered hand. Had he forgiven me already or merely forgotten in his excitement in solving the case? Perhaps politeness was so ingrained in him too that it was merely an act of a well-brought up man.

My hesitation cost me and he withdrew his hand before I could accept it. He left and I could hear him speaking to his mother in another room.

I sighed and stood. Next time I wouldn't spend so much time trying to work out what an offered hand meant. Sometimes it meant nothing more than he was polite.

I met him in the hall as he buttoned up his jacket. He

plucked a hat and coat off the stand and opened the front door for me.

"What did you tell your mother?" I asked.

"That I have something to tell my father that might help him solve the murder."

"We're going to Scotland Yard?"

"Without evidence?" He scoffed. "He won't accept our theory without proof."

"He won't want us to confront Mr. Hookly."

"We're not going to. We'll avoid him at all costs." He turned up his coat collar and thrust his hands into his pockets. "We'll find out if there's any possibility that a key to Mrs. Warrick's room could have gone missing on the night of the murder. Our entire theory hinges on Mr. Hookly stealing one."

"The fake Mr. Hookly." I quickened my step to keep up with his long strides as we walked along the street. "I wonder who he really is, and if he truly has just come back from Africa."

"If he has, I doubt he just sold a gold mine or he wouldn't be trying to swindle everyone."

"Diamonds," I said.

"No, gold. That's what he told me."

I stopped. When he realized, he stopped too. "He hasn't just come from southern Africa at all!" I said. "Otherwise he'd know that diamonds are mined near Cape Town, not gold."

"How do *you* know?"

"I read about it in a book I borrowed from the hotel library."

He smiled as we started walking again. "Your bloody visit to the library," he muttered.

I glanced at him sideways. "What do you mean?"

He remained silent.

"Mr. Armitage, if you won't answer, I'll tell your mother that you just used a vulgar word in front of a lady."

"I thought you were the silverware thief."

I burst out laughing.

He smiled too, but with a measure of chagrin in the lopsided tilt of his lips. "I thought you were sneaking about in the sitting room. In hindsight, of course you couldn't have been the thief. You didn't arrive until after the thefts started."

"Why would I steal from my own uncle?"

"I thought you liked to stir up trouble."

I laughed again. "This is rich. You've been punishing *me* for accusing you when all this time, you suspected me of being a thief."

"First of all, I'm not *punishing* you. Any guilt you feel is entirely of your own making. And perhaps my mother's."

"And your father's. You have very loyal parents."

"Second of all, I never actually accused you. Thirdly, you accused me of *murder*, Miss Fox. I merely thought you were a troublemaker. And finally, I lost my job thanks to your wild theory."

"It might have been wild, but at least it wasn't stupid."

He shook his head and huffed out a breath. I wasn't quite sure if he was amused or exasperated. Perhaps both.

The train journey followed by the hackney ride to the hotel felt long, with many awkward silences between us. Our easy banter turned polite and dull; he asked me about Cambridge and I asked him about London. We avoided sensitive topics of his childhood, my family, and where he was going to work next.

I was so relieved to see the hotel that I alighted from the carriage without waiting for Frank to open the door.

"Mr. Armitage!" the doorman said. "What're you doing here, sir? And with Miss Fox, too…" His curious gaze shifted from me to Mr. Armitage and back again.

I simply smiled.

Mr. Armitage placed a finger to his lips. "Don't tell anyone. I came to see my uncle."

"And I wish to see mine," I said—and meant it. If Uncle Ronald was in a good mood because plans for the ball were going well, I would ask him again to reconsider hiring Mr. Armitage.

"Why do you need to see Sir Ronald?" Mr. Armitage asked as we entered the foyer. "If it's because of me, I meant it the other day. I won't accept my old position back, even if he begs me."

"Oh," I said on a breath. "Isn't it wonderful?"

I turned around to take in all of the decorations in the foyer. A half dozen potted large ferns added some greenery, while garlands of fresh flowers and leaves brightened up the front of the counters and above doorways. A closer inspection revealed a string of small lightbulbs woven through each of the garlands. It would look marvelous as darkness fell.

"Isn't it wonderful, Mr. Armitage?" I said again.

But he'd moved away. He was talking with Mr. Hobart near the entrance to the vestibule. I went to join them but was waylaid by Goliath.

"Is Mr. Armitage back permanently?" he asked.

"It's just a brief visit," I said. "Have you seen Mrs. Kettering? Is she in her office?"

"I think so."

"It doesn't look terribly busy here anymore." There were several gentlemen chatting to one another but few ladies. "Has everyone arrived who is going to stay overnight for the ball?"

"Most. The women have retired to their rooms to get ready." He shook his head. "I don't know why it takes you ladies so long to put on a frock."

Mr. Armitage crossed the foyer and joined us. "Goliath, go and help Mr. Hobart. He needs someone tall in the dining room."

"It's the ballroom for today, sir." Goliath grinned. "Nice to have you back, sir."

"I'm not," Mr. Armitage said as Goliath walked off.

"Mrs. Kettering is in her office," I told him. "Shall we speak to her first then go in search of Edith?"

"I just checked with my uncle," he said as we headed towards the senior staff corridor. "He's adamant his spare set of keys weren't touched that night or any other night. They're kept in a locked drawer and he and I are the only ones with a key to the drawer. Mine didn't go missing and he keeps his on his person. The drawer's lock hasn't been tampered with."

"Did you tell him we're investigating the murder?"

"No. He didn't ask why I was asking about the keys. He's under a lot of pressure right now and his mind is focused on the ball going smoothly."

We found Mrs. Kettering enjoying a cup of tea at her desk

while she looked over some paperwork. The clashing of her eyebrows suggested she was cross. Or perhaps that was their usual position. I didn't know her well enough to know if she ever looked anything other than cross.

"We need to ask you questions about your set of room keys," Mr. Armitage began. "Is it possible that one went missing on the night of Mrs. Warrick's murder?"

She blinked rapidly. "Why are you asking questions about the murder? You are not the police."

"We're helping them," he said.

"Nonsense. Scotland Yard don't enlist the help of the public." She picked up a pencil. "I don't have to answer your questions, Mr. Armitage. You are no longer assistant manager."

I opened my mouth to invoke the name of Uncle Ronald, but Mr. Armitage got in first. "I'm working here as a private detective, at Mr. Hobart's behest. You can ask him, if you like. He's in the vestibule. Be quick, however. He's very busy, as you can imagine."

Her nostrils flared. "My keys did not go missing on that night or any other. I am not in the habit of losing them."

"Could someone have stolen one and returned it without your knowledge?"

"No," she ground out.

"Where are your keys kept?" I asked.

Her nostrils flared again. "Is Sir Ronald aware that you're interrogating staff, Miss Fox?"

"This isn't an interrogation," I said evenly. "We're simply trying to get to the bottom of a mystery. There's no need for you to be so defensive. Unless you have something to hide, of course." I hoped that honesty and directness would get through to her. She seemed like someone who appreciated frankness.

Or she might throw us out.

"They're kept in that locked box at all times." She pointed to a wooden box on the shelf behind her. "I keep the key to it on my person." She picked through the bunch of keys attached to the chatelaine at her hip until she found the one she needed and proceeded to use it to unlock the box. "These keys remain with me in my room overnight and I lock my door while I'm asleep." She slammed the box lid shut. "Satisfied?"

"Thank you for your co-operation," I said. "We have to check all the keys, as I'm sure you understand."

She pressed her lips together.

"Was Edith the only maid with a key to Mrs. Warrick's room?" Mr. Armitage asked.

"Yes. Are you going to question her now?"

Neither Mr. Armitage nor I responded.

"If you happen to find her, tell her she's supposed to be assisting Lady Royston with her hair."

"She's missing?" I asked.

"Not missing, just not where she's supposed to be. Typical of girls like her," she added in a mutter.

I was glad to leave the dragon's lair behind, but it seemed as though we were about to come to a dead end in our investigation if we couldn't find Edith. It worried me more that it was her key that might have been stolen. When Mrs. Kettering and Mr. Hobart found out, she'd lose her position, even though it wasn't her fault.

"We'll start in the staff parlor," Mr. Armitage said in answer to the unspoken question of where to look for Edith.

The parlor was empty, however. Considering all the maids would be busy helping ladies prepare for the ball, and the porters were assisting new arrivals with their luggage, it wasn't surprising. But it left us uncertain where to look for Edith next. She could be anywhere. She might not be in the hotel at all.

Mr. Armitage touched the side of a teapot that had been left behind. "It's still warm."

I fetched two cups from the cupboard and he poured. I accepted a cup and sat. "Something Mrs. Kettering said got me thinking. She said girls like Edith. I suppose she meant shy, nervous girls."

Mr. Armitage shrugged. "Go on."

"Edith's nature would make her easier to bully than someone like Mrs. Kettering. The killer may not have had to steal the key from her. He could simply have bullied her into giving it to him."

He nodded thoughtfully.

Now that I'd said it out loud, I doubted my own theory, however. "But Edith has friends among the other staff, if a guest bullied her into giving up the key, she would have told one of the other maids. She seemed to trust Harmony."

"True," he said. "Knowing Harmony, she would have encouraged Edith to tell Mrs. Kettering immediately."

"If not immediately, she would have come forward after the murder. She might be timid, but she's not a fool. So we're back to the stolen key theory."

Mr. Armitage's teacup clanked back into the saucer. "Unless Edith was in love with him."

"With the murderer? Don't be ridiculous."

"It's feasible, particularly when you know what I know."

I arched my brows. "Go on."

"We both assumed Mrs. Kettering was referring to Edith's timidity when she said girls like that. But if she's the maid Mrs. Kettering suspected of having a lover among the guests, then her comment takes on a different meaning."

"Edith have a lover? One of the guests?" I scoffed. "Come now, Mr. Armitage, you know her. She's a shy little thing. She finds it difficult to even make eye contact with me, and I'm a woman. I hate to say it, but men don't usually notice girls like that."

"Just because she's a mouse, doesn't mean she's not capable of taking a lover," he said.

The more I thought about it, the more I liked his theory, but for different reasons. "He seduced her precisely because he knew a girl like Edith would welcome the attention. Indeed, she probably craved it. If he paid her pretty compliments and promised her a future life out of servitude, she would have taken the bait along with the entire hook. It's a sad fact that shy girls are easy prey for unscrupulous men."

"Which Hookly clearly is."

"Are you sure Edith is the maid Mrs. Kettering suspected of having a lover?" I asked.

"She never named her to me, but we can ask her now."

We set down our teacups at the same time and hurried out of the parlor, across the foyer to Mrs. Kettering's office. She wasn't there.

Mr. Armitage thumped the doorframe. "Damn."

I sighed. "Now we have two people to find."

"I remember when Mrs. Kettering told me about the maid she caught on the wrong floor once, and how she suspected she was having a liaison with one of the guests. I told her the maid probably made a mistake and went to the wrong floor, but she insisted it meant more."

I frowned, recalling a conversation between the two women I'd overheard. "What floor is Mr. Hookly on again?"

"The fifth. Why?"

I met his gaze. "Because Mrs. Kettering confronted Edith in the stairwell as they were both leaving level five on the day of the murder. Mrs. Kettering told Edith she was supposed to be on the second floor turning down the beds. Edith offered a poor excuse, saying she lost count of the levels. She was clearly lying."

Mr. Armitage frowned back at me. "Are you sure Mrs. Kettering told her it was time to turn down the beds? And this was Christmas Eve?"

"Yes, the day I arrived. Why?"

"Because Mrs. Kettering should have been checking the linen supplies in the dining room all afternoon on Christmas Eve to make sure there were enough clean napkins and table-cloths for luncheon the following day."

"You think *she* was having a rendezvous with Mr. Hookly?" I pulled a face. "It's not inconceivable, I suppose. She was also very close to Mrs. Warrick's room on the morning of the murder. Edith says she came across her quickly. She could be the murderer and have stayed close by to watch the aftermath." I shook my head. "But I can't believe that old dragon took a lover."

"Not Mrs. Kettering. I think *Edith* was having the liaison with Hookly. I think Mrs. Kettering is the silverware thief and she's hiding the stolen items somewhere on the fifth floor before she smuggles them out of the hotel."

CHAPTER 13

"*I* suspected either Mrs. Kettering or Mr. Chapman was the thief," Mr. Armitage said. "But I admit I favored Chapman. He has more access to the silverware than Mrs. Kettering, and he's never liked me."

It was such an odd conclusion to make that I couldn't help a bubble of laughter escaping. "Do you suspect everyone who doesn't like you of theft?"

His gaze narrowed. "It was a reference to his character. Everyone likes me. I'm very likeable."

"When you want to be."

"What does that mean?"

"Can we focus on the task at hand? Namely the murder?"

"I think the theft should become our task. We've hit a brick wall with the murder since we don't know where to find Edith. We'll telephone my father and tell him what we know about her and her possible relationship with Hookly." He strode off in the direction of the foyer.

I picked up my skirts and raced after him. "I don't think she had any knowledge of the murder."

"Why not?"

"Because Edith was outside Mrs. Warrick's door at seven AM with a cup of tea in hand. If she'd known Mr. Hookly murdered her during the night, would she have gone there at all the following morning?"

"If she wanted to appear innocent, she'd keep to her routine."

"But the guest in the room opposite who saw her didn't comment that she acted nervously. Not as far as we know, anyway. We've already established that she has a nervous constitution."

"Perhaps he didn't comment about her behavior because he wasn't asked. Or perhaps he did mention it to my father." He strode into the vestibule, only to be shouted at to step aside. He just managed to dodge a red carpet being rolled out from one end to the other.

"We could ask the witness staying opposite," I went on.

Mr. Armitage turned to me. "Trust my father, Miss Fox. Ask Peter to call him and tell him what we know about Edith." He walked around the carpet to speak to Mr. Hobart who'd been watching the unrolling from the other end.

I asked Peter at the front desk to call Scotland Yard and leave a message for Detective Inspector Hobart to come to the hotel. "Also, do you know the name of the guest staying opposite Mrs. Warrick's room?" I asked when he hung up the receiver.

"Mr. and Mrs. Sellen." He leaned over the counter. "You haven't given up, have you?"

"Not yet, Peter. Not yet."

I met Mr. Armitage at the stairwell after he gave up waiting for the lift to arrive at the ground floor. "You're coming with me?" he asked.

"Yes, of course." After a moment, I said, "Where are you going?"

He eyed me sideways. "To tell Sir Ronald I solved the silverware theft. My uncle is too busy to leave the dining room at the moment, so he asked me to do it."

"I believe I solved it too," I said. "Without my eyewitness account of Mrs. Kettering on the fifth floor that afternoon, you would still be in the dark."

"I would have worked it out."

"How, when you no longer work here?"

"So why *are* you heading this way, Miss Fox?"

"To join you. I want to see the confrontation between you and my uncle."

"I see. That's interesting, since I only just told you where I'm going. You're not still investigating the murder alone after I suggested you telephone my father, are you?" He gave me a look that implied he knew I was doing precisely that.

"Peter left a message with Scotland Yard for your father. I really am coming with you to see my uncle. There ought to be a witness present."

He grunted. "I would prefer an impartial one, but you'll have to do."

Uncle Ronald looked up from his desk when we entered and scowled. "What are you doing here, Armitage?"

"I know who the silverware thief is."

Uncle Ronald paused then returned the pen to the inkstand. "And you want your position back in exchange for telling me, is that it? You're manipulating me?"

Mr. Armitage's eyes darkened. "I don't want my position back. I have no interest in working at the hotel again. It's time I moved on. In fact, I should thank you for giving me the push I needed, although your timing could have been better. My uncle is run off his feet."

"He brought that on himself." Uncle Ronald looked to me. "Cleo, why are you here?"

"I want to hear what Mr. Armitage has to say."

He indicated we should sit. I did, Mr. Armitage didn't. "So who is the thief?" Uncle Ronald asked.

"Mrs. Kettering," Mr. Armitage said. "She's been hiding the silverware somewhere on the fifth floor until she can smuggle it safely out of the hotel. All we have to do is catch her in the act."

Uncle Ronald smoothed his moustache with his thumb and forefinger. "Are you sure it's her?"

"Almost, but I prefer to catch her in the act of moving the stolen goods before I accuse her."

Uncle Ronald nodded. "And I suppose you want me to hire you to catch her?"

"I'll do this task for you gratis, if you stop punishing my uncle."

"I'm not punishing him."

"Then let him know you forgive him."

"But I don't."

"Pretend," Mr. Armitage all but growled.

Uncle Ronald stroked his moustache again. "I can order one of the staff to watch Mrs. Kettering. I don't need to hire you, gratis or not."

Mr. Armitage blew out an exasperated breath.

"He is the best choice," I said to Uncle Ronald. "All the staff are currently too busy to be taken away from their regular duties. Besides, Mr. Armitage is very good at talking his way out of tricky situations. If Mrs. Kettering spots him following her, he'll think of something to deflect her suspicions."

Uncle Ronald's gaze shifted to Mr. Armitage. "He is very good at lying."

Mr. Armitage bristled. "Do you want to catch her or not?"

Uncle Ronald hesitated then nodded. "She'll probably act tonight while the hotel is busy and everyone's attention is focused on the ballroom. If anyone asks, say I've hired you back for the evening. That will give you a legitimate excuse to be here."

"Thank you for your faith in my abilities, sir."

"I never doubted your abilities, Armitage. You could have been manager one day."

"He still can be," I said, hopeful.

"No," both men said at the same time.

I could say something about stubborn men, but it wouldn't have achieved anything. I simply sighed and rose to leave.

"Did Cleo help you discover the culprit?" Uncle Ronald asked. "Is that why she's here?"

Mr. Armitage stared at him for a long moment. "She—"

"No, I didn't help," I said before he could tell the truth. "Mr. Armitage returned to the hotel earlier and spoke to Mrs. Kettering alone. I saw him come out of her office with an odd look on his face, and that's when he told me he'd solved the crime."

Mr. Armitage turned his glare onto me. I lifted my chin and glared back.

"So how did you discover it was her?" Uncle Ronald asked Mr. Armitage.

I opened the door and ushered Mr. Armitage out. "There's

no time to explain now. He has work to do." I closed the door, but not before I noticed the amused gleam in my uncle's eyes.

"You can't come with me," Mr. Armitage said. "Two of us watching her will be too obvious."

"I don't plan on coming with you. The theft is your mystery to solve, not mine."

His eyes narrowed. "You're not going to attempt to solve the murder alone, are you?"

"I believe we agreed to leave it to your father. Peter really did just telephone Scotland Yard."

We parted ways at the staircase. He headed up and I went to my suite. But I didn't stay inside for long. I couldn't stop thinking about the murder and Edith's involvement. Had she been complicit? Did she willingly hand over the key to her lover so that he could poison Mrs. Warrick in the night? Or had he stolen it from her? Had she known Hookly intended to kill Mrs. Warrick, or had it come as a shock?

Despite promising I wouldn't investigate, I felt compelled to. After all, there was someone close by who could give me a clue as to Edith's reaction on the morning she discovered the body. The guest opposite Mrs. Warrick had seen her both before she went in and immediately after. If anyone could speak about her initial reactions, it would be him. And he was just one floor below.

* * *

MR. AND MRS. SELLEN didn't have a suite with a sitting room, and since Mrs. Sellen was getting ready for the ball inside, her husband agreed to talk to me in the corridor, but only after I introduced myself and explained that I was assisting hotel management and Scotland Yard to find the murderer. Mr. Sellen said he was happy to help as he was worried the murderer had not yet been caught. He and Mrs. Sellen had decided to stay on for the ball because Sir Ronald spoke to them personally and offered them a free night's accommodation.

"It was definitely seven," Mr. Sellen said in answer to my question. "I checked the clock as I got out of bed." I was pleased to see he wasn't an old man, nor did he wear glasses.

He should have been able to see the clock face as well as Edith's expression.

"You told the police that you saw the maid with the cup of tea for Mrs. Warrick as you collected your newspaper," I said, recalling what Edith herself had told me. "Is that true?"

"Yes. She was standing right there." He nodded at the door numbered three-two-four. The room had remained unoccupied ever since the police removed Mrs. Warrick's body. "She saw me, nodded, and turned away."

"Did she seem nervous to you?"

"In what way?"

"Did her gaze meet or avoid yours? Did her hands shake or did she seem pale?"

"Nothing that can't be attributed to shyness."

That sounded like Edith. As much as I wanted to solve this crime, I didn't want to find out that Edith was involved. She had certainly played a role in the murder, but I dearly wanted it to be an unwilling part.

"Did you see anyone else in the corridor?" I asked.

He shook his head. "It was too early for most, I suspect. I'm not usually up at seven, but a noise awoke me that morning."

"What kind of noise?"

"A bang, like something knocking the door or wall." He indicated the closed door behind him. "It must have been loud to wake me. I sleep like the d—" He cleared his throat. "I sleep heavily. My wife does too. The knocking woke her as well."

"So it wasn't a scraping sound? Or voices?"

"It was definitely a knock or bump. Is that important?"

"It might be," I said, thinking it through.

It was odd for there to be a bump at that time. Edith hadn't mentioned it. She'd been alone, carrying a cup of tea. She didn't carry anything that could make a knocking sound if dropped, and there was no reason she'd walk into the wall along a straight corridor. The knock was out of place.

Unless it was done on purpose.

The only reason to make the sound was to encourage Mr. Sellen to come out of his room to investigate, and thereby be a witness to Edith delivering a cup of tea at seven AM, a full hour or more *after* Mrs. Warrick had been poisoned.

Oh lord. Edith had made the sound that woke Mr. Sellen. She had knowingly been involved in the murder after all.

I thanked Mr. Sellen and raced off, my mind reeling. It was sickening to think that I'd been completely wrong about Edith. I thought back to all the times I'd spoken to her. I didn't think the mousy act was entirely false. She couldn't have duped all of the staff so thoroughly. But she'd lied numerous times, and tried to learn what I knew about the police investigation at every turn.

I cursed myself for discussing theories in front of her. Had she passed them on to Hookly?

I paused at the stairs, not sure whether to go up to the fifth floor and find Mr. Armitage or down to the foyer and once again ask Peter to call the police. In the end, I did neither. I stopped the maid coming towards me carrying a dress.

"Do you know where Edith is?" I asked.

"No, Miss. She hasn't been seen for hours. Mrs. Kettering is furious."

"What about Harmony? Have you seen her?"

"She's with Miss Bainbridge in her rooms."

I thanked her and raced up the stairs. Harmony answered Flossy's door when I knocked.

"I knew you'd change your mind at the last moment," she said, smiling. "That's why I waited here."

I blinked at her. "I don't understand."

"I knew if you changed your mind, you'd come straight to your cousin's room and ask about a dress. I thought if I waited for you here, I wouldn't miss you. Everything's all ready. I'll get the dress while you tell Miss Bainbridge. She'll be so pleased."

I stared at her. "What are you talking about, Harmony?" I shook my head. "Never mind. Just tell me, have you seen Edith this afternoon?"

She frowned. "She seems to have disappeared after she cleaned her rooms. She's supposed to be helping one of the ladies get ready. I hope she has a good excuse because Mrs. Kettering'll dismiss her if she can't give a reason for being absent."

I swore under my breath, earning a blink of surprise from Harmony. "Sorry," I muttered. "Now what is all this talk about a dress?"

"Harmony, who is it?" came Flossy's voice from beyond.

"It's Miss Fox," Harmony said over her shoulder.

Flossy emitted a squeal of delight. "Oh, Cleo, do come in! I'm so thrilled you've changed your mind."

Harmony took my hand and pulled me into the bedroom where Flossy sat at the dressing table, a maid behind her, arranging Flossy's hair.

My cousin put out her hand to me. "We are going to have such fun tonight."

"I can't go," I told them. "I have nothing to wear."

For the first time since hearing about the ball, I actually wished to attend. Not for the festivities. I wouldn't enjoy dancing so soon after my grandmother's death; I *couldn't* enjoy it. But Mr. Hookly was going to be there to speak to the banker friend of Lord Addlington's, and I wanted to observe him. I also wanted to see the police pull him aside to speak to him about his involvement in Mrs. Warrick's murder after I informed the inspector how he'd manipulated Edith into giving him the key.

Flossy and Harmony exchanged glances in the mirror's reflection. They smiled.

"You do have something to wear," Flossy said. "Harmony and I have been conspiring to make sure you had a suitable gown."

I stared at her. "When? How?"

"These last few days. I gave her one of mine and she's been altering it to fit you."

"We can make some last-minute adjustments if we need to," Harmony said as she headed for Flossy's wardrobe. "But I think it should be about right."

"And don't worry about the style or color," Flossy went on. "It's gray, which I think is entirely appropriate for a young lady in mourning. The hairpiece is jet, as you know."

I gasped. "You bought that hairpiece from Harrods'? Flossy, that must have cost a fortune!"

"Shhh. Don't tell Father."

"I'm not wearing it. You will return it tomorrow."

"The shops aren't open tomorrow." She sniffed. "Besides, I'm Florence Bainbridge. I don't return things. If I change my mind, I simply give it away." She suddenly smiled. "Now go and get ready. I'll see you in the ballroom in an hour and a half. Don't forget the matching gloves, Harmony!"

Harmony insisted that I eat something while she did my hair so I ordered a salad down the speaking tube. While we waited, she played with different arrangements, but couldn't settle on one thing. I was acutely aware of the clock ticking.

"We need to do something with your face," she said, frowning at my reflection in the dressing table mirror.

"What's wrong with it?"

"Nothing, really, but you could be prettier with a little color on your cheeks and lips, and perhaps a dash of powder on your nose and brow for the shine."

"My face will have to stay as it is. I don't have any powders of rouges."

Grandmama wouldn't have approved of me wearing makeup. According to her, only a certain type of woman used it. Times had changed, however, and this was London. I'd noticed some of the younger ladies with a little color on their cheeks and lips, and Flossy had some pots on her dressing table.

"I don't have anything for your coloring," Harmony said. "I'm sure Miss Bainbridge will let you use hers."

The knock on the door signaled the arrival of my salad, carried in by Danny. He deposited the tray on the dressing table as directed and regarded me with a critical eye.

"She needs something to bring out her eyes," he told Harmony.

She agreed. "Can you fetch some makeup from Miss Bainbridge's room?"

He returned a few minutes later with seven small pots which he laid on the table in front of me, and some blotting papers. "Miss Bainbridge didn't know which would suit Miss Fox's complexion best so she gave me all the ones she had." He left us to return to his duties, although he seemed disappointed to be going.

Harmony insisted I try on the dress before we finished hair and makeup. She assisted me into the gown then stepped back to study it. "I think it fits well enough. How does it feel?"

I fidgeted with the low-cut neckline, but nothing I did would cover more of my décolletage. "It's very low and a little tight."

"Can you breathe?"

"Yes."

"Then it's perfect."

I turned to the mirror and had to agree with her. The gown was indeed lovely. The dove-gray silk would have been plain on its own, but the black beading drew the eye. The beads were sewn into a vine-like pattern growing up from swirls at the hem to a denser canopy across my breasts. The capped sleeves clung to the very edges of my shoulders. Coupled with the low neckline, there was quite a lot of skin on display. I'd never worn anything so daring.

Harmony pulled my hand away as I once again tried to tug it higher. "Don't touch. It makes you look self-conscious."

"I am self-conscious."

"Don't let on that you are. That's the key."

"The key to what?"

"To being a sensation."

I laughed. "I am hardly that. Anyway, the rest of us will look drab next to the two actresses and opera singer."

She snorted. "I'd like to see them look at you and *not* feel jealousy."

"Besides, I'm not going to the ball to dance and flirt. I'm going to watch the police arrest Mr. Hookly for murder."

Her eyes widened. "You continued to investigate?"

"Yes, and I have some things to tell you. Some of them are quite troubling."

"Then you'd better sit down and tell me while I do your hair and face."

Harmony listened in horror to the evidence against Edith, and the theories Mr. Armitage and I had developed that indicated she was involved in the murder, to some extent.

But when I finished, she rejected the notion that Edith was the killer. "I think you're right when you say Hookly manipulated her into giving him the key and covering up the crime. She's a mouse, and if someone like him paid her attention, she'd do almost anything for him. Not murder, mind. She wouldn't do that."

"If she helped him, it's as good as doing it herself. Harmony," I said gently, "she showed no remorse those times we talked about our theories in the staff parlor. She *is* involved. There's no doubt in my mind."

Her lips flattened. "It would seem so." She closed her eyes and a look of pain crossed her face. It was still there when she opened her eyes and her gaze connected with mine in the mirror. "I should have looked out for her. I shouldn't have let Hookly take advantage of her."

I caught her hand. "It's not your fault."

"I knew she was having a liaison with a guest, but I didn't know who."

"And you didn't know it could lead to this."

She sighed. "She needed guidance from a friend, and I failed to give it to her." She continued with my hair, only to stop and frown. "I'm worried about her, Miss Fox. I haven't seen her for a while. No one has. She's not at the hotel or the residence hall."

I nodded gravely. Edith could very well be in danger if Hookly thought she knew too much and might talk. "The inspector's men will find her."

He ought to have arrived by now, yet he had not come searching for me. Perhaps Mr. Armitage had spoken to him so there'd been no need to seek me out. I would check with Peter before I entered the ballroom, and ask him to telephone Scotland Yard again if the police hadn't arrived.

Harmony finished doing my hair and face then stood back. The frown that had settled onto her pretty features when I'd told her about Edith smoothed away. She smiled. "There. You look lovely."

She had done very well with my hair, sweeping it up high on my head with a few artfully placed curled strands at the sides. The jet and diamond headpiece went perfectly with the dress and there was just enough color contrast with my light brown hair.

I touched the bare skin of my décolletage, still unused to being so exposed.

"A necklace with a large pendant would look nice nestled

about there," Harmony said, indicating where my fingers rested above my breasts.

I withdrew my hand. "I don't have anything suitable."

"Then you'll just have to go to the ball without one." She gave me an impudent smile. "Hopefully a rich gentleman agrees that a pendant would look very fetching and gives you a ruby necklace when he asks you to marry him."

It was so ridiculous that I burst out laughing. Harmony did too. "Rubies?" I managed to scoff while still grinning. "I won't accept anything less than diamonds."

* * *

HARMONY TOLD me she planned to sneak a peek into the ballroom from the service corridor near the back of the dining room-turned-ballroom. She wanted to see what the other ladies wore, particularly the very modern and very fashionable actresses and opera singer, but she was reluctant to do anything until she'd found Edith. I warned her not to let on what we suspected about the maid's involvement in the murder if she did happen to find her. She agreed, and wished me luck.

I wasn't sure why I needed luck. I was simply going to find the inspector and tell him everything I could about Mr. Hookly and Edith. It was up to him what to do next. I doubted he would make an arrest tonight in the middle of the ball. He would want more evidence, something that left no doubt in his mind. At least by telling him our theories, he could make that judgement. It wasn't up to me, and I couldn't be more relieved. I could simply watch Mr. Hookly and gauge for myself whether he was acting guiltily or not.

I went immediately to the front desk when I stepped out of the lift. Peter was not on duty, however. He'd already left for the day. The night porter didn't know anything about the detective inspector, and he hadn't seen him arrive. He let me use his telephone to call Scotland Yard.

"Please tell Detective Inspector Hobart that it's an emergency," I said down the line. "He needs to come to The Mayfair Hotel at once and ask for Miss Fox or Mr. Armitage." Hopefully by using Mr. Armitage's name, the inspector wouldn't dismiss the message lightly. He might think I was wasting his time, but he would pay attention to his son.

Music from the ballroom drifted into the foyer where some guests were chatting. According to the clock on the wall behind the front desk, the ball started an hour ago. Flossy must be wondering where I was.

I rushed into the vestibule, only to slow down again. I'd already seen the red carpet, but the rest of the room looked quite different. As with the foyer, large potted palms had been brought in to flank the double doors leading to the dining room—now ballroom—and a floral garland hung above them. The lights woven through it sparkled in the otherwise dim room.

Two footmen stood on either side of the entrance with trays of champagne flutes. I didn't recognize either of them but they both greeted me by name. I plucked off a gold-stemmed flute with the M enclosed in a circle within the stem, and admired my surroundings.

The room was unrecognizable as a dining room. There was no sight of the tables or chairs, except for a few lining the walls where older ladies sat chatting. The first thing to catch my eye was the enormous clock on a dais towards the front. That must have been what I'd seen the delivery men wheeling through the foyer that morning. It was the size of a small carriage.

The garlands of flowers and greenery continued in here. They were draped above windows and across doorways, their small lights sparkling. But even more spectacular was the ceiling. It was covered in swathes of ribbons in the hotel color of burgundy with touches of gold and black. There must have been hundreds of them. Each end was tied either to a chandelier or to a ribbon cluster, depending on where it finished on the ceiling, and the other end was fixed to the edge of the room, high up on the wall. I could clearly see silver balloons above them, trapped between the bed of ribbons and the ceiling.

"Cleo, you made it!" Flossy caught my hands and looked me over. "You look lovely."

"So do you," I said, and meant it. She wore a pink gown that suited her complexion, and the seed pearls sewn into it somehow caught the light so that she seemed to sparkle. She had more bosom showing than me, but that was because she had more to show off. The expanse of her décolletage was broken up by a necklace of pearls and amethysts.

Flossy led me further into the ballroom, chatting excitedly all the way. I searched for Mr. Hookly but could not see him. The crowd was rather thick and I wasn't overly tall.

"There seem to be a good number of people here," I said to Flossy over the music.

"It's a success, Cleo! Father is so pleased, and Mother too. Look, there they are. They asked me to bring you to them when I found you."

Somewhat reluctantly, I approached my uncle and aunt. I was suddenly too aware of everything about my person. They would think I showed too much décolletage for a woman in mourning. Or they wouldn't like that I wore Flossy's dress. And what if they knew the headpiece had been bought at their expense?

But their welcoming smiles banished my reservations.

"You look lovely, my dear," said Aunt Lilian as she kissed my cheek.

Uncle Ronald kissed my other cheek. "Your mother would be immensely proud," he said quietly.

I drew in some deep breaths to banish the tears welling in my eyes. Harmony had given me strict instructions not to cry or the coal and beeswax mixture on my lashes would run.

My aunt whisked me away to introduce me to several of her friends, dragging a reluctant Flossy along with us. Meeting so many people in a short space of time proved to be confusing, but it gave me an opportunity to find Mr. Hookly. I spotted him talking to a group of gentleman near the clock. I wondered if one of them was the banking friend of Lord Addlington's.

"Mother, I was in the middle of a conversation," Flossy whined when Aunt Lilian moved us along to speak to friends she'd just spotted. "Can we not stay in one place longer than five minutes?"

"Cleo must meet everyone, and as you can see, there are quite a lot of people here." Aunt Lilian beamed at a lady with two young women of almost identical appearance on either side of her.

Flossy was soon rescued by a gentleman who asked her to dance while I chatted to the young women. When others joined us, I searched for Mr. Hookly again. I couldn't find him.

I did, however, glimpse Mr. Armitage standing in the shadowy exit to the service area. He was watching me. When he realized I'd seen him, he quickly looked away.

He would know which fellow was the banker. I gave my excuses and headed towards him, only to be waylaid by Floyd and two of his friends.

"Dearest cousin!" Floyd clasped my gloved hand and kissed it. "Meet my closest companions, Jonathon and Arthur. We met at Oxford."

"And he's been leading us astray ever since," said the blond-haired, blue-eyed Jonathon, bowing over my hand. Of the three of them, he was the most handsome. A small scar on his cheek added interest to a face that could have otherwise been considered delicate.

Arthur looked positively ragged beside him, although I suspected he'd spent quite some time trying to conjure the right amount of raggedness for tonight. His dark hair fell across his forehead, but did not quite hide the receding hairline.

Uncle Ronald joined us and shook the hands of both men. He was then pressed with questions by Floyd about the actresses and opera singer.

"Hopefully they'll arrive soon," his father said with a worried glance towards the door. He turned back to Floyd's friends with a smile. "You know what these ladies are like. They love to make a spectacular entrance. But never mind them when there's a beautiful jewel right in front of you." He gave me a light push towards Jonathon before going on his way.

Jonathon's eyes shone as he smiled at me. "What actresses?" he said.

I laughed softly.

"The ones who're supposed to be coming tonight," Arthur

said. "Idiot," he added in a mutter." He bowed to me. "I'd be delighted if you'd dance with me, Miss Fox."

He swept me onto the dance floor for a quadrille. He would have been quite a good dancer if his gaze didn't constantly drop to my décolletage.

Jonathon intercepted us before I could dance a second dance with Arthur, and we enjoyed a pleasant waltz while we chatted amiably. He was a good conversationalist and dancer, and I enjoyed my time with him. So much so that I forgot to look for Mr. Hookly.

I danced twice more with Jonathon during the night. My dance card became quite full, something for which I blamed my uncle, aunt and cousins. Every time I saw them they were pointing me out to someone new. Indeed, I gathered so much interest that it became too obvious what was going on. Everyone must think I was an heiress. Aunt Lilian had inherited a fortune, after all, and my mother had been her sister. It was natural to assume the fortune had been equally split between them and that I had inherited it upon my mother's death.

How sorry they'd all be when they discovered the truth. The men would wish they hadn't spent so much time with me, and their parents would wish they'd asked more questions of Uncle Ronald and Aunt Lilian.

All of the attention came to an end when a flurry of activity near the entrance had heads turning in that direction. The names of the actresses and opera singer were passed between guests in loud whispers. Gentlemen craned their necks and women nudged their way through to get a better look.

I took the opportunity to speak to Mr. Armitage. I searched the service rooms, even heading down to the kitchen, before being shooed away by one of the chefs. I finally found Mr. Armitage standing near a palm in the hotel foyer.

His eyes widened when he saw me. "What are you doing here?" he whispered.

"Looking for you."

He grabbed my elbow and pulled me behind the palm. When he let me go, I found I was standing very close to him. I did not move away. I didn't want to, not when he gazed down at me with those smoldering eyes of his. It suddenly became very warm in the foyer.

"Why are you looking for me?" he asked in a low, rumbling voice.

"I, er…" I lowered my gaze and stared at his cheek instead. "I wanted to ask you if that banker is here, and what he looks like. I want to see if our theory is correct and Mr. Hookly is trying to speak to him."

He glanced towards the senior staff corridor. "Come with me. It's easier to point him out to you."

"Are you still watching Mrs. Kettering?" I asked as we crossed the foyer.

He nodded. "She's in her room. I don't think she's planning on moving the stolen silverware tonight, after all. Why are you here, anyway? I thought you weren't coming to the ball."

"I changed my mind."

"Stay away from Hookly," he said as we walked along the red carpet in the vestibule.

"I will. I've been waiting for your father to arrive. He should have been here by now."

"I just telephoned. He's on his way."

"Why has it taken so long?"

"He hasn't been at the Yard all afternoon. He's been following up information about the mercuric cyanide. I telephoned him at home. He wasn't aware you'd been trying to reach him."

"Scotland Yard need to review their messaging system."

We skirted the edge of the ballroom until Mr. Armitage found the man he was looking for. "The short fellow with the monocle," he said with a nod towards a group of gentlemen that included Mr. Hookly. "It looks like Hookly found him."

"Should we warn the banker not to promise him a loan?"

"We say nothing. My father will take care of Hookly when he gets here."

"At least he's still here," I said. "Thank goodness he hasn't got wind of our suspicions. Speaking of which, I'm very worried about Edith. She's still missing."

"I'm worried about her too." He touched my elbow and I

looked up to see him staring down at me. "Don't leave the ballroom until the ball is over, then only return to your room when your family retires. We don't know what Edith has told Hookly."

"As far as either of them are aware, we don't have any solid evidence against them."

He dragged his hand through his hair. If any other man in the room had done that, he'd have a palm slicked with hair oil. The lack of it made Mr. Armitage stand out from them. Indeed, he looked out of place compared to the gentlemen with their formal eveningwear of white tie and stiff shirt. Instead of making him seem less than them, however the difference highlighted his masculinity. More than one female's gaze followed him and it wasn't because she was horrified by his casual attire.

"I have to go," he said. "I don't want to lose Mrs. Kettering."

"You don't want to see the actresses and opera singer before you go? They're here somewhere."

He smiled. "I can meet an actress or opera singer whenever I want." He walked off and was quickly swallowed up by the crowd.

His confident smile stayed with me for quite some time.

I watched the banker and Mr. Hookly until the banker moved away. Mr. Hookly watched him go, looking pleased.

A woman bumped me and apologized, her words slurring. The gentleman with her laughed as he led her onto the dance floor. I glanced at the large clock. Fifteen minutes until midnight. The excitement for the countdown to the new century had started to build in my absence. The dancing was more vigorous, the music seemed louder, and the chatter too. A woman nearby squealed with delight over something her companion said, and a couple twirled past me on their way to the dance floor without looking where they were going. Guests had to quickly step out of their way or be barreled over. Girls without partners danced with one another and drunken men watched on from the sidelines.

I searched for a friendly face but couldn't find Flossy, Floyd or their friends. I moved away from the wall into the throng where the air felt hotter, closer.

"Dance with me, Miss Fox."

I turned to see Mr. Hookly standing very near, his hand extended. My heart leapt into my throat and beat a warning rhythm.

"Dance with me," he commanded. "I've been waiting for this moment all evening." His lips might be smiling, but the cold gleam in his eyes told another story.

He wrapped his fingers around mine and pulled me onto the dance floor, leaving me with no doubt.

He knew.

$\mathcal{M}$r. Hookly's grip on my hand loosened as we settled into a waltz. I could have got away, but there seemed no point. We were in the middle of the dance floor. He couldn't harm me here.

I wasn't sure he wanted to anyway. "I need to explain some things to you," he said. "I think you have the wrong idea about me."

"What idea is that, Mr. Hookly? Or whatever your name is."

He looked unsurprised that I knew. "My name isn't important. Truly, it's not. It never has been. Not to me or to anyone else. Because *I* wasn't important." We twirled for a few steps before he continued. "I was a footman in Hookly's household. That's how I knew him."

"Is that where Mrs. Warrick recognized you from?"

"No. She knew me from a prior engagement as the footman in the household of one of her friends. I was surprised to learn she recognized me. Usually people like her look right through the staff. We're as insignificant as a chair or vase. I don't expect someone like you to understand, Miss Fox."

I ignored the taunt. I didn't care if he thought I was as wealthy as the Bainbridges. "Mrs. Warrick confronted you on Christmas Eve, didn't she? She asked why you were in the hotel, and how you could afford a room here when you are a mere footman."

His fingers tightened at my hand and waist. "She could have ruined everything."

"You mean your plan to live off credit for as long as possible here at the hotel? To use the letter you stole from a dead man's desk to secure the trust of a banker? You learned the banker was attending the ball so you needed to remain at the hotel even after you killed Mrs. Warrick so you could speak to him."

He smiled. It wasn't cruel. It was the smile of a content man who thought himself safe. "You can't jeopardize this opportunity, Miss Fox. Not now. He's gone."

"The banker?"

"He left early as he suffers from gout, but not before he promised to give me the loan. I have a signed agreement from him in my pocket. I can take that to any branch as soon as the banks re-open after the holiday."

"You won't get away with this. The police are almost here and they know everything about you." Well, they would once I told them.

His smile widened. "I'll be sure to set them straight at the first opportunity. You see, I didn't kill Mrs. Warrick. My hands are clean. I don't know who did it, although I have my suspicions. A word of advice, Miss Fox. Don't trust the staff here. They're a bad lot."

"I know all about Edith," I said, just as benignly. "You needed someone with a key so you courted her. What did you promise her? A life out of servitude? Love?"

A muscle in his jaw pulsed and his breathing quickened. He hadn't known that I knew about Edith. He merely thought I suspected him, and he meant to shift the blame onto her as we danced. But I'd drawn a connection between them, and that worried him. It confirmed what I'd suspected—that Edith had gone to him after I'd spoken to her about my concerns. She'd told him that I suspected he was the murderer. At that point, I hadn't suspected her.

"Edith and I were together before Mrs. Warrick spoke a word to me," he sneered. "So that destroys your theory."

"Not really. Did you initially court her because you planned to use her keys to break into rooms and steal valuables? But you changed your mind when you got a better idea after learning about the banker, didn't you? Either way, you knew you needed keys, and Edith could get you some. She was the perfect victim."

"She's not a victim," he snarled. "She's a murderer! She orchestrated everything."

"Nonsense. She's not devious. More importantly, she wanted attention. She craved to be noticed by a man, and you sensed that the way a hound senses a hare's fear. You told her what she wanted to hear and she fell in love with you. She was prepared to do anything for you. You took advantage of her and manipulated her; you made her give you the key so you could enter Mrs. Warrick's room and poison her."

His eyes hardened. His mouth set firm and his grip became bruising. There was no shock or horror on his face, only cold acceptance. I needed no other confirmation of his guilt than that.

"Where's Edith?" I asked. "What have you done with her?" When he didn't answer, I stopped dancing. "Let me go."

His grip tightened. I tried to jerk free but he held on. I tilted my chin, determined not to show fear. This man thrived on it. He used it to his own advantage, just like he'd used Edith's nervousness.

The music stopped and the crowd counted down the last ten seconds until the new year. I glanced around and found we were near the edge of the dance floor, close to the service area. But no servants came and went. They were probably counting down the seconds to midnight in the kitchen, their attention focused on a clock, just as the revelers in the ballroom directed their gazes forward, not back to us.

"Let me go!" My shout was drowned out by the counting. Nobody took any notice of us.

"SEVEN! SIX!"

Mr. Hookly glared at me. He did not move. He did not try to hurt me, except for his firm grip on my wrist.

"FOUR! THREE!"

"Let me go!" I shouted again.

He did not, and nobody paid me any attention. The new

century was almost upon us and they didn't want to miss a moment of the celebration.

"TWO! ONE! Happy new year!"

The musicians struck up the tune of *Auld Lang Syne* as revelers clapped. Applause soon turned to gasps and squeals of delight as the ribbons above their heads gave way and the silver balloons rained down.

Mr. Hookly continued to smile at me as I continued to try to break free. I even called out for help, but the applause, music and loud chatter drowned me out. And then the slowly sinking balloons reached us. In the moment before they drifted past our faces, Mr. Hookly's smile thinned.

"Let me go!" I shouted in a last ditch effort to be heard.

"Who's that?" came a gentleman's voice nearby. "Everyone all right?"

He couldn't see me and I couldn't see him with the hundreds of balloons floating to the floor. A balloon burst, then another and another. Guests squealed in fright and delight.

I opened my mouth to scream, but Mr. Hookly pulled me against him and clamped his hand over my mouth. Before the balloons had completely sunk out of the way, he ushered me out of the ballroom.

We were in the service area. There would be footmen coming this way very soon with more champagne and food. They would see me struggling with Mr. Hookly and come to my rescue.

But before we'd got far, he opened a door and shoved me through.

My back slammed into shelves, rattling what sounded like crockery and cutlery. Mr. Hookly had let me go to lock the door, but he hadn't turned on the light. It was so dark I couldn't even make out his silhouette.

He couldn't see me either.

I crouched low, and just in time too. The contents of the shelves rattled again, louder this time, and something fell, breaking on the floor. He must have lunged in my direction but missed.

I reached out and realized how small the storeroom was. My fingers brushed shards of a broken vase or bowl. The fingers of my other hand touched Mr. Hookly's leg, alerting him to my position.

I scampered away just as his hand swiped down, knocking my cheek.

"I'll get you, Miss Fox. There's no way you can get out."

That meant he stood between me and the door now. But he couldn't hurt me if he couldn't capture me. And he couldn't capture me if he couldn't find me.

I had to remain silent long enough to draw him away from the door to come looking. I remained low to the floor, cursing the tight bodice. I held my breath, but it might not have mattered. His own breathing would have drowned mine out. His breath came hard, as if he'd just run up and down all of the hotel's stairs. The sound filled the small space, as well as my ears along with the thumping of my blood in my veins.

The door handle rattled. "Is someone in there?" came a man's voice.

"Yes!" I cried. "Help!"

My voice gave away my position. Mr. Hookly reached out and grabbed my hair. He pulled me up, dislodging my head-piece and Harmony's elegant arrangement.

I hissed in pain and clasped his wrist in an attempt to ease the burn across my scalp.

"Miss Fox?" came the voice outside. "Mr. Armitage, I think she's in here!"

I went to call out again but Mr. Hookly's hand clamped over my mouth. He pulled me back against his body.

"Don't say a word," he growled.

Someone banged on the door. "Miss Fox!" It was Mr. Armitage. "Miss Fox, are you in there?"

My heart pounded, trying to burst out of my chest. I closed my eyes. Not that it mattered. I still couldn't see in the dark.

"Get a key!" Mr. Armitage shouted. "Someone get a damned key off Chapman!"

Something cold and hard pressed against my throat. "I've got a knife!" he called out. "Let me go or I'll kill her!"

The doorknob stopped rattling. The voices outside lowered. Beyond them, I could hear the music playing in the ballroom. Inside the storeroom, the only sound was Mr.

Hookly's and my hard breaths and the scent of his sweat. The edge of the knife scraped my skin.

My body was up against Mr. Hookly's, my back against his chest, the heel of my shoe against the toe of his. It was unpleasant to be so close to this disgusting man, but it gave me the advantage I needed. I tightened my grip on the shard of vase I'd picked up when I'd been crouching, and stabbed it into his thigh.

He cried out, but more importantly, he relaxed his grip enough for me to slip free. I lunged for the door and fumbled for the lock. The precious second it took to find it cost me. He caught me and shoved me back against the shelves.

But I'd managed to flick the lock back.

The door opened and enough light filled the storeroom for me to make out Mr. Armitage charging in. Mr. Hookly swiped at him with the knife, but Mr. Armitage blocked the strike by grabbing Hooky's wrist. He pinned Mr. Hookly to the shelves.

The storeroom light went on, revealing Detective Inspector Hobart standing in the doorway, a constable behind him. My uncle peered over his shoulder.

The knife clattered to the floor near my feet. Mr. Hookly bared his teeth in a snarl at Mr. Armitage. Mr. Armitage gave him such a cold look in return that I shivered.

"Cleo?" Uncle Ronald pushed past the inspector. "Cleo, are you hurt?"

"I'm all right," I said. "Just a little shaken."

He patted my shoulder. "Take him away, Hobart."

The constable escorted Mr. Hookly, or whatever his name was, and my uncle ushered me out of the storeroom. The ball sounded like it was still going strongly and I sensed Uncle Ronald wanted to return to his guests.

"Go," I told him. "I can talk to the inspector alone."

He looked over my head at the inspector. "You can speak to her tomorrow. She should rest. She's had an ordeal."

"Of course," Inspector Hobart said. "Tomorrow, Miss Fox."

"I prefer to speak to you now," I said. "While it's still fresh in my mind."

"Is there somewhere we can go?"

"My office," Mr. Hobart said. I hadn't noticed the manager there. He gave me a gentle smile. "I'll have someone bring you tea."

"And something stronger," I added.

They all looked at me.

"For Mr. Armitage," I said. "He looks as though he needs it more than me."

Mr. Armitage's chest expanded with his deep breath. My attempted joke fell flat. His features didn't so much as twitch with mirth. His face was all hard, angular planes and his eyes darker than ever.

My uncle glanced towards the ballroom again then back at me. "I would send your aunt to be with you, but she just retired, taking Flossy with her."

"It's all right," I assured him. "I'll speak to the inspector then make my way to my rooms."

"Someone should escort you." He looked to Mr. Hobart and Mr. Hobart nodded.

After another pat on my shoulder, Uncle Ronald bade me goodnight and went to rejoin his guests.

Mr. Hobart handed his keys to Mr. Armitage then departed for the service rooms. Mr. Armitage led his father and me to his uncle's office. The inspector sat in Mr. Hobart's chair while Mr. Armitage stood by the door.

I shivered, partly because the office was cool but also because my blood no longer pumped through my veins. Mr. Armitage removed his jacket and settled it around my shoulders before stepping back to stand by the door.

"Thank you," I said. "Did you capture Mrs. Kettering?"

He simply nodded.

"My men have already taken her away," Inspector Hobart said. "It was fortuitous that Harry caught her in the act of removing the stolen goods when we arrived at the hotel. We met him in the foyer as he confronted her."

I congratulated them. "It's been a good night's work all around."

"We then went looking for you in the ballroom," the inspector went on. "Sir Ronald was none too happy about us mingling with his guests, although I felt we were very discreet. Don't you agree, Harry?"

"We stood out like nuns at a Tattersalls bloodstock auction," Mr. Armitage said.

"Very amusing, Harry. Now, come and sit down." The inspector indicated the chair next to me. "There's no need to stand sentinel by the door. All the bad eggs have been arrested."

Mr. Armitage did as his father directed, but he didn't sit comfortably. He held himself like a tightly coiled spring, ready to leap into action at any moment. "We arrived in the ballroom just before the midnight countdown," he told me. "When we couldn't see you, we made inquiries of Sir Ronald and the footmen on duty then went in search of you. It was an age before one of the footmen overheard you in the storeroom."

"Not an age," the inspector said. "A minute or two at the most. How did you find yourself in the storeroom with Mr. Hookly, Miss Fox?"

Harmony arrived with a tray of tea things as well as a silver flask marked with the hotel's emblem. "I'm so glad to see you!" She set the tray down and closed her hands into fists at her sides. She bit her lip.

I put out my hand to her and smiled. She took it and squeezed. "I think I need a dash of whatever you've got in that flask," I said.

"Mr. Hobart said you might." She poured the tea then tipped a small measure of the flask's contents into the cup. She handed it to me. "So what happened?"

I started at the beginning for the inspector's sake, explaining how I'd suspected Mr. Hookly then discovered he wasn't the real Mr. Hookly. "I still don't know his name. He told me he was a footman in Mr. Hookly's household, but Mrs. Warrick recognized him from his previous employment."

"And how did he get into and out of her room without breaking in?" the inspector asked. He did not take down notes, but merely sipped his tea and listened.

"Edith, one of the maids, gave him hers. Either that or she delivered the poison herself. I'm afraid he manipulated her by pretending he loved her."

"It's not her fault," Harmony added.

"Has she been found?" Mr. Armitage asked.

Harmony shook her head. "I'm very worried about her. What if he…" She swallowed.

"I'll make inquiries," the inspector said. "I'll do my best to locate her."

He drained his teacup and set it down on the tray. "I must return to the Yard and question Hookly, or whatever his name is."

"It can't wait for morning?" I asked. "It's New Year's Eve. Your wife would probably want you at home."

"Mrs. Hobart is used to me being out at all hours. She was going to enjoy a quiet evening with her sister-in-law and should be fast asleep now. Tomorrow is a busy day for her, with calls to make."

He left with a promise to keep us informed of his progress in the search for Edith. I was glad he didn't lecture me about investigating the murder. I wasn't up for it. I was suddenly rather tired.

Harmony offered to see me settled in my room before she retired for the night.

I shrugged off Mr. Armitage's jacket and handed it back to him. "Thank you again. For the jacket and…everything. If you hadn't come when you had…" I blew out a ragged breath.

He offered me a weak smile. "You seemed to be doing quite well on your own. I only came in at the end to take the glory."

I returned his smile, although we both knew if he hadn't tackled Mr. Hookly I would have been stabbed. "We make a good team, Mr. Armitage."

"Goodnight, Miss Fox. And happy new year." He strode out of the office, throwing his jacket on as he walked.

Harmony gathered the teacups on the tray, only to leave it on the desk. She picked up the flask instead.

"I don't need any more," I told her. "I've warmed up and calmed down."

"It's not for you, it's for me," she said. "My nerves are as jangly as a jester's bells."

* * *

I SLEPT WELL but lay in bed for some time in the morning after waking. The events of the night before continued to swirl through my head. I finally rose late-morning when Harmony arrived with breakfast. I'd been too busy to pre-order it the day before, however.

"Did you pilfer another guest's breakfast?" I asked, inviting her in.

"There's plenty in the kitchen. No need to steal anything." She set the tray down on the table in the sitting room and lifted the lid. It smelled delicious. "I wasn't sure what you'd want so I got a little of everything."

She certainly had. I could never eat it all. "You'd better join me or it'll go to waste."

"I can't do that. I've got to work."

"We'll say you're tidying up my room." I patted the chair. "Besides, who will care? Mrs. Kettering no longer works here."

"Mr. Hobart will care."

"I'm sure he's far too busy taking down decorations and restoring the hotel to its usual state to worry about you spending twenty minutes with me."

She poured coffee and I gratefully took the cup off her hands and sipped. The bitter taste was just what I needed. "How are things among the staff today?"

"We hardly slept a wink last night. Most worked late and had to get up again early today, but in between we were all a-twitter. Between Mrs. Kettering's arrest and Mr. Hookly's too, and Edith's disappearance, and of course all the gossip from the ball, nobody wanted to sleep."

"Any news on Edith from Scotland Yard?"

She shrugged as she plucked off a strip of bacon from the platter. "Not that I've been told. Poor thing. I hope she's not… you know."

"I know," I said darkly. "I hope so too."

Flossy arrived after Harmony departed and invited me to afternoon tea in the hotel's main sitting room with her mother and several friends who'd come for the ball and were staying on.

"Everyone's so relieved the murderer has been caught," she said.

"Your father spread the news?"

"It's all over the hotel." She frowned. "He says you had a part in discovering the murderer. Is that true?"

"Yes."

Her eyes widened. "Cleo, you're so brave and clever."

"Not really. I'm just curious to a fault."

She patted my knee. "Father asked me to tell you not to tell anyone. He doesn't want Mother knowing."

"I understand." I didn't want Aunt Lilian knowing the full story either. I didn't want to be responsible for a further decline in her nervous state.

"And don't let any of the guests know, or our friends. It'll just be between you, me, Floyd and Father."

"And the staff."

"Yes, them too. We don't want any ugly gossip about the Bainbridges in the newspapers."

I refrained from pointing out that I was not a Bainbridge and I didn't consider catching murderers to be "ugly gossip." But my relationship with my relatives was still very new and I didn't want to have a disagreement over something that I had no intention of discussing with their friends or journalists anyway.

I sat through a pleasant afternoon tea with Flossy, Aunt Lilian and a room full of their female friends. Despite her gaunt features and hollow eyes, Aunt Lilian held court in the sitting room like a queen, and she even made a speech thanking them all for attending the most successful New Year's Eve ball in all of London. The enthusiastic applause widened my aunt's and cousin's smiles, and mine too. I was immensely relieved that my tussle with Mr. Hookly hadn't ruined the evening.

My aunt didn't dine with us that night, but I ate with my cousins and uncle in the dining room. All the tables and chairs were back in place, and there was no evidence of the previous night's revelries. The dining room was rather full, and a stream of guests constantly came up to my uncle to congratulate him on a wonderful ball.

"Did you enjoy it?" Floyd asked me while Uncle Ronald was engaged with a guest. "Aside from your little adventure late in the evening, I mean."

Flossy glared at her brother. "It was hardly an adventure."

"My apologies, you're right, Floss. Cleo, how did you enjoy the evening before you were almost killed by a murderer in the storeroom?"

Flossy choked on her salad.

Floyd passed her a glass of wine.

"I enjoyed it immensely," I said, although it wasn't quite true. I'd been too intent on watching Mr. Hookly to truly enjoy myself. "I met some lovely people."

"Lovely, eh? I'll tell Jonathon you said that."

Flossy set down her wine glass and shot him another glare. "Don't go foisting your idiotic friends on Cleo."

"Jonathon is not idiotic. He's very intelligent, as it happens."

"He can't be or he wouldn't be friends with you. Anyway, Cleo can do better than Jonathon."

"Do better than a Hartly?" Floyd snorted. "You do know what he's worth, don't you?"

Flossy turned up her nose at him. "I don't care. He's a scoundrel."

"The love of a good woman will tame him."

She rolled her eyes. "Don't listen to him, Cleo. Dance with Jonathan if you have to, but don't believe a word he tells you. He'll speak sweet things in your ear then repeat them into the ear of the next girl, and the next and next. He doesn't mean a word."

It reminded me of Mr. Hookly and Edith. She wasn't the first girl in history to fall in love with a man who told her what she wanted to hear, and sadly she wouldn't be the last.

* * *

I HAD DECIDED to pay a call on Detective Inspector Hobart at Scotland Yard to learn if there'd been any progress in the search for Edith when a message arrived from him the following morning. It stated that she had been found and he wanted a woman to be present when he questioned her. I was to meet him at eleven at Westminster Hospital.

She was alive, thank God. It was an immense relief, and I

made sure to let Harmony know too. We'd both been so worried.

"Why do you think he needs you to be at the hospital when he questions her?" she asked.

"I don't know. But I'm glad he wants me there. I'm very keen to hear her side of the story."

CHAPTER 15

etective Inspector Hobart was waiting on the steps at the front of the hospital when I arrived. "There are a few things you ought to know before going in," he told me. "First of all, I'd like you to ask Edith a series of questions. I wrote them down."

"Me?" I said, accepting his list. "Shouldn't a policeman ask them?"

"I've tried. She wasn't very forthcoming. Some women naturally respond better to other women, and I suspect she is one of them. Usually I ask Mrs. Hobart to aid me in situations like this, but since Edith knows you, I think you are the better choice in this instance."

I read over his questions and committed them to memory before returning the paper. "I'll try my best. Is she badly hurt?"

"She has broken ribs and is bruised after being trampled by a horse. She was extremely lucky that a passerby saw the incident as it was occurring and pulled her out of the way before the carriage wheels got her too. The witness said a man pushed her into its path."

"Not knocked her accidentally?"

"Definitely pushed."

"But Mr. Hookly has been in your custody since New Year's Eve. It can't be him."

"It occurred that afternoon, before the ball, and the

witness has since identified the man you know as Hookly. His name is Lawrence Conrad, by the way. Edith was brought here but seems to be suffering from the shock of her ordeal. She won't say a word, not even give her name. The administration staff notified the police when she arrived but it took some time for word to reach me that a woman matching Edith's description was here."

"Shall we get started?"

"There's one more thing you should know. Lawrence Conrad is married. His wife is on her way to London now."

The nurse at the front desk nodded at the inspector in greeting and didn't stop us from going through to the ward. Dozens upon dozens of beds were lined up in rows, some with curtains drawn all the way around. Only one had a constable standing guard.

"Is that necessary?" I asked.

"Until I think her innocent, I must treat her as guilty." The inspector nodded at the constable who pulled the curtain aside for us. The constable removed a pencil and notepad from his pocket and waited.

Edith lay on her back, her swollen eyes closed. Although the inspector had told me she'd suffered bruising, it still came as quite a shock to see her face all black and blue.

I sat on the edge of the bed. "Edith," I said gently. "It's me, Cleo Fox. Can you hear me?"

Her eyes opened to mere slits before closing again. Tears slipped from the corners onto her pillow.

I went to touch her hand but they were both covered in bandages. I settled my hands on my lap. "Edith, I know you did some terrible things, but I also know what happened isn't your fault. He manipulated you. You just have to tell Detective Inspector Hobart so he knows too."

She gave a slight shake of her head.

"Why not, Edith?" When she didn't answer, I said, "He tried to kill you. You owe him no loyalty."

"That wasn't him. He wouldn't do that."

"We have a witness," the inspector said. "He saw a man matching Lawrence Conrad's description push you."

"Who?"

"Mr. Hookly's real name," I said. "You recall that I

mentioned he was impersonating Mr. Hookly. I told you in the parlor that day that the real Mr. Hookly was dead. You weren't surprised, so I suspected you knew."

She turned away from me. "I won't say anything that'll make him look guilty. He loves me, and I love him."

Behind me, the inspector shuffled his feet. I suspected he disliked leaving the questioning up to someone else, as used as he was to doing it himself.

"He's married," I told her.

Her lips parted then closed again and her throat moved with her swallow. I expected more tears but there were none and her voice was surprisingly steady when she spoke. "He must have stopped loving her. She can't have been a good wife to him."

"If he stopped loving her, he would have told you all about her. He didn't. Nor did he tell you his real name. And did he tell you he was a footman?"

"You're wrong, Miss Fox. He's a gentleman. He just fell on hard times."

"He's a footman. Mrs. Warrick recognized him. He used to work in her friend's household."

She closed her eyes again.

"Did he not tell you *why* he had to poison her?" I asked gently.

"She was a previous lover who was going to kill him."

"She wasn't his lover, Edith, and I doubt she threatened to kill him. He planned to murder her from the moment he realized she recognized him."

"We didn't plan it!"

Something at the back of mind told me she was lying, but I couldn't place my finger on why I thought so. "He was kind to you, wasn't he?"

Edith nodded. "He gave me gifts and sweets, and he told me he was going to marry me just as soon as the money came through on the sale of his mine."

I hated taking away the one good thing in her life, but it had to be done. That good thing didn't exist. It never had. "It was just an act, Edith. Not only was he married, but he flirted with me too before he knew I suspected him."

In hindsight, I wasn't entirely sure if he didn't know when

I met him in the smoking room. It had been the same day that I'd mentioned my suspicions in front of Edith. It was possible she'd informed him and that was why he'd readily told me about the letter from Lord Addlington. He'd tried to divert my suspicions away from him.

Tears slipped from beneath Edith's closed eyelids again. My words were finally getting through to her. It was time to exert more pressure.

"He'll blame you," I told her. "He'll say you poisoned Mrs. Warrick and that he had nothing to do with it."

Her eyes opened. The inspector handed me his handkerchief and I dabbed her tears away. "It *was* me," she said. "I gave her the poison."

My heart did a little flip in my chest. "You?"

"He told me I had to do it because she wouldn't accept a cup of tea from him. I *had* to do it, you understand. If I didn't, she would have killed me first. Or him, or both of us."

I shook my head. "That's not quite true, is it? They dined together in his room. If she didn't trust him, she wouldn't have gone there alone."

She swallowed heavily and eyed the inspector behind me.

"Mrs. Warrick confronted Mr. Hookly that afternoon," I said, thinking as I spoke. "Is that when he invited her to dine with him?"

"He told me she wanted to resume their relationship, but because she was the jealous type, and he was worried about me, he couldn't refuse right away. He was scared for me, you see. Scared she'd fly into a jealous rage if she found out about us."

That was not how their confrontation would have transpired, but I didn't tell her. She was talking, and that was the main thing.

"He had to try to convince her to leave him alone but do it in a way that wouldn't anger her," Edith said in high voice. "He said if he couldn't convince her over dinner then we'd have to do something more drastic or she'd never stop pursuing him." She held my gaze. "He says she became angry with him when he told her about me. She said she'd kill me in the morning when I delivered the tea. We thought about it all night, but we knew the police would believe her and not us.

The only thing we could do to stay safe and be together was to kill her before she killed me or him. So we decided to poison her by bringing her tea early. It wasn't planned, you see. It was kill or be killed. That's self-defense, isn't it? The jury will let us go, won't they?"

"She just let you in?" the inspector said flatly. "Even though you weren't due to bring her the tea until seven? Wasn't she suspicious?"

I shot him a glare over my shoulder.

He pressed his lips together and stepped back.

But his question brought my own doubt to the forefront again. Edith's story didn't ring true. Mrs. Warrick hadn't threatened Mr. Hookly out of jealousy, although Edith might believe that. But she certainly didn't believe the murder was a spur of the moment idea. Yet there was no way to prove it.

The inspector sighed. "Constable, what time is it? I have to be back at the Yard by one."

The constable removed his pocket watch. But I didn't hear his response. I'd got it! I knew when Edith had poisoned Mrs. Warrick, and I knew it had been planned.

It was all about the time.

"When did you change the clock, Edith?"

Her lips parted.

"The clock in Mrs. Warrick's room," I prompted. "Did you change it while she dined with Hookly? Is that when you let yourself into her room and moved the clock by her bed forward an hour?"

Edith's face crumpled. "The murder wasn't planned," she whispered.

I touched her arm. "No more lies, Edith. It's over."

"What about the clock, Miss Fox?" the inspector asked.

"It had been changed the day before. The time had been put forward an hour."

"How do you know?"

"Mrs. Warrick scolded Danny for bringing her hot chocolate late. It was eleven PM, the usual time for her chocolate to arrive, but she *thought* it was midnight because that's what the clock in her room showed. The following morning, Edith brought Mrs. Warrick her cup of tea at the usual time of seven. But it wasn't seven, it was really six. Her clock showed seven so she accepted Edith's arrival at her door with the teacup without question. The poison was in that cup." I turned to Edith, looking broken and fragile in her bruises and bandages. I felt sorry for her, but I couldn't let her get away with murder. She had to take some responsibility, if not all.

She gave a small nod.

"But the witness saw you at seven," the inspector said to Edith. "He saw you with a teacup then not even a minute later you emerged when Mrs. Warrick was dead. Did you change his clock too to fool him into thinking it was seven when it was actually six?"

I shook my head. "It really was seven when he emerged from his room. At six, after Mrs. Warrick drank the poison and died, Edith changed the clock in her room back to the actual time and took the cup with her when she left and locked the door behind her. She returned at seven with another cup of tea, just as she did every morning during Mrs. Warrick's stay. She made sure to bang on the wall or door of the room opposite to wake the guest. He emerged to see her and so bore witness to her being in Mrs. Warrick's room for a mere minute before she came out, upset over the scene she'd just witnessed. Your tests on that teacup came back negative for poison and your doctor's tests proved Mrs. Warrick was dead at least an hour before Edith was seen outside the room. You struck Edith off your list of suspects after that, even though she could have still done it earlier, because you had no motive for her to poison Mrs. Warrick."

"She wasn't struck off entirely," the inspector muttered. "But you're right. I could find no motive so I assumed her key had been stolen then returned to her without her knowledge. I wasn't aware of her relationship with Conrad."

"Nor was I, when I confided my suspicions to her. It was Mr. Armitage who made the connection."

"Mrs. Kettering told him I was with one of the guests, didn't she?" Edith asked.

"She suspected you were."

"I hate her," she bit off.

I didn't tell her the housekeeper's own crimes. It seemed irrelevant now.

"What did you do with the teacup that held the poison?" the inspector asked.

"Threw it away in a lane." Edith tried to sit up higher but hissed in pain. "So you see now that it was me who poisoned her, Inspector."

"You did it for him," he said. "He put the idea into your head, he gave you the poison, and the means to do it and cover it up later. He's just as guilty, if not more so. You can argue in court that he lied to you and that his charismatic presence put you under his spell."

She seemed to consider this. "But he won't hang, will he? Not when he didn't do the poisoning."

"It's not up to me to decide his fate."

She started to cry again. "I don't want my words to lead to his death."

"The inspector will speak to you again before the trial," I said before the inspector could answer. "Thank you for your help, Edith. You've been so brave in speaking to us today. Truly marvelous considering all you've been through. Everyone is very grateful."

Afterwards, when Detective Inspector Hobart and I were finally outside again, he turned to me. "That was a little thick at the end, wasn't it?"

"It was necessary if you want Edith to testify. The last thing you want is for her to retract her statement."

"Why would she?"

I blinked up at the pale glow of the sun, trying to pierce through the gray clouds only to fail. "Edith did what Conrad wanted because he knew how to make her feel worthy. He made her feel good about herself after years of being overlooked. If you make her feel important, and that she is central to the investigation, then she might turn her attention to you. She might want to please you instead of him."

He looked up at the sun too then at me. "If that's your way of asking me to go gently with her, then I will, if it'll get her to testify at Conrad's trial. I want him to be found guilty."

He didn't mention Edith's guilt, and I didn't ask. It was impossible to know if a jury would sympathize and let her off or would consider her to be just as guilty as Conrad.

I shook off the melancholia that had descended upon me

when I first saw Edith lying bruised and battered in the bed. The horrid events were over and it was time to move forward. It was a new century after all, full of possibility. I couldn't wait to see what it held for me.

I smiled at the inspector. "You policemen might be good at detecting, but you'd be even better if you combined that with a knowledge of human nature."

"I understand something of human nature," he said defensively. "Just not women." He smiled. "Don't tell Mrs. Hobart I said that."

I laughed. "If what you say is true, then it's quite likely she's already well aware."

He chuckled. "She'd like you, Miss Fox. You should come to tea."

My laughter faded. "I'm afraid she hasn't forgiven me for getting your son dismissed. I can hardly blame her. I'd be furious with me too."

"She'll come around. As a matter of fact, she invited you to join us for tea this afternoon."

I eyed him with suspicion. I doubted she'd invited me but it wasn't polite to question him.

"Harry will be there," he added.

"And you?"

"I have a few things to finish at the Yard after hearing Edith's confession, but the investigation is largely wrapped up now, so I can manage it."

At least there'd be one friendly face there, although I wasn't entirely sure if the inspector had forgiven me yet, despite appearances to the contrary.

"Three o'clock," he said, walking off. "I'll tell my wife to expect you."

"I thought she already was," I called after him.

* * *

AFTERNOON TEA WASN'T AS AWKWARD as I thought it would be, mostly because Detective Inspector Hobart filled the silences by talking about the investigation. I thought Mrs. Hobart would object, but she listened to his account and even asked her own questions. She was probably used to him talking about his work. Or perhaps it gave her an excuse not to talk to me directly. She could hardly meet my gaze, after all.

Mr. Armitage sat listening too, not saying much. It was difficult to know what to make of him today. Who was he? There were so many facets to his character, I was no longer sure if one of them was more dominant than the other, or if one or more were an act. He could be the charming assistant manager who made the guests feel at home, or the brooding fighter who'd tackled Conrad, or the unforgiving, argumentative fellow who wanted to punish me for getting him dismissed.

Worse still, I didn't know if I liked or disliked any or all three of those facets. Just when I thought I understood him, he changed. And just when I thought I liked him, he said something to make me dislike him, or vice versa.

But not today. Today, he was contemplative as he let his father carry the conversation. That is, until I asked him how his hunt for work was progressing. It was the only way I could be sure to poke him into speaking. A more sensible woman would have chosen a less controversial topic, but I wasn't always sensible and I really did want to know how he'd fared.

"Yesterday was New Year's Day and everything was closed," he said. "I haven't progressed very far since the last time we spoke on the subject."

"I saw an advertisement in this morning's newspaper for a bookkeeper. You're good with numbers and have experience with the hotel's books."

"How do you know what I'm good at?" he asked mildly.

"Your uncle told me."

"I asked him, and he said he's never spoken about my private business to you."

Oh, that wasn't fair. Mr. Hobart had told me a little about Mr. Armitage, although not about his abilities with numbers.

Mr. Armitage gave me an earnest, somewhat mocking, frown. "Did you somehow discover that I was once apprenticed to a bookkeeper? Perhaps my file from the orphanage fell out of the cabinet and into your pocket."

Ohhhh. It seemed the vicar had guessed what I'd done after finding the piece of paper slipped under the orphanage door. I couldn't admit to the crime. Not in front of the detective inspector. I didn't want to get Victor into trouble. "Don't be ridiculous. I was with the reverend the entire time when I was in the boys' home. I would have had to break in during the night and where would I learn to do that?"

His frown turned to a scowl. He clearly didn't believe me innocent but he couldn't prove I'd broken in, either.

"You have a fanciful imagination, Mr. Armitage. Perhaps you should be a novelist."

"Or a journalist," he added with a hard edge. "Since they make up a lot of what they report on."

"Not all of them," his father said, thoughtfully. "Some are good at uncovering things. You should consider it, Harry."

Mr. Armitage set down his teacup. "I might as well tell you both," he said to his parents. "I wanted to think about it some more first, but Miss Fox has forced my hand, as she has a habit of doing."

"You can't blame me for this too," I said.

He ignored me. "I've decided to become a private detective."

His mother pressed a hand to her throat. "No, Harry."

His father shook his head. "They're a nuisance."

"Until the police force changes its criteria and allows for the recruitment of reformed felons, this is my best option. Besides, I'll be one of the respectable ones."

"There's no such thing," the inspector growled. "They trawl for clients in the most unseemly places."

"I won't have to trawl. I'll have Uncle Alfred put it about among the hotel guests that I'm available. I'm known to be reliable and discreet among that set. I've kept their secrets for years and I'll continue to do so. Once they're aware that I'm available for investigative work, they'll come to me instead of an unknown person advertising in the papers."

The inspector seemed to lose some of his bluster, but he hadn't given in yet. "Private detectives get their information from lowlifes and by tricking their suspects into confessions."

"How is that different to what you do?" Mr. Armitage asked.

The inspector set down his teacup with a thud. "I have the law on my side." He shook his head. "Think about it, Harry."

"I have. I'll use my savings to set myself up." He turned to his mother. "I want to do this. I've realized I like investigating, and I'm quite good at it."

"Modest too," I muttered into my teacup.

Mr. Armitage's jaw hardened. "Did you say something, Miss Fox?"

"I said it was me who discovered the murderer."

He gave me a tight smile. "I found the silverware thief."

"I believe I discovered the final piece of that puzzle."

"You *helped*, Miss Fox."

I smiled back. "I'm rather good at helping, aren't I? And didn't we just agree a few days ago that we make an excellent team?"

His gaze narrowed. "What are you getting at?"

I softened my smile and turned it onto his mother. "I think the private detective business is a wonderful notion. While Mr. Armitage made an excellent assistant manager, he needed to step out from his uncle's shadow. And, if I'm honest, he always struck me as someone who shouldn't be taking orders. He should be the one to give them, and if he begins his own business and hires assistants, then he'll be manager of his own empire, not someone else's."

"I know you're buttering me up, Miss Fox," she said, not unkindly. "But it so happens that I agree with your assessment of Harry's character. I've always thought he could be so much more than manager for *that* fellow." Too late, she realized the fellow she was referring to was my uncle. She blushed but did not apologize.

I pretended not to notice. "It's a new century," I said. "It's the right time for beginning a new adventure. And becoming a private detective is much better than joining the army."

Her eyes widened in alarm. "The army! Good lord, Harry, don't you dare."

"So you agree it's a good idea?" he asked her.

She got up and patted his cheek. "I do, as long as your father agrees."

The inspector put his hands in the air. "I think it's already been decided."

It would seem the decision maker in their relationship was Mrs. Hobart, and their son knew it.

"Now, if you'll excuse me, Miss Fox, I have dinner to prepare," she said.

I assisted her to pick up the teacups and placed them on the tray then handed the tray to her. "Thank you for the pleasant afternoon, Mrs. Hobart."

The inspector rose after his wife left. "Nicely done, Miss Fox. Nicely done."

"I don't know what you're referring to."

"Human nature." He tapped the side of his nose. "Harry, see Miss Fox to the door. I'd better talk to your mother."

Mr. Armitage signaled for me to walk ahead of him into the hallway. "I feel as though I owe you a debt for convincing my mother," he said as he reached for my coat on the stand by the front door.

Now *that* was what I wanted to hear. "In that case—"

"But if you try to call in the debt, I'll be reminding you that you cost me my position at The Mayfair." He handed me my coat but did not let go. He leaned down and spoke in a low voice. "We're even."

He let go of the coat, smiled tightly, and opened the door.

I took the hint and stepped over the threshold. He closed the door behind me.

I walked off, feeling lighter than I had since my grandmother's death. He hadn't slammed the door in my face, so that was a good sign. Now all I had to do was convince him I'd make an excellent assistant in his new venture.

No, not assistant. A co-investigator. We could call ourselves Armitage and Fox Investigations. I'd let him think his name was first because he was a man, but in truth, it was simply because A came before F. His pride wouldn't let it be the other way around.

Yes, Armitage and Fox Investigations had a nice ring to it. Now all I had to do was convince him and my family that it was a marvelous idea for me to join him.

Available 1st June 2021:

MURDER AT THE PICCADILLY PLAYHOUSE

The 2nd Cleopatra Fox Mystery

A MESSAGE FROM THE AUTHOR

I hope you enjoyed reading MURDER AT THE MAYFAIR HOTEL series as much as I enjoyed writing it. As an independent author, getting the word out about my book is vital to its success, so if you liked this book please consider telling your friends and writing a review at the store where you purchased it. If you would like to be contacted when I release a new book, subscribe to my newsletter at http://cjarcher. com/contact-cj/newsletter/. You will only be contacted when I have a new book out.

ALSO BY C.J. ARCHER

SERIES WITH 2 OR MORE BOOKS

Cleopatra Fox Mysteries

After The Rift

Glass and Steele

The Ministry of Curiosities Series

The Emily Chambers Spirit Medium Trilogy

The 1st Freak House Trilogy

The 2nd Freak House Trilogy

The 3rd Freak House Trilogy

The Assassins Guild Series

Lord Hawkesbury's Players Series

Witch Born

SINGLE TITLES NOT IN A SERIES

Courting His Countess

Surrender

Redemption

The Mercenary's Price

ABOUT THE AUTHOR

C.J. Archer has loved history and books for as long as she can remember and feels fortunate that she found a way to combine the two. She spent her early childhood in the dramatic beauty of outback Queensland, Australia, but now lives in suburban Melbourne with her husband, two children and a mischievous black & white cat named Coco.

Subscribe to C.J.'s newsletter through her website to be notified when she releases a new book, as well as get access to exclusive content and subscriber-only giveaways. Her website also contains up to date details on all her books: http://cjarcher.com She loves to hear from readers. You can contact her through email cj@cjarcher.com or follow her on social media to get the latest updates on her books:

facebook.com/CJArcherAuthorPage

twitter.com/cj_archer

instagram.com/authorcjarcher

pinterest.com/cjarcher

bookbub.com/authors/c-j-archer